INTO THE UNKNOWN

Corrie radioed the orders, knowing why Ben was doing this. If he could have six burning tanks blocking the two-lane road, they had a chance of holding until help arrived.

"We've got to get across the St. Bernard Bridge and hold it from the other end; keep Bottger's men from blowing it," Ben said. "We've got to keep that bridge intact."

But he had no way of knowing whether or not the twisting bridge was wired to blow.

The rainy night suddenly boomed as anti-tank rockets were fired—right on target. The darkness was briefly illuminated as tanks rolled onto ATs and set them off. Two more explosions were heard and Ben was up and running out of the tunnel toward the bridge, yelling for his people to follow him—Jersey, Beth, Corrie, and Cooper keeping pace with him.

"Goddamnit, General!" Lt. Bonelli hollered. "Will you wait for the rest of us? Goddamnit!"

Ben shouted, "Come on, people. Come on. Let's take this bridge and do it now!" He disappeared into the rain-swept darkness.

Rebels surged forward out of the tunnel, following Ben into the unknown.

SMOKE JENSEN
IS
THE MOUNTAIN MAN!

THE MOUNTAIN MAN SERIES
BY WILLIAM W. JOHNSTONE

Available wherever paperbacks are sold, or order direct from the Publisher. Send cover price plus 50¢ per copy for mailing and handling to Penguin USA, P.O. Box 999, c/o Dept. 17109, Bergenfield, NJ 07621. Residents of New York and Tennessee must include sales tax. DO NOT SEND CASH.

BETRAYAL IN THE ASHES

WILLIAM W. JOHNSTONE

ZEBRA BOOKS
KENSINGTON PUBLISHING CORP.

ZEBRA BOOKS are published by

Kensington Publishing Corp.
850 Third Avenue
New York, NY 10022

First Printing: April, 1996
10 9 8 7 6 5 4 3 2 1

Printed in the United States of America

Let the chips fall where they may.

—*Roscoe Conkling*

Book One

At first . . .

. . . it was just a thought in the back of the minds of a few, just a dream. A place where people of like mind could live and work and play and raise their children without fear of crime.

"Impossible!" cried the socialist-leaning liberals who controlled the government of the United States.

"Bullshit!" said Ben Raines, pointing his finger at yet another pair of federal agents who had come to his home to harass him again for his articles attacking the government. "I have committed no crimes. I am a tax-paying, law-abiding citizen who has the right to address the problems I believe are destroying this nation. And I'm looking at two of them."

"Mr. Raines, we're only doing what we were ordered to do," the senior agent said. "Personally, I agree with you. But you're advocating violent overthrow of the government. Tone it down just a little bit."

"No. I won't do that. The policies of the present administration are destroying this nation. You gentlemen had better get a firm grip on the edges of the commode, 'cause this nation is going right down the toilet."

The younger of the two, a blow-dried fanatical devotee of President Blanton, flushed and said, "Now, you listen to me, Raines. There are charges we could bring against you. You—"

"Go sit in the car," the senior agent told his younger partner. "Right now!"

Alone with Ben in the living room, the older agent said, "I've got one year to go, then I pull the pin, Mr. Raines. I want my retirement." He sighed. "Look, what I'm about to say, I didn't say. OK? Hey, I agree with you—one hundred percent. But you're fanning the flames of insurrection through your writings. You have too many people ready to pick up a gun and start a revolution. This administration is out to get you, Ben. Not just you, but every writer who advocates change through violence." He jerked a thumb toward the outside, where the younger agent was sitting pouting in the car. "You see the type of men we're actively recruiting now. They kiss the ground around President Blanton's feet. And they're dangerous, Ben. The liberals have firm control of the government, and they're not about to turn loose."

"Death will make them turn loose."

"Goddamnit, Ben, don't say things like that in front of me! You've got to tone it down, Ben. If you don't, it's going to get rough. And I mean that." He walked to the door, then turned to face Ben. "Tone it down, Ben. If you don't, they'll silence you. And I'm telling you straight."

It wasn't about to get rough, it was already rough. Several writers of popular fiction, those men and women who were openly scornful of the present administration and were demanding change through

their writings, were getting hassled by federal
agents and agencies in an attempt to shut them
up. They were making the liberals in power (the
touchy-touchy; kissy-kissy; disarm-and-stomp-on-
the-rights-of-the-law-abiding-taxpaying citizens,
take-a-punk-to-lunch bunch) very nervous.

Ben and others could clearly see the writing on the
wall. And it was being written by hands who, politically, leaned so far to the left it was nothing short of
a miracle they could even stand up straight.

Thanks to liberals, conditions in America had de-
teriorated to the point of anarchy: discipline in public schools was virtually nonexistent; the juvenile
justice system was a joke; teachers lived in fear of
their lives; law-abiding, tax-paying citizens were
afraid when they went out shopping, out for a drive,
even sitting in their homes. The land of the free
and the home of the brave had become the land
of the frightened and the home of the powerless.
The liberals in control were so terrified that some
decent, law-abiding taxpayer might actually use a
gun to defend or protect self, family, home, or possessions against some slobbering, quasi-literate, shit-
for-brains asshole, carefully orchestrated programs
were put into motion to disarm the American public . . . and the majority of the nation's press went
right along with it.

According to liberals, criminals, you see, were really not bad people. That was a terrible ol' ugly myth
started by Republicans and other conservatives.
Criminals, you see, had all been forced into a life of
crime by an uncaring society. If you leave your keys
in your car and someone steals it, it's your fault, not

the fault of the thief. That is wisdom from the mind of a liberal. Not exactly what one would call on a par with Solomon.

Thanks to liberals, the hands of cops trying to do their jobs were not just tied, they were chained and locked.

"Ooohhh!" cooed the liberals to the men and women who wore the badges. "You must protect us." And when the cops tried to do just that, the liberals moaned, "Ooohhh! But don't you dare hurt that poor unfortunate criminal while protecting us."

The cops found themselves between a rock and a hard place.

The average time served for murder was about eight years; for rape, about two-and-a-half years; for stealing a car, about six months; and for home burglary, the criminal got a lecture. If you beat somebody's head in with a tire iron, that was assault with a deadly weapon. However, if you used a brick during a riot, the charge was less.

Ben Raines had a simple solution for crime: Allow the hard-working, law-abiding, tax-paying citizens to protect family, self, home, and possessions by any means possible without fear of arrest, prosecution, or civil suit.

"Ooohhh!" moaned the liberals. "That's a big No-No!" It had begun to appear to many that a liberal would rather see a law-abiding taxpayer get raped, mugged, assaulted, robbed, or killed than have just one lawless punk get shot while committing a crime. "Besides, we're going to take all your guns away from you so only the criminals will have guns."

As the last decade of the millennium began to

wane, that prophecy came true and the liberals got their way: All pistols and most rifles and shotguns were gathered up by federal agents, and the citizens of the United States were left defenseless against the lawless.

"I told you so," Ben Raines said, among others who had been prophesying that once the anti-gun crowd got their feet in the door, they would never be content until they totally disarmed American citizens. The law-abiding ones, that is. The criminal element was delighted with the new law. They never had worried about going to jail if they were caught with a gun, and now they didn't have to worry about getting shot by some law-abiding citizen while committing a crime.

"Oh, goody!" the liberal gun-grabbers and punk-ass-kissers said as they danced with joy. "Now we can all be safe in our beds and on the streets. Those big ol' horrible nasty guns have all been collected from Americans."

"From law-abiding Americans," Ben said, watching the news one evening. "Not from the criminals, you goddamned fool!"

It was all moot anyway, for shortly after the greatest gun-grab in the world's history, the whole world blew up.

Ben had been predicting that, too; and so far, he was right up there with Nostradamus in his predictions. And he had also predicted that thousands of Americans, rather than giving up their guns, would seal them up tight and bury them. And many of them did just that.

Although those citizens did not realize it at the

time, in that single act, the Rebel movement had been born.

After a very limited nuclear-and-germ war, and the collapse of every single government around the world, Ben roamed the countryside with the intention of writing about the fall. He began seeing billboards asking him to call in on a certain frequency. After encountering about a dozen of them, he found a radio and called in. Startled to learn that he had been named a general in some sort of army, he laughed and signed off. But the billboards kept appearing, and finally he met with some people.

The Rebel movement took another step toward full-blown reality.

A year later the Tri-States were born: three states in the northwestern section of the nation that the Rebels seized and settled. They held on for a few years, and then the newly restored federal government launched a full military assault against the Tri-States and smashed them. But the Rebel movement would not die. Ben rebuilt his forces and when they re-emerged, the movement simply could not be stopped.

The Rebels moved their base of operations into the south, first claiming the northern part of Louisiana. As the movement gathered strength, the Rebels branched out until they now claimed eleven southern states. Ben, head of the largest standing army in the world (as far as anyone knew), petitioned the newly formed United Nations for official recognition.

Over the heated and often-quite-profane objections of President Blanton and his newly formed liberal Congress, now headquartered in Charleston,

West Virginia, the Secretary General of the U.N. agreed to give the SUSA—the Southern United States of America—sovereign nation status if Ben and his Rebels would do just one little job for the U.N.

"Just one little job," Secretary General Son Moon told Ben.

"Little job, my ass," Ben muttered in response.

After meeting with the elected President of the SUSA, his old friend Cecil Jefferys, the first black man to be elected to this high an office anywhere in the northern hemisphere, and meeting with all his Batt Coms, Ben agreed to take the job.

And what a job it was: Stabilize the world.

"Is that all you want us to do?" Ben asked, his tone martini-dry.

"That's it," Son Moon replied, his usually unreadable eyes holding a definite twinkle.

"OK," Ben agreed casually. "You've got a deal!"

One

Ben had gone off to sit by himself on the roof of the newly remodeled and refurbished hotel in the city. He had just had his head filled with a lot of facts—and they were facts—that he really didn't want to hear.

He sat for several hours on the roof of the building before returning to the designated conference room in the hotel. He met the President of the United States, Homer Blanton, on the way, and the men walked silently together for a time down the long hallway. General Bodison, Chairman of the Joint Chiefs, joined them on their walk.

"How's the First Lady taking all this grim news, Homer?" Ben asked.

"Badly."

"I'm sorry to hear that. I really am. I know she doesn't like me . . ."

Homer waved that off with a curt slash of his hand. "That's her problem, Ben. Don't worry about it. We have more important things to concern us."

General Bodison caught Ben's eyes and smiled

knowingly as they walked. Both men knew Homer Blanton had matured dramatically. He was still a Democrat, and always would be. But hard reality had slapped him right in the face more than once over the past year, and many of his liberal views had gone flying right out the window with each slap . . . much to the chagrin of his wife, Vice President Harriet Hooter, and many members of Congress. Homer would probably never adopt the hard-line political views of the Rebels, but he would never again return to the totally liberal outlook he had brought with him into office.

The three men sat down in the conference room and were silent for a moment, occasionally looking at one another. General Bodison finally broke the silence. "Mr. President, if you will allow the law-abiding citizens of the United States to use force to protect what is theirs against the criminal element, without fear of arrest, prosecution, or civil suit, I could free up several more full battalions of troops to aid General Raines over here."

Blanton shook his head. "I don't have the power to do it. That would be up to the courts and Congress, not necessarily in that order."

"The people could vote on it, sir," the general said.

Blanton smiled, a rather sad curving of the lips. "And how do you suppose the vote would go, General Bodison? Ninety-nine percent of the lawyers who survived the bad times are living in the states that still fly the stars and stripes. Ben ran most of them out of the SUSA. When we reestablished the Supreme Court, Congress stacked it with liberals . . ." He grimaced. "With my help. I have to admit that. Besides, how can we have elections when we don't even know how many voters are in what district? All the records were lost—destroyed, probably. It's going to take months—years, perhaps—to get things back to some sort of normalcy. The only smoothly running part of the world is the SUSA and those states that aligned with them."

Ben kept his face expressionless and drew little doodles on the yellow legal pad in front of him.

"That wasn't meant as a criticism, Ben," Homer said.

"I know, Homer. I didn't take it as such."

"What the hell are we going to do about Bruno Bottger and these hideous threats of his, Ben?" Homer asked.

Bruno Bottger now controlled all of Germany, and half-a-dozen other countries. He had a standing army of a quarter of a million men and a reserve of over a hundred thousand, and his scientists were close to perfecting a drug that would make any who consumed it sterile. Bottger had laid it all right on the line to those attending the meeting in Geneva: He planned to control all of Europe before he was through; and if the Rebels were not out of Europe within twenty-four hours, Bottger's men would drive them out.

Secretary General Son Moon had joined the men in the room, and they talked quietly for several minutes. Coffee and sandwiches were brought in.

"We can't clear Europe in twenty-four days," Ben said. "Much less twenty-four hours. Bottger knows that. He's just looking for a fight. Besides, I've talked to my people about this. They don't like the idea of running—unless it's straight ahead."

Blanton looked at Ben. "Bottger said he'd use that serum if we didn't get out."

"I'm betting he doesn't have that stuff. I don't think he's even close to having it. He's bluffing."

"You are betting the lives of millions and the possible extermination of an entire race, General," Son Moon said.

"I'm open to suggestions."

"If Bottger is not stopped here, he will continue to overpower other nations on the continent," Blanton said. "In a few years, he'll be so strong nothing or no one will be able to stop him. He'll conquer the United States—I believe that is his ultimate goal."

"I agree," General Bodison said.

"Yes." Son Moon spoke softly. "I concur."

Ben reheated his coffee and added sugar. He stirred the murky liquid for a moment and said, "Homer, I'm going to get my thoughts together here and then tell you something, and you're not going to like it—"

"What else is new?" the President asked with a genuine smile.

Ben chuckled and took a sip of coffee. He looked at General Bodison. "Is the military willing to back the President, one hundred percent and all the way?"

Bodison hesitated for a second, then nodded his head. "I'll play this game," he added, "Yes. One hundred percent and all the way. Whatever it is."

"It's something that any sitting President could have done, should have done thirty years ago. I'm sure several Republican Presidents have considered

t, or at least entertained the thought. I doubt if any
Democrat ever did . . ."

Blanton sighed.

"Certainly sounds interesting," Bodison said.

"Homer, when you get back to the United States,
you call the major networks and set up a nationwide
radio-TV hookup to be followed with the entire text
of your speech in the newspapers. Publicize it for a
couple of weeks. When you feel that as many people
as possible have heard about the broadcast and will
be listening, you get on the air and you tell the American public that from that moment on, they control
their own destinies . . ."

Blanton leaned forward, his coffee and sandwich
forgotten.

". . . No citizen has to fear being arrested, prosecuted, or being subjected to a civil lawsuit for protecting family, self, home, or possessions against
thieves or intruders. Criminals have no constitutional
rights until they are arrested by a duly constituted
officer of the law or the military, which will be assist-
ing the police and sheriff's deputies. In short, Homer,
just take a page from the Rebel philosophy and apply
it to the United States. I give you my word that crime
will drop by seventy-five percent within sixty days of
your broadcast."

"But the lawyers—"

"Fuck the lawyers and the liberals and the Congress and the Supreme Court. They won't be able to
do anything because the entire nation will be under
martial law. The instant you get back, start a recruiting drive to beef up the military. You've got millions

of people out of work; you should have no trouble finding good men and women to fill the ranks."

"Ben, what about those fifty thousand or so armed men and women who have surfaced in the Midwest ready to attempt to overthrow the nation?"

"Use as many of them as you can in the military."

"What? Ben, they're racists!"

"Some of them, yes. But I'll wager not the majority. You don't have a choice in the matter, Homer. You've heard the reports from both your intelligence people and mine. Your nation is on the verge of collapse until you do something and do something damn quick. I'm telling you how you can keep your nation intact, Homer. I can't force you to do it; I can only suggest."

"What is my alternative, Ben?" the President of the United States asked.

"After we finish up here, I return to the United States and start kicking ass and picking up the pieces. Before long, the Rebels will be in control of the entire North American continent and you'll be out of a job. You want that?"

"You're not serious, Ben!"

"The hell I'm not."

Homer Blanton slowly shook his head. "All my life I have wanted to be President of the United States. Now I have to say it is the shittiest job on the face of the earth. You say those people in the Midwest are not racists, Ben. They want to round up all the blacks and put them on reservations. Now, if that isn't racist, will you kindly tell me what is?"

"I said some of them were racist, Homer, and some of them are. But the majority are just plain ol' Americans who will give anybody a decent shake if they think they deserve it. They were frustrated before the Great War; they've managed to live through the hard times, and now they see the government in Charleston going back to the same old dog-and-pony show they had to endure before the world fell apart a few years ago. They're not going to put up with supporting what they perceive as an entire underclass. You might as well get that through your head once and for all."

"I might, Ben. But many of those around me won't."

"Then they're going to be in deep trouble. Oh, hell, Homer. Americans are probably the most compassionate and giving people on the face of the earth. You know that. But you also know that just before the Great War, many believed America was teetering on the brink of a race war."

"If that is true, and I think it probably was, it was due entirely to racism," Homer said stubbornly.

"On both sides of the color line, Homer. On both sides."

General Bodison and Son Moon had both sat silently, keeping their expressions neutral as the President of the United States and the commanding general of the Rebel Army argued.

"Bullshit, Ben!"

"No, Homer. Fact."

"Time, gentlemen, time," General Bodison finally said since both men were getting a little hot under the collar. "You are both right to a degree. But this is not the place to discuss it."

Homer struggled to get his famous temper under

control and Ben nodded his head and leaned back in his chair.

"Being who and what I am," Son Moon said softly, "I am certainly not unfamiliar with racism. But I have never experienced the terrible racism that so many blacks say they have to endure. I wonder why that is?"

Ben smiled, and that smile infuriated Homer Blanton. General Bodison sighed, knowing the argument was not yet over.

"Perhaps, Mr. Secretary General," Homer said, "it is because of your education."

"In part. But only in part," the Secretary General retorted. "I think by and large it is because, while I am quite proud of my heritage, as all people should be, I do not flaunt it in the face of others. My God is how I perceive Him to be. I do not sit on television shows and tell others that their God is Oriental and they must accept that as fact. I can prove my heritage; I have no need to engage in half-truths and pure myths."

Son Moon leaned back in his chair, folded his arms across his chest, and half closed his eyes. The inscrutable Oriental.

Ben chuckled; General Bodison exhaled, and Homer Blanton got up and started for the door, clearly angry.

"Homer!" Ben said. Blanton turned and faced him. "We still have a war to fight and decisions to be made. And we either make them right now or everybody goes down the toilet. Including those who put you in office and whom you believe can do no wrong."

"Goddamnit, Ben!" Homer flared. "You wanna get off my ass?"

"Are you going to sit down and work with us on this matter?"

Homer walked around the table twice, getting his temper under control, and then returned to his seat. He stared at Ben for a moment. "Have you been playing devil's advocate in this discussion, Ben?"

"No, I have not. I'm just trying to get you to face facts. Not myths, not lies, not half-truths, just facts."

But Blanton wasn't through. "Facts as you see them, Ben."

"Ah, shit!" General Bodison muttered.

Ben shrugged his shoulders. "Are you going to declare martial law and give the people the right to defend themselves against criminals, Homer?"

"No," Blanton said.

"That's firm?" Ben asked.

"That's firm. How you conduct this war over here is your business. How I choose to run the United States of America is my business."

"Do I still get those four battalions of troops?"

"Yes." He looked at General Bodison. "Get them moving, General."

"Yes, sir."

Blanton left the room.

"I suppose we should be grateful for small favors," Ben said.

"The man can separate the trees that make up the forest," Son Moon said. "But he cannot see that each tree is different."

Son Moon stood up. "I fear for the world," he said, and then walked out.

"I'll get those troops moving, Ben," Bodison said. He pushed back his chair and left the room.

Ike McGowan, the ex-SEAL who commanded two battalions of the Rebels, entered the room and sat down, noting the glum look on Ben's face. Ike and Ben had been friends for years and kept nothing from each other.

"How bad is it, Ben?"

"Just about as grim as we've ever faced, ol' buddy."

"This push have a name?"

"Yeah. Operation Hopeless."

Two

President Homer Blanton flew back to the United States, his feathers still ruffled. Ben started shifting battalions around and beefing up the areas he thought would be the hot spots in the upcoming days.

Bruno Bottger launched no attacks against the Rebels. But Ben's intelligence people reported that Bottger was making no efforts to hide the massive movement of troops, all heading straight toward Rebel-held positions. And just before nearly all of Mike Richards' deep-cover people in Bottger-held territory were rounded up and shot as spies, Mike received one more communique, and it shook Ben down to his jump boots.

"Bruno is fielding an additional ten thousand troops a month, Ben. That's why he's holding off attacking us."

"Ten *thousand* troops a month?"

"You heard it right. He's getting them from the countries he occupied. My people tell me that this movement has been going on for years. He started with the young children, just like Hitler, and force-fed them his racial hatred bullshit in the schools. About the time you were setting up your old Tri-States, years ago, Bottger was on the move. He's been at this a lot longer than we first believed. He also took a page from you, Ben."

"Military training in school."

"Right. But while you don't start until middle school, Bruno was starting the kids in pre-school. Four and five years old. Love of Bruno Bottger and his twisted philosophy is all they know. He went into gang-ravaged and lawless countries and stabilized them. He controls everything from the Baltic down to the Black Sea. The adults despise him while their kids love him. Just like the old Germany of sixty-odd years ago."

"Kids turning in their parents for treason?"

"You bet."

"Drop the other boot, Mike," Ben told his chief of intelligence.

"I have several more boots to drop, Ben. Bottger's movement has spread out of Europe. He has a lot of supporters in both South and . . ." Mike paused and stared at Ben. ". . . North America."

"Son of bitch! How much support in America?"

"Can't get a fix on it as yet. But he's got at least a toehold in North America. Maybe more than that."

Mike stood up and walked around the room for a moment. He turned to face Ben. "At first, and for a long time, those groups in America loved you. They thought you were hard right-wing all the way. About a couple of years ago, they finally began to realize that you were really interested in protecting the rights of people of all colors as long as those people subscribed to the Rebel philosophy. The hidden groups began to slowly turn against us."

"So once more," Ben said, "we have enemies front and back and on both sides of us."

"That's about the size of it."

After Mike had left, Ben muttered, "How in the hell did those race-hating groups ever get the idea I was one of them?"

The deadline that Bruno had laid down had long passed and still he made no effort to attack the Rebels' positions. But he did continue to move troops up near Rebel positions. The four battalions of troops from American forces arrived and were being held in reserve, far back from the front. Ben flew back to the staging area to meet with their commander, Colonel Lee Flanders, a man who had been a professional soldier since he enlisted in the army as a teenager and had worked his way up the ranks. He was a mustang, starting out as an enlisted man, and that brought him and Ben even closer together.

Ben laid it out for the colonel, with no whitewashing of what they were up against.

Colonel Flanders had but three words to say when Ben finished. "Jesus Christ, General!"

Ben was amused at Lee's reaction. "We're only outnumbered about forty or fifty to one, Colonel. The Rebels are used to that."

Colonel Flanders studied Ben for a moment. "I was informed that you were a right-wing racist, General. Yet I have personally seen and spoken to men and women of all races, all creeds, and all colors in your army."

"Let's just say that over the years I have gotten a lot of bad press, Colonel."

Grim soldier humor surfaced in both men, and they laughed. "Right, sir," Lee said. "I do know the feeling."

"I've ordered half-a-dozen senior Rebels back here to start briefing your people on the situation and to begin indoctrination on the Rebel way of doing things, Colonel. Have you ever fought against us?"

"No, but I have talked with men who have. To a person they all agreed that they would rather stick their hands into a sack full of rattlesnakes than tangle with Ben Raines' Rebels. Are you really that mean, General?"

"Let's just say we don't believe in taking many prisoners, Colonel."

"After capture, my men are trained to be as compassionate as possible to the enemy, General Raines."

"Have they ever fought Creepies?"

"No, sir."

"Your men are going to change their minds after their first encounter with those bastards. Providing the Creeps don't eat them before they can."

Colonel Flanders grimaced. "Then all the things we've heard about the . . . ah . . . Night People are true?"

"Everything you've heard and ten thousand times more. And don't get yourselves captured by any of these punk gangs that Bottger has recruited. In their own way, they're just as bad. They have nothing to lose, Colonel. Nothing at all. They're all under a death sentence by one government or another. My intelligence people believe that any who might have surrendered, have done so. Now, Colonel, I want some information from you."

"Sir?"

"Tell me what you know about this rather large group of people who have surfaced out in the Midwestern section of the United States who have this wild plan to round up the nation's blacks and put them on reservations."

"I'll tell you what my people have found out about them, General. I know the leader is someone called Billy Smithson and that is his real name."

"Billy Smithson," Ben repeated the name. "That has a familiar ring to it."

"He was a TV preacher before the Great War."

"Ahhh! Right." Ben had a puzzled look on his face. "And he was a good one, too. There was never a breath of scandal about him. He wasn't a ranter or raver and he was universally liked. But I seem to recall he was a moderate on the subject of race."

"Not anymore, General. He did a hard one-eighty."

"Why?"

"You might recall his family was slaughtered by a gang of punks about a year before the balloon went up. His wife, kids, and mother and father."

"That's right. Now I remember. It was a two- or three-car caravan. They were going to services and got caught up in a crossfire between rival gangs. Yes. The punks were caught, but Smith wasn't happy with the sentences handed down."

" 'Not happy' is an understatement, General. He left his TV ministry and dropped out of sight. Now we know what he's been doing."

"Then you think he's serious about all this?"

"About as serious as an iron lung. We know now that he's the one who spread the rumors about a certain section of the Midwest being hot with radiation. Even you bought the rumor."

"I sure did. So that's where he's been headquartered, building his army."

"That's right, sir. And he's got one hell of an army, too. My people tell me they are as professional as anything they've ever seen. It took them about six weeks to clean out Missouri, General. And I mean turn it totally white."

"All this was done while we've been over here?"

"Smithson started his purge about two months ago . . . started it very quietly and finished it very quietly."

"So he's got people in my organization?"

"I'd bet on it. Hell, sir. He's got people on *Blanton's* staff. Why haven't you been informed of this, General?"

"I already knew part of what you've told me. But not all of it. My chief of intelligence thinks his group has been penetrated."

"Probably has. This Smithson is a smart one. He's not one of these pus-gutted, pig-eyed, shit-ignorant cross-burners. He's a highly educated, very intelligent man."

"You think he would throw in with Bottger?"

Colonel Flanders' brow furrowed in thought for a moment. He shook his head. "I don't think he would, General. Bottger is a bloodthirsty savage. Smithson is not. When he purged Missouri, his orders were to move the blacks out, not kill them. There were very few casualties."

"You think he would agree to fight alongside me?"

The colonel was clearly startled at that question. "Goddamn, General, you don't mind stepping up and shaking hands with the devil, do you?"

"Not if it helps me defeat Bottger."

Flanders thought about that for a moment and then smiled. "Of course, if you could get Smithson to split his forces—say, half over here and half back home—then when this is over here, he'd be more easily defeated, right?"

"Why, Colonel, what a terribly devious mind you have!"

Ben sent Mike Richards back Stateside to try to set up a meeting with Billy Smithson, but he did not inform President Blanton of his plans. Ben was having serious doubts as to how long Blanton and his government were going to be able to stay in power. There were dangerous cracks already appearing in Blanton's hold on the new White House.

"I feel sorry for the man," Ben said to Ike. "He's basically a really decent person who was handed a lot of bad advice over the years."

Ike grunted. The ex-SEAL was not nearly so taken with Blanton as Ben was. Ike not only didn't trust liberals, he had absolutely no use for them.

Ben smiled at his long-time friend. "I've seen you risk your life many times to get a dog or a cat or a horse out of the line of fire, Ike."

"That doesn't make me a liberal, Ben. Just an

animal-lover. Besides, I've seen you do the same damn thing."

Ben laughed and looked at the room full of Batt Coms and resistance leaders from more than half-a-dozen countries. "This is probably going to be the last meeting for a long time, people. Bottger is gearing up for a push." He sighed. His smile faded, and his shoulders slumped for a moment. "And there is no way in hell we're going to be able to hold against over a quarter-of-a-million troops."

"Have you heard anything from this Billy Smithson, Dad?" Tina asked.

"No. Well . . . only that he doesn't really trust me."

The room rocked with laughter. "I certainly can't imagine why that would be," Dan Gray, the former British SAS officer, said.

"Me, neither," Ben said innocently. "After all, I was a Boy Scout."

"Before you got kicked out for stealing a boat and trying to navigate your way down the river to the Girl Scout camp with two cases of beer and several quarts of whiskey," Dr. Chase said.

"Not true," Ben said. "It was six cases of beer and no whiskey."

"Did you make it, Dad?" Ben's son, Buddy, asked.

"No. The damn boat hit some rocks and sank."

"Damn landlubber," Ike said. "Can't even navigate a rowboat down a river."

Colonel Flanders smiled at the easy camaraderie among the men and women. It was easy for his soldier's mind to grasp why the Rebels were such an effective fighting force. In the short time he'd been on the continent, he'd watched them closely. The

Rebels moved with the precision of a ten-thousand-dollar watch. Lee Flanders would admit to anyone that he was in awe of them.

But could they stop a quarter-of-a-million fanatics? No. Even Ben Raines readily granted that.

"You're deep in thought, Lee." Ben's voice cut into his musings.

"Yes," the colonel acknowledged. "I was thinking about Bottger and his troops."

"As we all are," General Vanderhoot of the Free Dutch said.

René Seaux of the French Resistance Forces looked at Ben, standing on the stage of the hotel meeting room. "When we are pushed back to the sea, General . . . what then?"

"You would think of that," General Matthies of the German Resistance said acidly.

Seaux and Matthies held a very deep and profound dislike for one another.

Seaux looked at him and said, "Fuck you!"

The two men started for each other and had to be physically restrained. That ended the meeting.

"You're wanted over at the comm shack, Chief," Jersey told him.

Ben looked down at the diminutive and very lovely Jersey, his self-appointed bodyguard. How many years had it been since she, about seventeen or eighteen at the time, showed up one day out of the ranks and took her position beside him? Seven years, at least. "Lead the way, Jersey."

The rest of his team fell in with them as they walked along. Cooper, his driver. Beth, the records-keeper.

Corrie, who handled the radio. She had Ben's husky, Smoot, on a leash.

"What urgent message is awaiting me now?" Ben tossed the question out.

"Cecil Jefferys, Chief," Cooper said.

His long-time friend—and SUSA's first black President—didn't engage in much long range chitchat, so Ben knew the call must be important.

In the communications room, Ben took the mike and said, "Go, Cec."

"Ben, things are turning chaotic over here in a hurry." Cecil's voice came through as calm as always. "Outside our borders, that is. Blanton's government is shaky. Real shaky."

"Could we prop him up?"

"Yes—if he'd ask. But he hasn't."

"I'll call him and volunteer our help. How many battalions can you let him have for domestic use?"

"Four with no sweat or strain. We've got a new cycle coming out of boot right now. But I'm not so sure it's troops he needs. It's organization and revamping of his administration, top to bottom."

"He's not going to take the hard line, Cec."

"Then he's fucked, Ben—hard. There simply is no other way to put it."

"You've got to find a way to help him, Cec. If his government crumbled, we'd have to go in and take over. That would spread us too thin; and besides, I don't want to have to listen to all those goddamn liberals pissing and moaning twenty-four hours a day. It's bad enough now. As long as Blanton is in power, they'll stay with him . . . even though he has leaned a bit more to the right than they care for."

"This Billy Smithson is going to be a problem, Ben."

Everything was on scramble so the men were speaking their minds. Ben's reply was prompt. "If he doesn't fall in line with us, Cec, we can send K-Teams in to ice him."

"That's pretty extreme, Ben."

"Cec, I can't have Blanton's liberals taking constant potshots at me, Bottger at my front and Smithson at my back. Smithson is either going to fall in line with me or he's going to grab six feet of earth. That's it."

"He would never agree to talk to me, Ben. He thinks all black people are ignorant and savage. In case you haven't noticed lately, I am of a somewhat darker hue."

Ben laughed for a moment—keyed the mike. "Then that makes him either a fool, a dangerous crackpot, or a man who is badly misinformed. Let me make one more attempt to talk to the man. In case that fails, you get teams ready to go in and take him out."

"All right, Ben. Now then, what about all these people who are massing at our borders demanding to be let in?"

Ben hesitated for a few seconds. "Cec, you run the SUSA. What are your thoughts on the matter?"

Cecil was quick in replying. "If they are qualified to work at the jobs we have open, let those people in. The others stay out."

"It's your call, Cec. You know I'll back you in whatever decision you opt to make."

"I just made it."

"Keep in touch."

"That's affirmative. Luck to you, Ben."

"Eagle out."

Ben walked out of the room and sat on the steps for a time, playing with Smoot. After a few moments, he looked up at Corrie. "Have some people take Smoot back to Thermopolis. Get her out of harm's way. I think Bottger is through waiting and will start his push very soon."

Ben let Smoot lick his ear for a moment, and then Corrie gently pulled the husky away and led her off to Lt. Bonelli's people, who waited a few yards off. Ben was constantly surrounded by Rebels, twenty-four hours a day.

When Corrie returned, Ben said, "Have all civilians evac'd, Corrie. Starting immediately. Radio all batt coms to go to high alert. I think this dance is just about to start."

Three

Bruno waited just one more day before turning his rabid hyenas loose on the Rebels. From Liege in the north to Nice in the south, the fanatical men and women of Bottger's Minority Eradication Forces slammed into Rebel-held lines. The Rebels held because they had had enough time to get ready; but there was no way they were going to hold for very long, for this time, Bottger was pulling out all the stops.

"Start blowing the major bridges," Ben ordered reluctantly. "They can be rebuilt. But if we lose ground, chances are we'll never retake it."

Beginning moments after Ben issued the orders, on a wavy line running north to south for hundreds of kilometers, the Rebels began blowing major bridges and the MEF was powerless to stop them.

"Exactly what I thought he'd do," Bruno said with a strange smile.

"He's playing right into our hands," one of Bruno's senior officers said.

"Yes," Bruno said, and then joined all his staff officers in a good laugh.

For the moment, Bruno and his MEF appeared to be stopped cold.

"They won't be for long," Ben said, taking off his reading glasses and rubbing his tired eyes. He had been scanning maps for hours. "But he's up to something and I don't know what it is."

"The Chinese have a saying, Chief," Beth said. "That one should only rub one's eyes with one's elbows."

"Thank you, Beth. I shall treasure that for ever and ever."

"Please do," Beth replied sweetly, and returned to her reading.

Bottger's forces were probing at more than thirty locations, looking for just one weak spot, and Ben knew the MEF would find it sooner or later. It would not be because of any laxness on the part of his people or those resistance forces aligned with him. It would come because of vastly superior numbers.

Numerically, Ben needed about four more divisions to come close to evening out the odds. He also knew he might as well wish for the moon and the stars.

He picked up his reading glasses and slipped them on, looking down at the map in front of him. Irritated, he shoved the map away. What was the point of it? The map would not change and neither would the numbers of troops lined up on the east side of the line. What the hell was Bottger up to? Why wasn't he infiltrating troops across the line? Why had he suddenly stopped?

Right now, it was a standoff; quiet . . . all quiet on the western front, Ben thought with grim humor. But it wouldn't stay that way for long.

He picked up another report and read it again.

His chief of intelligence, Mike Richards, had finally gotten a few people into North, Central, and South Africa. They reported widespread destruction, chaos, tribal warfare, a breakdown in civilized behavior, and everything else Ben had felt they would find. But no sign that Bottger had contaminated any water supply with his serum or vaccine or whatever the hell it was. But then, no one could know for sure because the continent was so vast.

"Casualty figures are in," Corrie called from across the room. Ben looked at her and waited. "Light on our side. But Bottger's people really took a beating because of those crazy suicide charges. Prisoners taken confirm that Bottger has more people in reserve than we do on the front lines."

"I think I know what Bottger is up to, and we've got to have some help," Ben said. "That's all there is to it. We've got to beat him over here. Corrie, get President Blanton on the horn. Tell him I'm going to make a deal with Billy Smithson: He can have his all-white state if he'll agree to send me twenty-five thousand men."

"Blanton will hit the ceiling," Corrie said.

Ben shook his head. "I can't help that. Blanton is going to have to face reality. We can't win this fight without some additional troops. He can either free up his existing army under the terms I laid out several weeks ago and get them the hell over here or bend to Billy Smithson and we'll use his men. Those are the only two choices he's got if he wants Bottger stopped. If he can't see that, then he's not as smart as I think he is."

"It's late in the States."

"Wake him up."

Blanton was furious at Ben's suggestion. "There is no way in hell I will agree to giving that damned racist his own state, General Raines. Absolutely not."

"Then Bottger is eventually going to force us back to the sea in retreat and he'll win over here, Homer. And the instant I set foot on American soil, I will take my Rebels and run your ass all the way to the North Pole."

"Are you threatening me, Raines?"

"Goddamn right I am, Homer."

"Defeat is not that distasteful if the rights of a free people are the basis for that defeat. I—"

"You're an idiot," Ben said. "I've shaken hands with the devil a dozen times as a means to an end. Goddamnit, Homer, can't you get it through your thick liberal skull that Bottger intends to rule the *world*? He must be defeated over here, on this continent. I think I know the reason he delayed so long in attacking us, and why he suddenly stopped. He just might be buying time in order to perfect that drug. So that means we've got to take the offensive and take it damn quick. You either make the deal with Billy Smithson, or I will. It's up to you."

"You don't have the authority to do that, Raines."

"You wanna bet?"

Blanton called for a meeting with his senior advisors and selected senators and representatives. A stranger gathering could only be found on the back lot of a carnival, where the geek shows are held.

"That dirty, rotten, honky, racist, right-wing, Republican bastard!" Rita Rivers said.

"I always knew he was a closet Klansman!" V.P. Harriet Hooter bellowed.

After the coffee cups stopped rattling, Representative Fox reminded the President, "I asked you years ago to temporarily suspend the Constitution and put all conservatives in prison where we could keep an eye on them."

"To arms!" Representative Immaculate Crapums shouted. "Invade Missouri and defeat the mongrel hordes."

"Where did we put all the arms we seized from the law-abiding taxpayers?" Senator Tutwilder asked.

"We stored them," I. M. Holey said. "In case we had to use them someday to defeat the Republicans."

"Where did we store them?"

"Doesn't make any difference. The Rebels stole them all years ago."

"Thieves and brigands!" Senator Benedict hollered. And he was a man who knew something about being a thief.

"Right on!" Senator Arnold shouted. And he was a man who knew something about being a brigand.

President Blanton listened silently. And once again, he wondered, for the umpteenth time, how and, more importantly, why in the hell he had ever openly supported and actually gone on the campaign trail for this pack of nitwits.

Blanton suddenly slammed his hand down on the table. "Shut up!" he shouted. "Goddamnit, shut up! I'm tired of this nonsense." The room stilled, became hushed. Stunned faces and shocked eyes turned to him. Blanton pointed a finger at the person on his left, then pointed at each person present until he had worked around the long table. "We have two choices," he enunciated carefully. "And only two choices. We must accept one of them. And you all know what the two choices are. Now stop this damn silly bickering and make up your minds. Or by God I'll do it for you." He stood up. "You have fifteen minutes to decide. Fifteen minutes," he repeated grimly.

When the door closed behind him, Rita Rivers said, "If we allow this Smithson racist son of a bitch his all-white state, while he sends half his army over to help that other racist son of bitch Raines, we might be able to send the army into Missouri and wipe him out."

"Good thinking, Rita!" Immaculate Crapums said.

"Outstanding!" Harriet Hooter hollered.

The door opened and President Blanton stuck his head in. "Oh," he offered sweetly, "in case you're thinking of invading Missouri, put it out of your minds. The army answers solely to me on this one. We've already agreed on that." He smiled. "Just thought you'd like to know." He closed the door.

"Shit!" Hooter said.

"I think," Representative I. M. Holey said solemnly, "it is time for us to consider getting rid of Homer Blanton."

"Billy Smithson on the horn, Chief," Corrie said, getting up so Ben could sit down at the table.

"Mr. Smithson. This is Ben Raines."

"General," Billy said from thousands of miles away.

There was a cautious note in his voice. "Are you fore-warning me about some invasion on your part?"

"No. I am telling you that I've cut a deal with President Blanton. You can have your all-white state; but in return, you are to send me twenty-five thousand of your best people to help me defeat Bruno Bottger. No doubt you are familiar with the name."

There was a long moment of silence before Smithson spoke. "What's the trick, General?"

"No trick, Billy. Blanton didn't want to tell you himself because I think it hurt his mouth to agree to it."

"Are you on the level, General?"

"On the level, Billy. Papers are being drawn up as we speak allowing Missouri to secede from the Union and become an independent nation if that is what you truly want and if you agree to the terms."

"Free of niggers?"

Ben sighed. "Yes, Billy. Free of black people."

"There has to be a catch to this. There must be. Those liberals traitors in Charleston would never agree to something like this."

"The only catch is that a certain percentage of those men and women you send over here to help me won't be returning. When you make up your mind about this offer, and it had better be damn quick, you level with your people. Lay it straight on the line with them."

"How much time do I have, General?"

"Twenty-four hours, Billy. No extensions. After that, the deal is off and when I get back to the States, then you deal with me and my Rebels."

"Is that supposed to strike fear in my heart and cause my knees to tremble, General Raines?"

"Billy, I don't care if it gives you diarrhea. I'll be waiting for your answer."

"You'll have it, General."

"Raines out."

"If he agrees, how are you going to keep our people and his people separated?" Cooper asked.

"One of us to the north, the other to the south, and the resistance between us."

"Hell of a way to have to fight a war, Raines." Dr. Lamar Chase spoke from the doorway.

Ben turned to look at the chief of medicine and his long-time friend. "You heard the conversation with Billy Smithson?"

"Yes. I seem to recall hearing his type before. Have you considered that once over here, he just might join Bruno Bottger and turn on you?"

"Oh, yes. But I'm betting that he won't."

"And betting the lives of a lot of Rebels."

"Yes, I know that, too. But tell me, what other choices did I have?"

Chase shook his head. "None, Ben. None at all. That's why I'm glad it's you having to make these decisions."

To Corrie Ben said, "Get me the President, please."

"Which one, Chief? Cecil or Homer?"

Ben stared at her and caught the twinkle in her eyes. The Rebels had that amazing ability to find humor under the most trying of circumstances. "Try Charleston, please."

"Yes, sir."

Once he had Blanton on the horn, Ben said, "I

spoke to the man, Homer, and gave him twenty-four hours to reach a decision."

"What was his initial reaction, Ben?"

"Disbelief. He thinks you must have some trick up your sleeve."

"I wish I did, Ben."

"I know, Homer. But what else could we do?"

"I guess nothing, Ben. But with the exception of the army, I'm standing alone in this one."

"You watch yourself, Homer. And I mean be very, very careful."

A moment's pause. "I know that sometimes the people I have surrounded myself with act . . . ah, a bit strange in your eyes, Ben, but I cannot believe they would harm me."

"Do you recall an article I wrote before the Great War, Homer, in which I wrote that the greatest danger facing the United States was liberal democrats?"

"Yes. I recall it."

"You just keep that in mind, Homer. Do you want me to bump President Jefferys and have him send some people up."

Another long pause. "I . . . think not, Ben. But thank you for the offer."

"You're sure?"

"Yes. I have to trust those around me."

"He's making a mistake, Ben," Chase said before Ben could key the mike. "A very grave mistake."

"I know it. But I can't force help on him." He opened the mic. "All right, Homer. I'll keep you briefed."

Cassie Phillips, one of the few reporters that Ben would allow to travel with the Rebels, walked into the room. Ben and Cassie had grown to both like and respect each other over the weeks since they'd met and often shared a bed. There was no love between them, but a great deal of like; and oftentimes that emotion is much more important than love.

"Cassie, get Nils and Frank, will you? I have something to tell you all."

Cassie Phillips, Nils Wilson, and Frank Service were the only three reporters that Ben had found on the continent that he trusted to tell the truth without slanting the story or pissing and moaning and sobbing about punks and street shit who got blown away while committing criminal acts, and they usually traveled with Ben's first batt. Since they were almost always right in the thick of things, they were the first to get the stories and the releases, which did not make them terribly popular with other reporters; but if that bothered any of the three, they did not show it.

Ben told them about the agreement in the works with Billy Smithson. "I'll ask you to sit on the story until he gives us his answer, one way or the other."

The three agreed, as Ben had known they would.

"What now, General?" Nils asked.

"Now we wait."

Four

Billy Smithson gave Ben his answer less than six hours after Ben spoke with him.

"All right, General. You're on the level."

And that told Ben that Smithson had people planted all over the place—close to Blanton for sure and probably in Ben's own intelligence system.

"How do you want to work the picking of troops to assist you against this Bottger nut?"

"You're certain about this, Billy? Be sure. I want to know that you understand Bottger's ultimate goals. He wants to wipe out the black race."

"General, I don't want to live with niggers. But that doesn't mean I want to see an entire race destroyed. We're all God's children, made, more or less, in His image. But even God could and did make mistakes. We have no way of knowing how many times God tried to make man in His own image and failed. Do you get my drift, General?"

"Oh, yes, Billy," Ben said drily. "Loud and clear."

"Bruno Bottger is playing God, General Raines. And no human has the right to do that. He must be stopped. Now, as to the troops from my army . . ."

"You pick them, Billy."

"You'd trust me to do that?"

"Yes. But Billy, try to put moderates in command. For if they mix it up with my people, there will be a bloodbath."

"I am fully aware of that, General. I will personally be in command. Is that all right with you?"

"Absolutely. I'll get transport planes on the move as soon as we're finished. Where do you want them to land?"

The two men quickly worked out the details. Ben turned from the radio and looked at the three reporters. "Do any of you think those people around Blanton who are opposed to this will leak it to the press?"

"I'm sure of it," Cassie said.

Nils nodded his head in agreement. "Are you kidding, General Raines? A liberal President just agreed to an all-white state. You bet it will be leaked."

"If it hasn't already been leaked," Frank Service added.

"File your stories," Ben told them.

But much to the chagrin of Rita Rivers, Immaculate Crapums, and their counterparts in Congress, no great hue and cry of alarm or dismay came from many sections of the battered country when the news broke the next day.

The residents of the SUSA—of all colors—shrugged it off and went right on living, as did many of the people who lived outside of the SUSA. Those who lived in the SUSA knew that it was people, not governments, who must live together. They also knew that if one group of people did not wish to live with another, no government on the face of the earth could pass enough legislation to make those groups like each other and, ultimately, it wouldn't work. Legislation alone cannot give birth to understanding and compassion. It takes people who are willing to give it everything they've got to make it work. It takes laws that a solid majority agree with and abide by—not some 51/49 percent split—and those laws must be administrated and enforced fairly and equally to all, regardless of social or economic status. It takes people of all colors and creeds and religion, each willing to go out of their way to respect the rights of the other, and not go whining and complaining to this or that group that it was society's fault because Jimmy or Jane or Leroy or José or Bubba or Billy Bob embarked on a crime spree.

Governments can't do it. But people can.

Transport planes began flying into Missouri just hours after Ben spoke with Smithson; and true to his word, Smithson had troops waiting on the tarmac, ready to go.

"How are they dressed?" Ben radioed.

"Standard BDUs, General."

"You were expecting them to be dressed in Confederate gray, maybe?" Chase asked, sitting by Ben's desk, drinking a cup of hot tea.

"It wouldn't have surprised me." Ben sat down and rolled a cigarette, conscious of the doctor frowning at him. But this time Chase let it slide without one of his acid comments about Ben's smoking.

The big transport planes being used to bring Smithson's people in were capable of carrying several hundred men and their equipment, and they would be flying night and day.

Ben's Batt Coms were coming in for another meet-

ing since the Rebels were going to be re-positioned
Ben opened a map case and stared at the map. He
shook his head. "This is going to be one hell of a
front, Lamar."

It sure was. Just over 800 kilometers in length.

Ben would have over fifty thousand troops under
his command against Bottger's several hundred thousand troops. Ben had been busy revamping his battalions. He was now adding a short company to each
battalion, about half-strength, making that Headquarters Company. Thermopolis' people could no
longer handle the strain of thousands of troops. Ben
had named Thermopolis' command to be a highly
modified Division HQ of the Rebels. The resistance
fighters would be 2nd Division; Smithson's troops,
3rd Division; and Colonel Flanders' men, a regimental combat team. Ben worked the rest of the afternoon positioning troops and then went to bed.

Ben threw a pencil on the desk. "Damn, I hate
paperwork!"

"I'll trade my job for yours," Thermopolis said,
walking in the room. "I want a frontline command,
Ben."

"You're too good at what you do to be replaced,"
Ben said. "Sit down and have a cup of coffee."

The hippie-turned-warrior poured a mug of coffee
and sat down. "I don't do jack-crap, Ben. That's my
wife that does all the tracking and plotting and detail
work. Rosebud, not me."

Ben shook his head. "I need you where you are,
Therm."

Thermopolis muttered under his breath and then resigned himself to the fact that Ben was not going to move him up front.

The Batt Coms began drifting in, coming from all over western Europe, greeting Ben and Therm and pouring coffee and finding seats.

"The first of Smithson's troops have landed," Ike said. "I was told they look pretty good. I just talked to Mike Richards. Most of the troops are between twenty-five and forty. Solid and steady."

"That's what I like to hear."

The Russian Bear, General Georgi Striganov strolled in, waved at everybody, pulled a mug of coffee, and sat down. Ben's kids, Buddy and Tina, were the last Batt Coms in. Tina sat beside West, the ex-mercenary and commander of Fourth batt. Tina and West were unofficially engaged to be married, some-day, when the wars were over. Buddy looked like he ate Jeeps for breakfast. The young man literally did not know his own strength.

Ben made certain that René Seaux and General Matthies were seated on opposite sides of the large room, as far apart as possible, and then tapped on his desk with a ruler, bringing the room to silence.

"Bruno Bottger knows all about the additional troops arriving. He's known ever since President Blanton and I agreed to this plan. So he's got people in deep. Why he hasn't made a move against us before we get beefed up is anyone's guess. I'm just glad he waited." He picked up a pointer and turned to face a huge wall map. "The Rebels First Division will be stretched out from here, at Besancon, all the way down to the Mediterranean Sea. Second Division, made up of the Resistance Groups and Colonel Flanders' regimental combat team, will be in the middle from Luxembourg to Besancon. Billy Smithson's troops, which are designated as Third Division, will stretch out from Luxembourg north to Nijmwegen. General Matthies, your people will be at the northernmost point of your sector, René Seaux and his people at the southernmost edge. Now then, I would like you all to meet Colonel Wajda of the Polish Brigade." A stocky man in a brown beret stood up and nodded at the group.

"Pleased, I am sure," the colonel said, then sat down.

"He and his people came out of Bottger's occupied territory a few days ago to join with us." Ben smiled. "I wish Colonel Wajda did have a full brigade, but he did bring a battalion-sized force with him. Colonel Wajda and his men have been waging a guerrilla war against Bottger's troops for over a year. A very successful campaign, I might add. Glad to have you with us, Colonel. All right, I have queried all the leaders of the resistance groups and they have agreed to an overall commander. And that is going to be General Georgi Striganov . . ."

"Chief." Corrie stuck her head into the room. "Billy Smithson is here."

"Show him in, Corrie."

All the Americans present knew the man on sight for he had been one of the most successful and popular TV ministers for years before the Great War. Billy Smithson was a man of average height and average built, with iron gray hair; but there was something about him, an aura, that commanded espect. His eyes were sharp and intelligent, his bearing erect. He had distinguished himself in combat during the Vietnam War as a company commander and was no stranger to bloody conflict or solid leadership.

His thousands and thousands of devoted followers were testimony to his ability to gather and keep supporters.

Ben guessed the man to be about his own age.

Ben left the raised platform and walked up to Billy, sticking out his hand. "Is it Mister, General, or Billy?"

Smithson smiled as he shook Ben's hand. "Just Billy, General Raines."

"Come on, I'll introduce you all around. But I don't expect you to remember all the names the first go-around."

Introductions over, Billy walked to the large wall map and stood staring at it for a moment. "This is the longest front I ever saw in my life, General. My people are designated Third Division?"

"That's right."

"And we will defend the northernmost section." Statement, not a question.

"That's correct."

"And we will be facing approximately how many enemy troops?"

"Between seventy-five thousand and a hundred thousand."

Billy studied the map, reading the unit names on the many tiny blue, red, and black pin-flags on the west side of the front. Bottger's forces were marked with yellow flags. "There was really no need to separate my division from yours, General. We are fighting a common enemy. My people are under orders not to start any trouble with your people. Anyone who started a fight would be dealt with most severely. The subject of race will not be brought up by any of *my* people."

"But it might be by mine," Ben countered. "Even though I have issued comparable orders. People don't like to be told they are inferior to others because of the color of their skin."

"Just as long as we know where we stand, General."

"Oh, I think we both understand that perfectly."

"Quite," Billy said, then turned away from the map and took a seat.

Bruno Bottger was furious. He had stomped and cursed around his field headquarters until he was out of breath. He finally sat down and pointed a trembling finger at one of his senior officers. "Billy Smithson, an avowed racist, a man who purged his own state of niggers, now shows up over here, fighting alongside Ben Raines, against *me!* The man should be over here on *this* side of the line, fighting with me, not against me."

"Billy Smithson is not a racist, General," the officer told Bruno. "He is a separatist."

"What the hell is the difference? Semantics, that's all. Nothing more than that."

"Yes, sir."

"If the goddamn Jews weren't busy fighting the goddamn Arabs, they'd be over here with Ben Raines. I suppose I should be thankful for that. What is the matter with this Billy Smithson? I'm trying to purify the races to make this world a better place. I was under the impression that's exactly what he wanted. Ben Raines promised him one lousy, crummy state. I could give him an entire *country!*"

The senior officer kept his mouth shut for he didn't understand it either.

Now somewhat calmed, Bruno stood up and studied a wall map. "A pity. A real pity. I could have used a man like Billy Smithson in America. Well, no matter. I'll destroy him just like I'll destroy Ben Raines."

"We should strike now," the senior officer urged. "Before all the troops get into place."

But Bruno was not listening. He was thinking of the latest reports from his laboratory in Poland. The latest run had looked so promising . . . but it had failed the last few tests, breaking down after only a few minutes' exposure to air. His scientists had promised him better results the next time. They were so close, so close.

He turned to face the senior officer. "Let's see how well Billy Smithson's men fight, Wilhelm. Order our troops to push past Aachen and take the ground between Maastricht and Liege. This should be amusing. But let's be sporting about it. Let Smithson's men get into place. After all, we are gentlemen, are we not?" He laughed. "And let's use what remains of those detestable street gangs to spearhead. No point in getting our own good soldiers killed and wounded. Besides, when Smithson's men are overrun by the dredges of society, those that remain will be clamoring to go back home."

* * *

Ben got Billy on the horn. "Bottger's troops are coming dead at you, Billy. They know how we fight; now they're going to test you."

Rebel advisors had worked furiously around the clock instructing Smithson's men in the use of long-range artillery, but that was not something that could be taught in a matter of a few days. Smithson's men were expert in the use of mortars, but had practically no expertise with long-range artillery or tanks. Ben had been forced to send some of his own people in to handle the tanks and artillery. And he had had to be very careful in picking the crews.

"This is going to be a real pain in the ass before it's all over," he bitched.

Finally, the blacks in the artillery and tanks crews picked a spokesperson to go see Ben.

"Hell, General," the man said, "why not just send the crews in as is? There is nothing that Smithson's men can say to us that we haven't heard ten thousand times before. We'll just ignore it and do our jobs. Besides," he added with a grin, "it will give us a great deal of pleasure to have Smithson's people depending on us for their lives . . . since we are supposed to be so inferior."

Ben returned the smile. "All right, Captain I'll send the crews in as is. Good luck."

Both Bottger and Smithson were about to learn something about the fighting abilities of Rebels . . . of all colors.

Five

Bottger's men were full of spirit as they left Aachen. When they hit the main bridge Ben had left intact at Maastricht, they died in bloody heaps and piles before they could get fifty feet across. They were piled up as high as the pedestrian guard railing before the commander realized he had made a terrible blunder.

The Rebel advisors with Smithson's men offered no comments or suggestions. Ben had told them to observe Smithson's tactics and to keep their mouths shut unless they were asked to comment. The Rebels watched with approval as Smithson's men quickly shifted their heavy machine guns to different locations before the men of the MEF could bring mortar and tank guns to bear on them.

"They're pretty good," a Rebel sergeant observed.

"One of the company commanders told me they've been studying our tactics for years," his friend replied.

"That explains it."

Bottger threw another attacking force at Smithson's men holding at a small town just south of Maastricht. Smithson's men not only held, but chased the MEF off the bridge and put them into a complete rout.

"I think we can go back to our units," one of the advisors said.

Ben was pleased by the field reports. "We can stop worrying about Billy's troops. They're fighters."

Bottger was busy putting together an air force, but he was not getting very far with it. Technology was again moving forward rapidly, but was still a long way from being what it was just prior to the Great War— due in no small part to the Rebels. Certain elements used to toughen steel and for the manufacture of high-speed aircraft could now only be found in certain areas of the country—and they were controlled, for the most part, by the Rebels or by countries or states who supported the Rebel movement. Vanadium, which used to come from South Africa, was, due to the violent clime in that part of the world and the collapse of South Africa's industries, no longer available in any quantities . . . but due to Ben Raines' farsightedness, the Rebels had stockpiled vanadium and titanium. The Rebels also controlled most of the major oil fields in North America and were friends with many countries south of the border who had huge oil reserves.

The Rebels possessed large quantities of raw materials and crude oil. Bottger had been forced to stockpile for years, and every gallon of fuel was precious. He did have oil fields in those countries he overran, but the equipment was old and constantly breaking down and most of the workers were solidly opposed to Bottger and his MEF. Bottger sometimes had to take harsh measures to make them work.

Bottger often said to his close inner circle that being a benevolent dictator was terribly hard work and awfully trying.

After Smithson's men stopped the MEF cold at the bridges, Ben knew that testing time was nearly at an end. Bottger would soon be throwing everything he had at them, and Ben felt beyond a doubt that his people would not be as lucky this time around.

At the last minute, the remaining gangs of street punks had dragged their feet getting to the battle sites, arriving late, arriving just in time to see the troops of the MEF slaughtered at the bridges.

"They learned their lessons the hard way," Beth said.

"So will Bottger's troops," Ben replied. "If they haven't already. Now it turns slow and mean and ugly . . . for both sides."

Rivers separated the Rebels from the MEF in many areas, but meadows, open ground, and forests also lay between the two, a deadly no-man's land.

It would be deadly for the Rebels if they were caught in the open, since Bottger's snipers were as good as any Rebel sniper. But the open meadows and dark forests would soon turn into a hideous killing field for Bottger's men, for the Rebels had laid out thousands of mines of all varieties.

Both sides now waited for the command to move out.

"We're as ready as we'll ever be," Ike, second in command of all Rebel forces, told Ben. "I've been up and down the line from Besancon to Nijmwegen, Ben. We're standin' tall.''

"It's all up to Bottger," Ben replied.

"Any word from President Blanton?"

"He's holding on. But it doesn't look good. I think his government is on the verge of total collapse."

"And?"

"He hasn't asked Cecil for help."

"Then he's a bigger fool than I thought he was," Ike said bluntly. Ike was no fan of Homer Blanton.

Ben didn't want to argue with his old friend, so he said nothing. Ben did not believe Homer was a fool, but that he was a man who had surrounded himself with liberal nitwits and who had listened to them for far too long. Ben was of the opinion that people who voted the straight liberal ticket fell into one of several categories. One: people who, for whatever reasons, wanted to live under a socialistic form of government. Two: people who were basically well-intentioned but could not separate reality from dreamland. Three: people who in the South were called yellow-dog Democrats; they would vote for a yellow dog if it ran on the Democratic ticket. Four: people who wanted something for nothing; those types made up a great portion of the liberal Democratic Party's constituents. And five: people who were so arrogant they felt they knew what was best for everybody and wanted to run everybody else's lives from cradle to grave.

Several million people now resided in the SUSA. If an adult were healthy, that adult worked . . . or that adult got out. Period. There were, of course, those who were sick, old, or handicapped who required help, and they got it, quickly and with no hesitation on the part of so-called public servants—which in the old USA had turned into a profane joke over the years. In the SUSA, planes and trains and buses ran on time; mail was usually delivered within two days anywhere in the SUSA. The judicial system was swift . . . if a criminal lived long enough to face a judge and jury, that is.

In the SUSA, Ben Raines had brought everything back to the basics, and it worked. The problem was, liberals just couldn't figure out how it worked without massive government interference in people's lives. The Rebel philosophy was so unpretentious it was baffling to liberals; they just could not or, as was probably the case, would not comprehend it.

Liberals just could not understand and/or accept the fact that all people, regardless of race, creed, or color, for the most part will control their own destinies if given the chance or are forced to take the risk.

When asked to explain the Rebel philosophy, Ben was fond of saying that after raking the leaves in one's yard, a considerate person will bag the leaves and put them out for pickup; an arrogant, stupid, and inconsiderate person will pile them up, set them on fire, and let the smoke drift into the neighbor's house. The latter wouldn't last long in the SUSA.

Then Ben would smile at the confusion on the questioner's face, and walk off.

Bottger opened up the dance on a warm summer morning. Just at dawn, his artillery began lobbing in shells and his troops started moving up behind the bombardment. But Ben had ordered his people out of buildings and dug into the ground in bunkers heavily fortified with sandbags and timbers scrounged from all over the countryside. Bottger's artillery could not reach Ben's biggest guns, the 203mm self-propelled, which had a range, using conventional ammunition, of twenty-five thousand yards. The M110A2 can hurl a rocket-assisted round almost thirty-five thousand yards. And the Rebels possessed nearly every large artillery piece that had formerly been in the hands of the U.S. government.

When reporters first asked where Ben had gotten all his artillery and heavy armor, he replied blithely, "We stole them, naturally."

The Rebels' towed 155mm could hurl a projectile almost twenty-five thousand yards, and five thousand yards farther using rocket-assisted rounds. Their 105mm towed could hit a target from three miles back and with rocket-assist could extend that range out to about eight miles.

Bottger soon realized he was out-gunned and no match for the Rebels' artillery.

When it came to rolling armor, Rebel tanks were far superior to anything Bottger had. Rebel tanks were all equipped with depleted-uranium armor plate called DU, which is almost three times more dense than steel. And Rebel tanks bristled with weapons. The Rebels' MBTs carried a main gun of either 105mm or 120mm, plus a driver-fired M-60 and two .50 caliber machine guns. One of the .50's could be fired when the MBT was buttoned up.

Bottger's tanks tangled head on with the Rebels'

MBTs only once. After that, they turned tail and ran when they spotted Rebel tanks heading for them.

"I'd sure hate to have to tangle with these Rebels," Billy Smithson told one of his batt coms.

"God forbid we should ever have to" came the reply.

Billy looked up as an MBT rumbled by. The black commander smiled and gave him a smart salute. Billy returned the smile and the salute, following the tank with his gaze until it rounded a curve.

"What's the matter, sir?" the batt com asked, noting the strange look on Billy's face.

"We made a mistake," Billy admitted. "We should have followed Ben Raines' lead and kept the best and booted out the rest—whites included."

"Some of the boys wouldn't like to hear you say that."

"Some of the boys can go right straight to hell," Billy replied. "And probably will."

The batt com watched him walk away. "No, sir," he muttered, frowning. "They are not going to like those words at all."

The artillery duel kept up for three days and nights, then the fire began to fade away from Bottger's side. Not one of Bottger's men had succeeded in breaching Rebel-held lines. Rebel P-51E's screamed over Bottger's lines and reported dozens of burned-out artillery pieces and tanks. And Bottger's troops were backing up, out of the scope of Ben's long-range artillery, crewed by highly trained experts who had honed their deadly skills on battle-fields around the world.

"Stalemate," Ben said. "He can't go west; we can't go east." Briefly he considered the only alternative. "Both of us have to push forward."

"This is boring, Chief," Jersey bitched. "Sure isn't like the old days."

Geneva had not had a round fired at it during the artillery duel. Bottger had troops a few miles outside of the city, but launched no assault. He held the town of Annemasse only a few miles away, and his troops also occupied the town of Nyon, just north and east of the city on the lake. But not one shot had been fired at the Rebels occupying Geneva, and that puzzled Ben.

"I don't think they want to mix it up with us," Cooper said.

Ben cut his eyes to his driver, a germ of an idea floating around in his brain. "Why, Coop?"

Cooper shrugged his shoulders. "Because every time they hit us before, we kicked butt."

"For a fact, Coop," Beth said. "But I think it's more than that."

"What do you think it is, Beth?" Ben asked, moving to the large wall map. He studied the division locations, waiting for her reply.

"I don't know, Chief. But it's strange. Up and down the line, not one major city attacked."

"So he wants the cities intact," Ben mused. "But why? Some noble thought on his part? I don't think so." Ben fell silent, deep in thought. He was flung back in memory to Vietnam.

"Now, why would I think of Vietnam at this juncture?" he mused. "It certainly isn't because of the terrain."

He picked up a disturbing report from Mike Richards. His intelligence network in Bottger-controlled Europe had been destroyed, with dozens of deep-cover agents ferreted out and killed.

One or two or three would have been acceptable . . . but dozens? And even had some of them broken and talked, they would have been unable to finger another agent, for Mike had set it up so one did not know the other.

Then what had happened?

Vietnam.

"What about 'Nam?" Ben thought, irritated at that constant that would not leave his mind.

Vietnam.

"Damn it!" Ben said aloud.

"What's the matter?" Jersey asked.

"I don't know, Little Bit. But something damn sure is."

Vietnam.

There it was again. But why now? He rarely thought of those terrible days in 'Nam. So why now?

He cut his eyes to Cooper, who was spreading something on a thick slice of fresh-baked bread. "What do you have there, Coop?"

"Honey from back Stateside. You want some?"

Ben shook his head. "Not now. Thanks."

Vietnam.

Honey.

"Now put it together," Ben whispered. "What does it mean? Why do you think it means anything?"

Honeycombed.

Tunnels.

He motioned for Jersey to come with him, and they stood outside in the street.

"What's up, Boss?"

"How many Southwest Indians in our ranks could you get ahold of, Jersey? Those that still speak the language?"

"Oh, 'bout a dozen or so, I guess. Apache, Navaho, Pima. What's the matter?"

"You get on a radio and bump them, in Apache. Tell them to reply only in their native tongue. Can you understand Navaho and Pima?"

"Enough to get by, sure."

"Tell them to get ready for an attack. Tell them to start moving all HQ's and CP's out of the city and to stay off the radios. Send out runners to the resistance leaders with instructions for them to do the same. Do it quickly, but without any panic or haste. We don't want to tip off Bottger's people."

"Tip them off?"

"Bottger has either made some sort of unholy alliance with the Night People or he's using their old tunnels. They're under us, Jersey. Right beneath our feet. That's why he won't shell the cities. The bastard took a page from the Viet Cong. That's how our intell people were found out. Every major city is honeycombed with tunnels. Get to it. Use the radio in the Hummer."

"The attack could come at any minute, Boss!"

"Any second. Move!"

Six

Ben walked back into his CP and whispered to Corrie. She nodded and stood up, holding a finger to her lips and motioning for the others to follow her. They did, with confused looks on their faces. Ben had waved to other Rebels outside and they quickly entered, walking silently, and began rigging charges to doors. As the news spread, the Rebels began working very fast booby-trapping the buildings they had occupied. Whether it be creepies or Bottger's men in the tunnels under the city, they were going to be in for a very rude surprise when they came up out of their holes.

The Rebels kept up a constant, meaningless chatter as they worked clearing out of the buildings and rigging booby traps as they went. Then they faded back toward the outskirts of the city.

What civilians there were had already been evac'd out of the city. Within an hour, those Rebels who were leaving, were gone.

The same scene was being played out up and down the Rebel front, and those in the tunnels beneath the cities did not have an inkling as to what was going on. They could hear lots of chatter, but no one among them spoke any Indian languages. They were thoroughly baffled.

The troops of the MEF radioed back to Bottger's HQ. "Something is going on."

"What?" Bruno asked.

"We don't know" was the reply.

"Idiots!" Bruno said. "If they don't know what is going on, how do they know *anything* is going on?"

But spotters in the mountains using high-tech equipment radioed to Bottger that something was definitely going on in the city.

"Ask them what," Bruno said wearily.

"Lots of activity."

Before Bottger could utter some sarcastic comment, reports began coming in from other spotters around other cities. Something was definitely wrong.

The consensus was that the Rebels were about to go on the offensive.

Bruno shook his head. "I don't think so. Raines is a chance-taker, not a fool."

"Then . . ."

"We wait and see. It may be time for *us* to take the cities. Yes. It just might be our time."

Ben, much to the disgust but not to the surprise of his batt coms, had not left the city for the safety of the countryside. He waited with his team for whoever was under the city to make a move.

Ben ordered the Indian talkers to stand down and the radio operators to return to English . . . and keep the transmissions military without giving away anything of importance. Empty Rebel trucks rumbled back and forth, giving the impression—Ben hoped—that all was normal.

"I think," Bruno said, "they were testing some new code. And if that was it, they had certainly succeeded. What damn language was that?"

No one knew.

The spotters reported that everything in the cities appeared to be back to normal.

Bruno paced the floor of his office. He was well aware that the longer he waited to use his underground troops, the greater the chances of their being discovered. After the Rebels' intelligence officers capture and execution, Raines certainly knew that Bottger had people in place within his organization and he would be testing those in the know. When nothing was found, he would look elsewhere and begin to put things together.

"Strike!" Bruno ordered. "Strike now! And kill that goddamn Ben Raines!"

Hundreds of Bottger's troops came charging up to the surface and went racing toward death's door. The troops were so glad to be finally getting out of those stinking damn tunnels, they were careless. The first ones rushed into the lower levels of buildings, threw open hidden passageways, hit ankle-high black wires, and were blown into bloody chunks of meat and shattered bone. Others entered rooms where no wire was stretched and ran up stairs and threw open doors and got blown into oblivion.

Ben and his team waited across the street from his command post. When the first explosions trembled the concrete beneath his boots, he knew he'd been right.

The troops of the MEF stepped over the bloody remains of their comrades and rushed onto ground level.

"Wait, wait," Ben cautioned his team. "Let them hit the sidewalks."

Bottger's men ran through the lobby of the old building and, meeting no resistance, raced outside, breathing deeply of the clean, fresh air.

Those were their last breaths.

Ben lifted his old Thompson and let it roar, the heavy .45 caliber slugs tearing into flesh and shattering bone. From Nijmwegen in the north all the way down to the sea, some eight-hundred kilometers away, the Rebels' surprise was successful.

In less than fifteen minutes, Bottger lost nearly ten-thousand troops.

Before the echo of the first shot fired had faded, P-51Es came screaming in right on the deck over Bottger's territory, unleashing a maelstrom of terror and death. The planes dropped napalm, fired cannon and rockets, and were shrieking off into the distance before the troops of the MEF could react.

Under cover of smoke and fire and artillery and utter confusion on the part of the enemy, Ben's Rebels surged across the rivers and streams and meadows and forests. Caught flatfooted, certainly not expecting that Ben would take the offensive, Bottger could do nothing except order a retreat that soon turned into a rout in many areas as main battle tanks spearheaded the drive, crushing and destroying anything and anybody that happened to be in their way.

Separatists and racists the men of Billy Smithson's division might well be, but they proved their courage in battle that day as Smithson's troops leaped out ahead of the rest of the long line. It was irritating to a small percentage of those troops that black tank-commanders were leading the way.

The highly vocal rancor among some of his men was mildly amusing to Billy.

Before Ben halted the push late that day, Ben's stabilization forces had advanced twenty-five miles into Bottger's claimed territory, pushing his troops back, killing, wounding, and capturing hundreds more.

"Shut it down and dig in hard," Ben ordered with about an hour of daylight left. "I want reports from all batt coms right now."

The field reports began coming in fast. Smithson had pushed off from Nijwegen, Eindhoven, Maastricht, Liege, and from just north of Luxembourg. His northernmost battalions, along with contingents of the Free Dutch and Free German forces, were on the road to Hengelo and Enschede when Ben called for a halt. His central and southernmost force had not made as good time and were fairly well lined up with Second Division.

Second Division had shoved off from Luxembourg, Metz, Nancy, Epinal, and Vesoul and had driven inward almost twenty-five miles.

Ben's command had jumped off from Geneva and southward all the way down to the sea and driven hard toward the east, making nearly the same distance.

But no one was under any illusions about their successes. Even the most inexperienced soldier knew that Bottger would stop, turn around, and make his stand sooner or later. Just when that would be was the joker in the deck.

"That's what all that goddamned jibber-jabber was about," Bruno said, angry to the core. "Setting up the offensive." He calmed somewhat, took several deep breaths. "I must learn not to attempt to second-guess Ben Raines."

Bruno did not linger long on how Ben had discovered his troops in the tunnels. It was done, over, and there was no point in dwelling on it. He also revised his opinion of Billy Smithson's troops, did a one-eighty on their fighting ability: They were almost as good as the Rebels.

Bruno's anger at his troops' retreat faded when he began reading field reports that evening. Half a division was missing, presumed dead, wounded, or captured. The Rebels' attack had been so unexpected, so swift and hard, Bruno could not sustain his anger toward his troops.

"Nor," he muttered, staring at a map, "can we make a stand here." Until reinforcements arrived, the MEF would have to continue giving up ground to the Rebels.

"Distasteful business," Bruno muttered, then turned off the field lamp and went to sleep.

"We'll continue pushing them," Ben ordered, "but we've got to be careful not to outdistance our supply trucks." He tapped the map. "And we've got to start spreading out north." He was talking to himself; something his team had long grown accustomed to. "We've got a hundred-kilometer gap between the North Sea and our troops advancing toward Almelo. And look at this mass of towns around Dusseldorf. That's where Bottger will turn and make his stand. Bet on it."

Ben took a grease pencil and drew a line, running north to south, from Dusseldorf down to Monaco. "Right there is where he's going to stop us. From that point on, our advance, if any, is going to be measured in feet, not miles."

"You think it's going to be that bad, Boss?" Corrie asked.

"Yes." He tapped the map. "Here, the MEF will be fighting on their own soil, and they'll fight to the last drop of blood." He straightened up and thanked Corrie for the fresh cup of coffee. "We've got to destroy or at least damage that underground lab in Poland to buy us some time. But I don't know how in the hell to accomplish that."

"Send Emil Hite," Cooper suggested.

Ben smiled. Over the years since Emil had linked up with Ben and the Rebels, the little con man and his followers had turned into a fine, tight fighting unit, if one could just put up with his antics. "He'd go if I'd suggest it, Coop."

"Yes, he would, Chief. But I don't know whether I'd wish Emil on the Polish people."

"Why don't *you* go?" Jersey suggested. "And take your mouth with you."

"Only if you go with me, my lovely little unplucked desert flower," Cooper responded, and took off for the door, Jersey right behind him.

"I said un*plucked*, Jersey!" Coop hollered on a dead run.

Doctor Chase stepped aside just in time to keep from being trampled.

He stepped into the room and said, "Someday those two will probably get married. They're made for each other. If she ever gets over her crush on you, Raines."

Corrie and Beth smiled at that. The entire Rebel Army knew that Jersey was in love with Ben Raines. But it was purely platonic and she and Ben both realized it and intended to keep it that way.

Chase waved off the offer of coffee and sat down. "The press has finally caught up with us. I thought you would enjoy that bit of news."

"I'm thrilled." He did not have to add that he hoped the press would stay the hell away from him. With the exception of a very few members, the media kept a wide berth from Ben, knowing that he did not like them. He did not trust most journalists to report a story fairly without resorting to a liberal viewpoint, pissing and moaning and stomping on hankies.

Cassie Phillips, Nils Wilson, and Frank Service—all major network reporters—traveled with Ben's One Batt . . . and they were the only ones he would allow to get close to him.

"Casualties are amazingly light, Ben," Doctor Chase said.

"They won't be for long, Lamar. In a couple of days, Bruno is going to turn and make his stand."

Chase smiled. "Did your crystal ball tell you that?"

"Something like that. Are your supply trucks pulling up with your MASH units?"

"My trucks are up even and we've got plenty of whole blood. Those captured troops of Bottger's we examined are all healthy as horses. Bruno Bottger may be a nut and something of a monster, but his followers are as fit as the Rebels."

"Then if we run short of blood, take it from them."

"Look, Ben. I—"

"Take it from them!" Ben said, his eyes flashing a warning that, as far as he was concerned, the subject was closed.

"If the press learns that we forcibly took blood from prisoners, there'll be hell to pay, Ben."

"Fuck the press. Not one in ten has the sense to understand that we're over here fighting this war, in part, so they can continue to spew and print their babble. If they get in my way again, I'll shoot the lot of them and have done with it."

Chase laughed and stood up. "You are a mass of contradictions, Raines. You know that?"

"So I've been told. By you. Often."

Chuckling, Chase left the room.

Panting, Cooper stuck his head through an open back window. "I finally lost her. Man, she can run!" He started to climb in, and Jersey grabbed him by one leg and started pulling him back out. "Oh, shit!" Cooper hollered. "Don't let this heathen get me. She's going to ravish my body!"

"Beat him up if you want to, Jersey," Ben called. "But don't ravish his body."

"Fat chance of that!" Jersey hollered, struggling to pull Cooper out of the window. But Coop had a death grip on the sill and wasn't about to turn loose.

Ben sat down and opened his map case. "It's going to be a long night," he muttered.

"Turn me loose, Jersey!" Cooper yelled.

Ben smiled. "And a noisy one, too."

Seven

Bottger raced troops in from the East to plug the gap between Groningen, and Almelo and Ben did some fast reshuffling and moved troops around to the west side to meet them. Now the line was complete.

Afterwards, deep in thought, Ben stared at map after map. He considered taking some of his Rebels to beef up Smithson. Then he decided to shift his own people around and take command up North. Then he rejected both options. Georgi had positioned himself close enough to see and correct any tactical errors that Billy might commit, although he sure hadn't made any thus far—except for being a bit eager—if that could be called a flaw.

Ben looked again at the map. Although Cannes and Nice had already been taken once by the Rebels, while the meeting in Geneva had been taking place, Bottger had moved troops up and the Rebels had backed away.

Ike was down near Marseilles, Dan just north of him. From there on, south to north, it was West, Rebet, Danjou, Tina, O'Shea, Greenwalt, Jackie Malone, Gomez, Nick Stafford, Jim Peters, and Ben at the far north of the Rebels' sector. Georgi was in command of the resistance groups; and Buddy and his special ops people, among them many ex-Air Force combat controllers, were held in reserve. Ben knew that sooner or later some dirty job would need to be done and Buddy's special ops people would be called upon to do it.

Corrie turned in her chair. "Bottger's forces have turned to make their stand, Boss. Exactly where you said they would."

"Bump Georgi in code and tell him to keep an eye on Billy and his people. Don't let them screw up."

"Right."

"Put everyone on high alert. Advise the batt coms we shove off at dawn. There is nothing to be gained by a lot of tiptoeing around. Bottger can see us and we can see him."

"Where are we going, Chief?" Jersey asked.

"Straight across just as hard as we can drive. Before we're through, our lines are going to resemble an elongated L-shape, the bottom angle just as long as the side. If we're successful with this maneuver, Bottger can only run one way: straight east into Russia."

Cooper was studying a map, being careful to hold it over his face to hide his grin. "I always wanted to visit Italy. Those Italian women will never be the same after I get there."

Jersey made a terrible gagging sound.

Cooper started singing, very badly, "Indian Love Call."

"Oh, God!" Jersey said, standing up, holding her M-16 like a club.

Cooper lowered the map and got ready to take

flight. "Did you say something, my lovely little cactus flower?"

And the chase was on.

"We have enough votes to impeach," Vice President Hooter said proudly, looking around the room.

"Wonderful!" Immaculate Crapums cried, clapping his hands.

"Right on, sister!" Rita Rivers bellowed, then jumped up and did a little dance.

All the rest of those present in the conference room nodded their approval. I. M. Holey could do little more than nod; he was drunk.

"What about the military?" Wiley Ferret asked.

"We'll order them disbanded and use that money for something else. I need some roads that go nowhere in my state," Senator Arnold said. "Some *more* roads that go nowhere, that is," he added.

"Let's use some of the money to hire more secret police so we can spy better on our constituency," another liberal suggested.

"Wonderful idea!" Zipporah Washington yelled.

"We'll use some of the money for an ad campaign," Senator Benedict said. "The slogan will be: Joining The Republican Party Is As Dangerous To Your Health As Smoking Those Ol' Terrible Nasty Horrible Cigarettes."

"Wonderful idea!" Zipporah Washington yelled.

"I have a better idea," another liberal said. "Let's use some of the money to outlaw the Republican Party. Once that is done, we can put a bounty on the head of any Republican left alive."

"Wonderful idea!" Zipporah Washington yelled.

"Yes," Senator Arnold said. "After all, everyone with any sense knows that only liberal Democrats know what is best for everyone."

"Wonderful idea!" Zipporah yelled. Zipporah was not widely known for her originality.

I. M. Holey grunted, belched, lifted his leg and farted, and went back to sleep.

"I have a question," Wiley Ferret said, looking nervously around him. "What happens when we tell the army that we are now in control and they tell us to go to hell?"

"They wouldn't dare!" Vice President Hooter said. Hooter hated the military. During a grab-ass party years back, hers was the only ass that hadn't been grabbed by a military hand. She had been deeply offended.

"Go to hell," General Bodison told the vice president. "And get out of my office."

"How dare you speak to me in such a manner!" Harriet Hooter hollered. "I am the Vice President of the United States."

"Carry your ass," the general told her. "Blanton is President and he's going to remain in that job until the people vote him out."

"Congress has spoken!" Hooter thundered.

Bodison waited until the ringing in his ears had subsided and said, "Leave or I will have you removed, Ms. Hooter."

"I'll have your job for this!"

"Out!"

Outside the new Pentagon, Rita Rivers asked, "Did he ravish your body?"

"No."

"Next time, send me. I have a way with men."

Yeah. For ten bucks. Five on a slow night.

Corrie woke Ben up. Ben looked at his watch: Nearly three o'clock in the morning. He had slept as much as he usually did, for Ben required only a few hours of sleep. He grabbed for his pants. "What is it?"

"Hooter and those aligned with her made their power play against Blanton just a few hours ago," she told Ben. "The military stood tall and backed the President all the way. But the politically correct gun-grabbers swear they are the ones in power and are rallying a lot of people."

"The police?" Ben asked, pulling on his boots.

"Most of them back the military."

"Consensus?"

"A lot of blood is going to be shed before it's all over."

"All right. Get me Blanton on the horn."

Ben pulled a mug of coffee and picked up a dough-nut from the tray while Corrie dialed the President. "Homer, I hope you realize that your back is up against the wall now."

"I do, Ben."

"You ready to play in my ball park now?"

"Do I have a choice?"

"No."

"All right, Ben. Lay down the rules."

"I'm sending you four or five battalions of Rebels from the SUSA—as many as Cecil can spare. Can you put a muzzle on Harriet Hooter?"

"I'd have better luck attempting to muzzle a grizzly."

"Make an effort. Advise the lady and her followers that you now have the full backing of the SUSA, the United States military, and most of the police. She'll have to think about that before making any rash moves, which will give us time to get Cecil's Rebels in place. You're running a shattered, fragmented, and demoralized bunch of states, Homer. And I do not mean any criticism by that remark. Only that those against you will have little or no real organization. Tell General Bodison to arm those citizens who support you and whip them into shape. You're going to need all the help you can get."

Ben could hear the President sigh. "If you say so, Ben. I guess you're right."

"You didn't think your friends would ever turn against you, right?"

"Are you a mind reader, too, Ben?"

"No, I'm just good at guessing. Homer, before this is over, we both are going to have friends turn against us. And when the dust and smoke finally settles, I firmly believe that North America will be the temporary home of anywhere from four or five to a dozen or more separate nations. I saw that coming back in the late '80's. Some of those nations won't last as long as it takes for the ink to dry on their constitutions; Billy Smithson's all-white state won't last. It won't last any longer than an all-black state or nation, and that's coming, too. There'll be Latins who want their own state or nation, and Indians, and so on down the line. None of them will be permanent. But your nation and my nation, Homer, they'll last. We've got a chance to start over here. We can either make something good out of it or fuck it up. But we can't start by massive give-away programs and pitting one race against the other. We've all got to be on equal footing. If we're not, it won't work. People have got to learn that they, and they alone, control their own destinies. And if they screw up, it's nobody's fault but their own. We have to stop allowing excuses for criminal behavior—or you have to, that is. In the SUSA, we've already put a stop to that nonsense. We've got to bring honesty back to government and law. And that means if I screw up or you screw up, we pay the price. It's hard to accomplish, Homer. And I won't say we've done it to my satisfaction in the SUSA, but we're close. I guess that's the end of the speech, friend."

"Friend," Homer said softly. "I like the sound of that, Ben. Friend. Are we friends?"

"I think so."

"Then we are. It was a good speech, Ben. A very good one." He took a deep breath. "Nothing is going to destroy what remains of the United States, Ben. I won't allow it. If I have to lock up my vice president and that entire pack of kooks she has around her, by God, I will."

"Hang in there, Homer. I'll talk to you later. I've got a war to fight."

"Good luck, Ben. And I mean that, friend."

"I know you do. Same to you, friend. Raines out."

"Well, I'll be goddamned!" Lamar Chase spoke from behind Ben. "The world's biggest liberal and the world's hardest conservative have made friends. This is one for the history books."

Ben got up from the radio and stretched. "What the hell are you doing up at this hour, Lamar?"

"Went to bed too early. I thought you'd be up and prowling around, so I walked over. I'm glad I did. That was a momentous conversation."

"It may surprise you to learn that back before the Great War, I had a number of liberal friends, Lamar."

"Nothing about you surprises me, Ben. Not after all the years I've known you."

Ben poured another cup of coffee and once more glanced at his watch. "Your people up and moving, Lamar?"

"I imagine so."

Ben sat down on the corner of a battered table he'd been using for a deck.

Chase smiled. "Are you about to say something terribly dramatic, such as 'This is it, boys'?"

Ben laughed. "I hope not, Lamar."

"Far Eyes reporting movement up and down the eastern side of the line," Corrie called.

"Get the people up," Ben said. "High alert."

Lamar drained his coffee cup. "I'd better get back to my boys and girls." He paused at the door. "It's down to the nitty-gritty now, isn't it, Ben?"

"Yeah." Ben's reply was soft. "I won't kid you, Lamar. It's going to be a bad one from here on in."

"Just how far is 'in' going to be, Ben?"

Ben shrugged his shoulders. "We've been attempting to make contact with some Russian resistance groups. But no luck so far. We know they exist, but they're hesitant to answer us. I sure would like to have them on our side. With their help, we could put Bruno and his people in a box and nail the lid closed.''

"What about this serum he's working on?"

"Mike's people were ferreted out and killed. We don't have anybody left there in any position to let us know anything. We're going in blind."

Chase nodded. "Is Blanton going to hang tough and stay in power?"

"I think so. I hope so. Cecil can only do so much; and Blanton would never, under any circumstances, accept any help from Billy Smithson's people."

"Ben, should Hooter and her bunch somehow manage to gain power, we could walk over them without a great deal of trouble."

"I know. I just want an end to the trouble back home, but I'm afraid that's not going to be for a long, long time."

Chase hesitated. "I'll see you down the line, Ben," he said, then walked out into the darkness.

Ben took a quick shower, then shaved and dressed. He slipped into his body armor and battle harness and picked up his old Thompson. "Pack it up, people," he said. "Let's get this show on the road."

Eight

There was no finesse to this battle. As if on cue, the two armies slugged it out, day after long, loud, and bloody day. Billy Smithson's forces were stopped cold on the outskirts of Dusseldorf and Koln. As Ben had predicted, this was homeland for the MEF and anyone who tried to take it was going to pay in blood.

Ben began shifting artillery batteries north and flew up to Smithson's sector. "Start throwing in HE and willie peter," he ordered the beefed-up artillery batteries. "Around the clock. We'll burn them out."

It had not taken Smithson long to realize that once the fighting ceased and he and his people returned to America, the one person in the world he did not want to tangle with was Ben Raines. While the artillery roared, raining death and fire down on the cluster of cities, Billy, his senior advisors, and Ben Raines withdrew for lunch and conversation.

"Your people are doing a damn good job," Ben told Billy.

"And when this is over?" Billy asked.

"You go back to your all-white state."

"And you don't approve of that, do you, Ben?"

"Not really. Running away from a problem is not going to solve it."

"Perhaps not. But if we're free of Negroes, then it is no longer our problem, is it?"

Ben grimaced. Billy was an intelligent man, highly educated and good at debating, while Ben was on shaky ground and knew it. He had personally chased people of all races out of the SUSA—although not because of their color—and he knew that Billy would pounce on that given the slightest opportunity.

"Billy," he said, choosing his words carefully, "if you will recall back a few years, when the world was more or less intact, I got in hot water more than once when appearing on various talk shows promoting one book or the other."

Billy chuckled and so did most of his men. A few did not. They disliked Ben and made little attempt to hide it. "Most of us couldn't quite determine which side you were on."

"Unlike most liberals—of any color—I know there is some difference—albeit slight—between a separatist and a racist. If a person bought a section of land, fenced it in, built a home, and was qualified to teach his or her own children and could thus be left alone, I saw no harm in the situation. And I also felt a great deal of sympathy for those people who had worked for years to afford a good home in a nice, safe neighborhood and one day looked up and saw strangers with low-interest loans and other government-sponsored financial help moving in and fucking up the neighborhood. It was all done under a federal mandate, and it was wrong. It was well-intentioned; but nevertheless, it was wrong. Many individuals were simply not ready for the move—on both sides of the line. No government

an or should pass laws in an attempt to force me
o like you or you to like me. It just won't work.
Never has and never will." Ben looked at Billy and
miled. "And those types of people cross all color
nes, Billy."

Billy returned the smile . . . faintly.

One of Billy's senior advisors stood up and threw
is fork onto the table. "I just flat don't like you,
aines." He cut his eyes as Jersey clicked her M-16
ff safety. "Relax, little lady. I ain't gonna hurt your
recious general."

"I know that," Jersey said. "And don't call me 'lit-
le lady,' you lard-assed tub of guts."

"Easy, Junior," Billy said. "Sit down and tell Gen-
ral Raines why you don't like him." He looked at
Ben. "If you're interested in hearing it, that is."

Ben shrugged. He had already pegged Junior as a
die-hard racist who would never change; he would
o to his grave unreasonably hating anyone not of
is own color.

"I just don't like niggers or nigger-lovers," Junior
aid. "Never have, never will."

"That's your right," Ben said, pushing his plate
way and taking out tobacco sack and papers.

Junior stared at him, astonished. "My right?" he
sked finally.

"Sure." Ben rolled his cigarette and lit up.

Junior sat back down. "I suppose you're goin' to
ell me that you're not goin' to invade us when all
his mess is over and we get back home."

"Not me, Junior. I gave you my word. And as long
s Blanton is in power, neither will he—provided any
erson of color can pass through your state without

harm or harassment. The old U.S. of A. is going t
get stronger. They'll probably never be as strong a
the SUSA, but they'll grow and prosper. And the
won't trade with your state, Junior. That is *their* righ
And the SUSA doesn't have to trade with you. We'r
totally self-sufficient. You people might last, probabl
will last for a few years. But not much longer tha
that. Where are you going to buy fuel? And all th
things that you can't grow or produce? You've iso
lated yourselves in a little world of hate and intoler
ance. Think about it. How are you going to get you
raw materials out to sell? You can pass our border
I would allow that. But you must remember that the
President of the SUSA is a black man. He might no
be as charitable as I am. Iowa, Kansas, Nebraska, I
linois . . . why, they're a part of the USA. You can'
go through those states.

"No, Junior. You're surrounded. You have your all
white state—but damned if I can figure out ho
you're going to survive now that you have it."

For the first time in a long time, Vice Presiden
Harriet Hooter and those who followed her foune
themselves powerless to do much of anything. Presi
dent Blanton had virtually suspended the Constitu
tion and placed the nation under martial law. Ceci
Jefferys, President of the SUSA, had sent troops t
back Blanton, and things were looking rather grin
for the liberal wing of the Democratic Party.

And, horror of horrors, Blanton was actually *arm
ing* the people.

"Oh, icky-poo!" Immaculate Crapums said, stamp

ng his foot. "How could he do such a terrible hing?"

Rita Rivers was less charitable. "Goddamned honky on of a bitch!" she cussed the President.

To protest his actions, the First Lady had moved out of their bedroom and cut Homer off cold. But as President of the United States, Homer could get ust about anything he wanted. Discreetly. Which he mmediately set about doing.

Ben and his team entered the smoking rubble of Dusseldorf with Billy and his people. The Germans— hose over twenty or so years of age—greeted them vith wild enthusiasm.

"We destroyed their city and their homes," Billy aid. "And still they cheer us."

"The adults," Ben said. "Not the younger ones. They're still solidly in Bottger's pocket. Look at the hate in their eyes."

"Sort of reminds me of the look in the eyes of some of my men." Billy spoke the words softly.

"Don't get too chummy with me, Billy," Ben warned him. "They're going to turn on you. And some of my people will mutiny, too. Not that it makes much difference how friendly we get, I suppose. It's already in the works—on both sides."

Billy gave him a sharp look. "Some of your troops are planning to betray you?"

"Yes. With some of your people."

"Fact or guesswork?"

"Fact."

"How many of your people?"

"Eight to ten percent of them."

"And mine?"

"Thirty to forty percent."

"Damn!" Billy swore, something he rarely did. "Because of our coming over here?"

"That's a small part of it. According to the information I'm getting, the betrayal in your ranks started even before you began purging Missouri of people of color. Those who are plotting against you want to spread out, to encompass more territory. About half of those thirty or forty percent support Bottger."

"We'll talk at length later, Ben. I just noticed that we're being followed."

Ben grinned. "Junior's bunch. We picked up on them the day I arrived. Don't worry. They're being followed by my people. Oh, that new bunch who just came over to join your battalion?"

"Yes. What about them?"

"They're Rebels. All of them raised in Missouri. I thought you'd like some people around you that you could one hundred percent depend on."

Billy chuckled. "We're going to end up on the same side yet, you know that?"

"I'm counting on it, Billy."

Billy had a frown on his face and a puzzled look in his eyes as he watched Ben stroll away, a security blanket surrounding him. Then he smiled. "The man never misses a trick," he muttered.

He did not notice when a man wearing sergeant's stripes and Rebel BDUs fell in beside Ben.

"Mike," Ben said, eyeballing the collar pins. "Have you been demoted?"

"I blend in better this way," Mike said. "We've got to talk, Ben. Big trouble brewing."

"I'll see you at my quarters in about an hour, all right?"

"I'll be there. And get ready to pull out in a hurry—we've got traitors all around us. More than even I first thought."

At his quarters, an empty house on the outskirts of town, Ben told Lt. Bonelli to prepare to evacuate when he gave the signal.

"My people are all loyal, General," Bonelli said. "I'd bet my life on it."

"That's exactly what we're both betting," Ben told him.

When Mike showed up, he had a worried look on his face. He spoke openly in front of Jersey, Beth, Corrie, and Cooper. "About half of Billy's boys are turning on him. There will be a sneak attack on his CP tonight; it'll be blamed on Bottger. The attack will coincide with an attack here. They're going to try to kill both of you . . ."

Ben opened his mouth to speak, and Mike waved him silent with a slash of his hand.

"There will be an attempt on Blanton's life and an attack on the northern and eastern borders of the SUSA within hours after the attacks over here. It's been in the planning stages for weeks—the attacks on Blanton and on our borders probably much longer than that."

"Billy doesn't have that many men left Stateside to pull it off," Ben said.

"They've recruited all those people who have been gathering at our borders. Of all colors. They'll be used as cannon fodder. And then disposed of. Any that are left, that is.''

Lt. Bonelli walked in. "Something weird going on outside, General. Smithson's men are throwing up a circle around his CP. They're doing it slowly and quietly, but we could still pick up on it.''

Mike quickly briefed the man while Corrie was busy on the horn, alerting all the Rebels attached to this contingent of Smithson's troops what was going down. She was using burst transmissions in code, so there was no way any of Billy's turncoats could understand the messages.

When she had finished, Ben said, "Corrie, get hold of Ike and have him bump Cecil. Tell Cecil to warn Blanton, personally. He's going to have to figure out how to do that. We don't know whom to trust in this, so everybody is suspect. Goddamnit!" Ben lost his temper for a moment. He took several deep breaths and forced himself to calm down. He turned to Mike. "How many of our people are involved in this treachery?''

Mike hesitated. "About twelve to fifteen percent, Ben. There were three attached to your personal company. Davis, Peterson, and Bosman. They have been neutralized," he added without change of tone or expression.

"Won't that alert Smithson's men?''

"No. The vehicle they were riding in was involved in an . . . accident The three were injured and air lifted back to our own lines. More or less," he added drily.

Ben didn't pursue that. Davis, Peterson, and Bosman would never be seen again.

Ben was thinking fast. "We're due to be resupplied this afternoon. The airport is clear. Instead of supplies, have those transports filled with Buddy and his special ops people. Get them moving right now, Corrie. And when you're finished with that, get me Smithson on the horn."

She nodded and went to work. A few minutes later, she handed Ben the mike. "Billy, those percentages we spoke of about an hour ago . . . you recall them?"

Billy picked up on it immediately. "Yes, I do, Ben. What about them?"

"Well, the ante's been upped quite a bit. I suppose you could say we're literally surrounded by facts and we're going to have to find a way to wade through them."

"I . . . see. Well, I don't like paperwork any better than you do, Ben. I always try to eliminate as much of it as possible. Sometimes it's unfortunate, but unavoidable."

"Oh, I agree with you. But with many of these papers, it's difficult to tell which are important and which are not. So I'm sending you some experts to help you sort through the maze."

"I certainly appreciate that, Ben. More than I can say. When might I expect them?"

"Momentarily, Billy. They are really quite good and, if you don't mind, I would suggest you follow their lead."

"I will do that, Ben. Without question."

"I'll talk to you later, Billy."

"Right. Good luck on your sorting through the maze, Ben. Billy out."

"I like that man, Ben," Mike said.

"So do I, Mike. He just lost his reason for a time. He blamed an entire race of people when it was the system at fault. I think he knows that." He turned to Corrie. "What is Buddy's ETA?"

"1500."

"Everybody in body armor and high alert. If Junior and his bunch get antsy, it's going to get downright nasty around here."

"In a hurry," Beth added.

Nine

Homer Blanton sat in his office and waited until the hot anger within him had cooled somewhat. He did not want to believe anything Cecil Jefferys had told him. But he knew Ben Raines would not alert him if he didn't have concrete proof of the betrayal.

But even Ben did not know exactly who in his administration was behind all the treachery or a part of it. But Homer thought he did—after some careful thinking. He picked up the phone and asked the chief of the White House detail of the Secret Service to come into his office. Then Homer Blanton, the most anti-gun President the nation had ever elected, opened a side drawer of his desk and took out a Colt Diamondback .38. He kept it in his right hand, out of sight of the Secret Service man. He waved the man to a seat using his left hand. Then he turned on a small radio and cranked up the volume. He leaned close to the man and began talking in low tones.

Homer laid it all out to the Secret Service chief, watching his facial expression closely. The man was either the greatest actor ever born or he was hearing of this for the first time.

The man's eyes widened when Homer lifted his

right hand, showing him the .38. He had not been aware the President even owned a gun.

"Jeff," Blanton said, "we've got to trust each other. But if you've turned on me, you will be the first one I plug. And that's a promise."

Jeff struggled to keep a straight face. "Plug, sir?"

"It sounded good at the time."

Then both men laughed and the tension and distrust was broken.

"This office is not bugged, sir. I swept it only a few hours ago."

"My phones?"

"The red one is secure. I'm sure of that."

"Good. That's where the call from Cecil Jefferys came in. How about the phones in your office?"

"One of them is secure. I know that for a fact."

"Use it and get in touch with General Bodison. Bring him up to date. I've got to trust Bodison. You two plan what we're going to do."

"You can trust him, sir. And I know a number of others you can trust. I'll start gathering the troops."

"Discreetly, Jeff. Very discreetly. I want those involved in this betrayal to show their hands."

"Yes, sir."

"Jeff?"

"Sir?"

"Get my wife clear of Charleston."

"Right away, sir."

"Jeff?"

"Sir?"

"Hit her on the head if you have to. Just get her clear."

Jeff smiled.

"You don't have to look so happy," Homer said with a small grin.

"No, sir. Of course not." Jeff managed to get out of the oval office without laughing.

Blanton punched a button on his intercom. "Is my vice president here yet?"

"She's in the building, sir. On her way up."

"Are the others with her?"

"Yes, sir."

"Send them right in."

"Yes, sir."

Homer checked the loads in the .38 and clicked the wheel closed. Suddenly he felt better than he had in years. Everything was sharp and clear in his mind. Ben's words came back to him.

We've all got to be on equal footing. If we're not, it won't work. We control our own destinies. If I screw up or if you screw up, we pay the price. We're no better than anybody else.

Homer looked at the pistol in his hand. What gave him the right to own a gun when most others could not? What gave him the right to have around-the-clock protection by highly armed guards and the entire military complex when ninety-nine percent of Americans (those living outside of the SUSA, that is) lived in fear of their lives? What made him so special that if his life were threatened—even by long-distance phone calls or by letter or E-mail—the person making the threat could be arrested immediately and then sent to prison for years, when the average citizen had no such protection or anything even remotely like it?

"I am no better than anyone else," Homer muttered. "If I can be protected by dozens of armed guards, everybody else should have that same right, or the equivalent thereof." He smiled. "Now I understand, Ben. It's taken me a year, but I finally got it through my thick skull."

"Vice President Hooter to see you, sir," his secretary said.

"Send her in."

"Now you see here, Homer," Harriet Hooter hollered before she even got through the door. "What you've done is unconscionable. Who the hell do you think you are? What gives you the right to . . ."

Outside the office, Blanton's secretary screamed. The door was slammed open and Harriet was knocked out of the way and onto the floor by two Secret Service men, both of them carrying pistols. They fired simultaneously, their slugs taking the President in the chest. Homer Blanton fell out of his chair and lay on the floor in a puddle of his own blood.

"Cecil says he spoke personally with Blanton," Corrie said, "but he can't reach him now. Something has gone wrong."

Mike ran into the room, out of breath. "Charleston reports that ambulances have been summoned to the White House following a volley of shots within the residence."

"Shit!" Ben cussed. "It's started. Any word on who got hurt or killed?"

Mike shook his head. "No. But I could take a guess and be right on the money."

"Buddy and battalion have landed and come under heavy fire from Smithson's contingent at the airport!" Corrie called.

"We're next," Ben said, picking up his Thompson. "And we're out of running room."

Corrie had slipped the headphones on to lessen the noise and confusion in the room. "Smithson's surrounded by troops loyal to him and they're holding," she called. "Our people are with him and say it looks pretty good. We're fairly evenly matched all the way around. If Buddy and his spec ops can bust out of the airport, we'll put the turncoats on the run."

"Here they come!" Cooper yelled. Coop had managed to wrangle a SAW—a 5.56 squad automatic weapon—along with half-a-dozen boxes, each containing 200 rounds in a belt—and was positioning himself at a window. "They've busted through our weak side!"

"Slow them up, Coop," Ben said, moving to a window just as Coop started rocking and rolling and screams of pain came from the side yard. Ben leveled the old Thompson and held the trigger back. The fat slugs tore into flesh and shattered bone, and the line of Smithson's turncoats went down like pins in a bowling alley. Ben fought the rise of the weapon until the clip was empty, then ejected the clip and fitted a drum into the belly of the weapon and knelt down.

Beth was kneeling behind a Big Thumper, the Mark 19-3 40mm automatic grenade launcher, and she had turned the other side of the yard into a slaughterhouse as the Big Thumper spat out anti-personnel grenades at about 40 grenades per minute. The anti-personnel mini-bombs had a killing range of about seventeen feet, and Beth was filling the air with shrapnel, shredding flesh from shattered bone. The bodies were stacking up in her perimeter and those troops who unwisely attacked her side of the CP were rapidly having a change of heart.

More than half-a-dozen Rebel MBTs came clanking and rumbling up, machine guns hammering. The tank commanders used no finesse in this fight. They just began circling the small battlefield and running over the turncoat troops, crushing them under the treads of the sixty-ton tanks.

It was anything but a pleasant sight, and the sounds were even less appealing.

The attack against Ben's CP was over. Ben had a cut on one cheek; Cooper had taken a burn on the left arm, and Mike had a splinter embedded in his right forearm. Other than that, no one among the Rebels had been hurt. The MBTs had assumed a defensive circle around the building.

"Get me a report from the airport," Ben called, coughing in the thick gunsmoke that filled the room.

"Say again, say again." Corrie was speaking into her mike. She listened, then turned to Ben. "Buddy's people broke through and put the turncoats on the run. Billy's troops at his CP held. The attack appears to be over." She grimaced as her headset filled with frantic calls. "All battalions, all battalions. This is Big Chick. Everything OK at the Eagle's Nest. We had a little trouble. It's over. Eagle to Shark, Eagle to Shark." She turned and nodded at Ben. "Ike on the horn."

Ben took the mike. "Ike, try to find out what's happening Stateside. We have reports that Blanton's been shot or killed. Looks like a revolution is starting over there. Give me a bump as soon as you know something."

Ben turned to his team. "Let's go find Billy."

Ninety percent of the Secret Service was loyal to Blanton. Jeff ran up the hall with two of his men and shot the turncoat agents dead in the doorway.

"Rebels are ringing the grounds with troops and tanks!" a Secret Service agent shouted.

"But what goddamn side are they on?" another agent yelled.

"If they're not with us, we're fucked!" Jeff called.

Jeff knelt down beside Blanton. "He's alive! Get an ambulance."

"I am in command," Harriet Hooter said. "Remove the Rebels from the grounds. Immediately!"

"Fuck you," Jeff told the Vice President.

"Now?" Rita asked.

"What did you say to me?" Harriet roared at the Secret Service agent.

"You couldn't command a gang bang," Jeff told her. "You're a joke. You've always been a joke—a very profane joke. Now get the hell out of my way and stay out of my way."

While Harriet sputtered and stuttered in shock, Jeff told an agent, "Get General Bodison over here. He's in charge."

"The fucking *military* in charge!" Harriet hollered.

"We're all doomed!" Immaculate Crapums shrieked.

"Done for," Senator Benedict droned.

"The nation is through," Senator Arnold said.

"We'll be in the hands of fascists!" I. M. Holey said.

Blanton opened his eyes and groaned. "Jeff," he whispered.

"Yes, sir?"

"If another one of those nitwits opens his mouth . . . shoot him!"

Jeff grinned at the President. "Yes, sir. With great pleasure."

"Did you get my wife clear?"

"Yes, sir. She's safe. And I didn't have to hit her."

"Good. On both counts. How bad off am I?"

"You took two good ones, sir. One high up in the shoulder and the other one in the side. But the bleeding is not excessive. I think you're going to be all right."

"You sure couldn't prove it by me. Any word from General Raines?"

"Nothing, sir."

Another agent knelt beside the President. "Sir, General Bodison is on the way. He'll be here in a few minutes. The grounds are secure."

"What about me?" Harriet squalled.

"Take a hike," Blanton told her.

"You want me to shoot her?" Jeff asked.

Harriet squealed and hit the door, followed quickly by her supporters.

The room filled with medical personnel and Rebels, and Blanton was lifted onto a stretcher and wheeled out. General Bodison entered and looked at the Rebel commander. "You on our side, son?"

"All the way, sir."

"Good boy." Bodison looked at the desk in the Oval Office. He shook his head. "I do not want this goddamn job."

"I'll take it!" Harriet shouted from the hall.

"On second thought . . ." Bodison muttered, and walked toward the desk.

"The United States of America is under martial law," Corrie told Ben and Billy. "General Bodison is now sitting in the Oval Office."

Billy Smithson had suffered a minor arm wound during the brief rebellion. Rebel medics had patched him up and given him two aspirin for pain.

"The fools should have known they couldn't pull this off," Billy said. "Here or back home."

"How many Rebels were involved in this, Mike?" Ben asked.

"Reports are still coming in. But it looks like each battalion had between seventy-five and a hundred turncoats. Some more, some less."

"Say two thousand all told."

"That's a good ballpark figure."

"About thirty-eight percent of your people turned on you, Billy," Mike said.

"About seventy-five hundred men," Billy said, his face tight with anger. "May God have mercy on their treacherous souls—for I don't intend to . . . if I ever find them."

"Oh, we'll run into them again," Buddy Raines said, appearing in the doorway.

"What do you mean, son?" Ben asked, looking his

son over. Buddy's face was streaked with dirt, but he did not appear to be hurt.

"Those who survived went eastward. I assume they joined with Bottger. One of the few prisoners we took told me he thought Bruno Bottger to be a very great man."

"I believe we discussed that very possibility, Ben," Billy said.

"Yes. We sure did." Ben sighed and sat down. "I felt there would be a few Rebels who would align with Bottger . . . but my God, not this many. How many senior people went with him, Mike?"

"None. And we can be thankful for that."

Ben stood up. "Let's start reorganizing and get ready for another push. We came over here to do a job. Let's get back to it. Corrie, order all Rebels being held in reserve to get to the front ASAP. I want full reports from all batt coms, reports from Cecil, and reports on the situation in Charleston. I want to be on top of things before they happen. Let's go, people."

Billy watched Ben as he strode out of the building, his team with him. He cut his eyes to Buddy Raines. "Does anything ever shake him up?"

Buddy smiled. "I've seen him shook up over a woman every now and then . . . but not for very long."

"The right one hasn't come along yet, hey?"

"Yes," Buddy said with a sigh. "She came along. They met shortly after the Great War, when conditions were chaotic. I really don't know all the details. But years later, my father buried her in the northwest part of the United States. Her name was Jerre. From what I understand, theirs was a relationship that was doomed from the start. But they did love each other in a strange way. He never talks about Jerre and he probably never will."

"This was your mother, son?"

"Oh, no. Good God, no. My mother was a perverted, crazed, evil woman. She hated Ben Raines. Her one goal in life was to destroy him. Then when I left her, she had two goals: To destroy both of us."

"What happened to her?"

"Her hate did her in . . . with a little help from Ike." He picked up his weapon and slung it over his shoulder. "What do you want done with the prisoners we took from your contingent?"

Billy's eyes went suddenly bleak and cold.

"You and my father do share a few things in common," Buddy said, then walked out the door.

Ten

The attack on the borders of the SUSA almost fizzled before it started. When the takeover in Charleston failed, Smithson's men in charge of gathering the rabble along the border ran for their lives. The mob made a few halfhearted attempts to cross the borders, but after being thrown back several times in bloody charges, they gave up and returned to their former vocations of bitching and whining and parading up and down in various locations throughout the nation.

Vice President Harriet Hooter resigned in a huff and took a dozen or so men and women with her. She started a new political party, calling it Americans Selected to Serve Honorably and Onward for the Liberal Endeavor. When it was pointed out to her that the name made absolutely no sense and the acronym was ASSHOLE, Harriet answered, "Only a very sexist, inconsiderate, unfeeling, politically incorrect person would make anything vulgar of it."

ASSHOLE started a registration drive and immediately began attracting hordes of people to its ranks. Their first convention, held a week after Homer Blanton was shot and General Bodison took over the running of the government, was something that had not been seen since Barnum and Bailey put together their first sideshow.

People showed up waving McGovern-for-President and McCarthy-for-President banners; and outside, people held placards that read: WHERE ARE YOU RONALD REAGAN NOW THAT WE NEED YOU? And GEORGE BUSH PLEASE COME BACK.

Inside, Harriet Hooter took the rostrum and immediately launched into a wild, screaming, arm-waving tirade against General Ben Raines and the Rebels; President Cecil Jefferys of the SUSA; President Homer Blanton; General Bodison, Acting President of the United States; the Republican Party; the National Rifle Association; Charlton Heston; the Army, Navy, Air Force, Marine Corps, and Coast Guard; all the cops everywhere, and anyone who didn't agree with everything Harriet said, while Rita Rivers worked the crowds and tried to pick up a few bucks turning tricks under the bleachers. She only had one taker, however, and he turned out to be a man who had gotten into the wrong line out front and was wearing a Gerald Ford-for-President button. But for twenty bucks and fifteen minutes, Rita could put political differences aside.

The convention broke up after putting forth these resolutions: One, the only way to solve America's problems was to immediately raise taxes. Two, cut the work week to twenty hours and set up medical facilities and build new welfare offices to accommodate all the uneducated, illiterate, unemployable new people who would arrive once the borders and coastlines were opened up. Three, take away their machetes as soon as they land—carrying a brick to bash someone's head in was all right, but machetes were a no-no.

Since they couldn't agree on a fourth resolution, the convention was adjourned until the following week, when they would meet again to discuss passing a resolution jailing anyone who was found with a terrible ol' handgun in their home or vehicle. We just have to put an end to violence, you know?

"ASSHOLE?" Ben said after reading the article in a Stateside newspaper. Hundreds of newspapers were flown over with the supplies every day from the States.

"The name fits that pack of nitwits," Cooper said.

President Blanton was recovering nicely from the assassination attempt and was expected to be back at work in a few weeks.

"I bet that was a shock to the V.P. when Blanton kicked her out of power," Beth said.

"She'll be back," Jersey remarked, reading the same newspaper. "This new party she started is attracting followers like flies to shit."

"What a feminine phrase," Cooper said with a grimace.

Jersey flipped him the bird.

"But nicely put," Ben said.

For reasons known only to the oftentimes fickle gods of war, the battle lines had not moved an inch either way in three weeks. There had been only a few shots fired from either side. Ben was taking the time to realign his troops, and Bottger was using the respite to rush reinforcements and supplies to the front.

Since the Rebels were now firmly established in Bottger's claimed territory, hundreds of French, Swiss, German, and Italian men and women had enlisted in the Free Forces of those countries fighting with the Rebels. But still the Rebels and the Free Forces were badly outnumbered as they waited for the assault to begin anew.

Billy Smithson had softened his attitude toward the black race, but not enough to open the borders of his newly claimed state. Not yet.

The Rebel troops rested up and down the long front, writing letters, reading, resupplying for the next push against Bottger's MEF.

Finally, after months of trying, Ben began getting some word out of Russia—the country was in total chaos. Norway, Finland, and Sweden were not much better, but the newly formed governments had their hands full attempting to bring some order and stability back to those countries and could offer only limited help to Ben and his troops.

The Balkan nations had exploded in war several years before the Great War that nearly destroyed the world, and they were still at war. Ethnic cleansing, it was called.

"Peacekeepers is what soldiers like us used to be called," Ben said to his team, laying his newspaper aside. "They were brave men wearing blue berets and got the shit shot out of them."

"Why didn't they shoot back?" Cooper asked.

"Most of the time they were under orders not to. That's why I made it perfectly clear to the Secretary General of the United Nations that we were most definitely not peacekeepers. Corrie, what is Bottger up to?"

"Whatever he's doing, he's keeping off the air," she replied. "But we do know for sure that those turncoat Rebels and Smithson's men did join with him. They were formed into one oversized battalion and positioned facing Billy's people."

"Interesting move on Bottger's part," Ben muttered. "Corrie, alert all battalions we jump off tomorrow morning at dawn. Let's get this show on the road. Get the HumVee ready, Coop."

An artillery barrage is a dead giveaway that an assault is on the way, so Ben stood his artillery down and began sending in teams of scouts and spec op people as soon as it was dark. Rebel radio operators kept up normal chatter, and the troops did not vary the day-to-day routines that Bottger's troops had grown accustomed to over the quiet weeks.

Ben was up an hour earlier than his usual time; but this morning, so was every Rebel troop up and down the line. There was no chatter and no movement unless it was absolutely necessary. Everything that might rattle or tinkle had either been stowed or taped. At three o'clock, the Rebels began moving out. At four o'clock, spec ops people silently cut the throats of Bottger's men guarding the tunnel at St. Bernard's Pass and Ben, leading his battalion, began moving into Italy.

"All you lovely and lonely Italian women, here I come," Cooper whispered.

"As soon as they see you, they'll run the other way," Jersey told him. "Now shut up."

Fortunately, the lights were out in the tunnel and

there was no traffic as the Rebels stealthily walked the dark length. Capturing and holding the tunnel and the bridge just beyond it was imperative—and it was chancy, for the Rebels would have no tank support for several hours. The lines were so close together that as soon as the tanks roared into life, Bottger's men would know something was in the works.

Ben's One Batt and the spec ops people with him had to hold the pass with only light weapons and mortars until the tanks and support troops could link up with them. Every Rebel in Ben's One Batt was carrying extra ammunition and mortar rounds. The fact that it was pouring down a cold rain was both good and bad. It helped hide the sounds of the Rebels' advance, but it also reduced visibility and the planes that were to have struck at dawn were now counted out because of fog and mist— they wouldn't be able to see the targets and might drop payloads on advancing Rebels . . . providing the troops got out of the tunnel at all.

Ben sent the spec ops people ahead when the main force was only a hundred feet from the eastern entrance. And it was a good thing he did, for the spec ops team still had about fifty feet to go when one of the guards suddenly sensed something and whirled around, lifting his weapon. The spec ops team cut him down, along with the three other guards who were out in the open.

"Let's go!" Ben yelled. "Go. Go. Go!" He took off running for the mouth of the tunnel. As he usually did when weight and ammunition was a factor, Ben was carrying an M-16, fitted with a bloop tube for firing 40mm grenades.

Ben reached the mouth of the tunnel and bellied down, waving Rebels on. "Both sides of the pass!" he shouted "Stretch out and get behind cover. And watch your footing in this rain. Those rocks are slicker than owl shit. Corrie! Get those tanks rolling."

Rebels were attacking at fifty different locations up and down the front, but this attack on the pass was different for this was a vital link and Bruno would have troops standing close by.

"Get those ATs out as quickly as possible," Ben called.

The anti-tank mines were rushed up and laid out as fast as the Rebels could work.

"And take it easy arming them," Ben added, knowing that the Rebels, when setting the single or double safeties on the timer (depending on the type of mine), sometimes cut it very short. "If we can cripple the lead tanks, they'll block the road and give us even more time," Ben said to no one in particular.

"And we're going to need some time," Corrie called. "MEF tanks are on the way in a hurry. I'm locked on to their frequency."

"Our MBT's are one hour away at top speed," Beth said.

"The roads are shit," Cooper spoke around a wad of gum. "Make it ninety minutes max for them."

"For once I agree with you," Jersey said.

"Thank you, my lovely little desert sandstorm," Cooper said, edging around so Ben was between him and Jersey.

"Dragons in place," Corrie said.

"Tell those gunners I want the lead two tanks to pass their positions," Ben told her. "When they set off the ATs, fire; then knock out any between the hits. Got it?"

Corrie radioed the orders, knowing why Ben was doing this. If he could have six burning tanks blocking the two-lane road, they had a chance of holding until help arrived.

"We've got to get across the St. Bernard Bridge and hold it from the other end and keep Bottger's men from blowing it," Ben said. "We've got to keep that bridge intact."

But he had no way of knowing whether or not the twisting bridge was wired to blow.

The rainy night suddenly boomed as anti-tank rockets were fired and were right on target. The darkness was briefly illuminated as tanks rolled onto ATs and set them off. Two more explosions were heard, and Ben was up and running out of the tunnel toward the bridge, yelling for his people to follow him—Jersey, Beth, Corrie, and Cooper keeping pace with him.

"Goddamnit, General!" Lt. Bonelli hollered. "Will you wait for the rest of us? *Goddamnit!*"

Ben shouted, "Come on, people. Come on. Let's take this bridge and do it now!" He disappeared into the rain-swept darkness.

Rebels surged forward out of the tunnel, following Ben into the unknown.

Far ahead of him, Ben could see dozens of headlights pocking the rain and darkness, the drivers pushing their trucks as fast as they dared in the rain; the trucks were carrying troops from Bottger's MEF.

"Who's got the M-60?" Ben yelled.

"Right here, sir!"

"Set it up and take out that first truck. Aim just above the headlights."

The M-60 roared and rattled, and the lead truck suddenly slewed to one side as the 7.62 mm rounds shredded the windshield and took out the driver and anyone else in the cab. The truck tipped over and the sounds of grinding metal against concrete was loud in the night; sparks flew for a few seconds. When the sparking and grinding ceased, the bridge was effectively blocked—at least for a short time anyway. Ben was running toward the lights, his Rebels right behind him.

They ran past the first of the burning tanks and the sickeningly sweet smell of seared human flesh coming from inside the hollow steel hulls. Not that far away, Ben could see other figures running toward them.

"Here!" he panted to the M-60 crew. "Take them down."

Cooper was carrying his SAW and he added his own .223 melody to the 7.62 mm song of the M-60. The first row of enemy soldiers crumpled and went down. Another truck began wobbling from side to side, banging against the heavy, steel-reinforced concrete barriers on each side of the bridge, and then toppled over onto its side, sliding to a halt.

Ben led the first wave of the Rebels into battle, going *mano a mano* with the lead troops of Bottger's MEF.

Bottger's troops had met many an enemy before this stormy, rainy night, but they had never faced the savage fury of the Rebels in hand-to-hand combat. It was no contest and it didn't take the MEF long to realize that.

When the magazines in Rebel weapons emptied, they either took the weapons away from the MEF and used them or started swinging their own weapons like heavy clubs, smashing heads and splitting skulls. Some Rebels pulled out long-bladed knives and went to work, cutting and slashing. The blood mixed with the rain on the long bridge.

"Verruckt leute!" more than one MEF troop yelled. Crazy people!

Twelve hundred yelling, screaming, shouting, and cursing Rebels now crowded onto the bridge, literally forcing the MEF troops into retreat. It was eyeball-to-eyeball fighting in the cold rain. The MEF had never seen anything like it, and they soon discovered they had no stomach for it. The MEF turned and began running eastward, trying to get away from the shrieking mass of crazy people on the bridge.

The Rebels gave chase and, for the first few minutes of the cold wet fight, offered no chance for surrender. Bottger would receive field reports from some of the survivors stating that Rebels bodily picked up MEF troops and hurled them over the side of the bridge. Others stated that the Rebels behaved like lunatics and fought like savages.

And it was not just at this one point where the Rebels showed the MEF what they were made of. All along the hundreds-of-miles-long front, the Rebels and the resistance forces slammed into Bottger's troops and put them into a rout, fighting with a seemingly wild fury and a cold dedication the enemy had never before encountered and simply could not withstand.

At the pass, Rebel tanks arrived and shoved the ruined enemy tanks and trucks over the side and rumbled across the bridge.

"Take a break," Ben finally ordered when his people were several miles deep into Italy and on the outskirts of a small town. "Let's find out where everybody else is north and south of us. Check the bridge for explosives. This day is ours."

Eleven

Just as dawn was splitting the skies, the rain ceased, the fog lifted, and the sun began breaking through, lighting the bloody morning. The mayor of the small town of Courmay rode out to meet with Ben. He was so happy to see the troops of the World Stabilization Forces, tears were running down his face. Ben thought for a moment the mayor was going to kiss him.

Bonelli stepped up and translated for Ben. "The MEF stopped running when they reached Aosta, the capital of this valley. It's called Valle d'Aosta. He says that Bottger's troops were badly mauled."

"You guys kicked the shit out of them, Joe," a boy of about ten said in English.

Doctor Chase walked over and looked at the boy.

"What the hell are you doing up here?" Ben demanded of the chief of medicine.

"Oh, shut up, Raines," the doctor said, inspecting the boy. "He's in pretty good shape. I'll start setting up for mass inoculation of the children."

"The mayor says his people have prepared a feast for us," Bonelli said.

"Can we trust him?" Ben asked.

"Oh, yeah, you betcha, General Raines," the boy said. "Everything's cool with us."

Ben laughed at the boy. "What's your name?"

"Mario."

"All right, Mario. You go with Doctor Chase here and do what he tells you to do, O.K.?"

"O.K., General. I'm hip."

Mario walked off with Chase. Bonelli listened to the mayor for a moment, then said, "The boy's family was killed by the MEF two years ago. They were all resistance fighters. He has no one and lives hand to mouth. The mayor said the boy is a savage. He's been known to slip into MEF camps at night and cut throats while the soldiers slept."

"Sounds like our kind of people," Ben said. "If he wants to go, we'll take him with us."

The press, in the form of Cassie, Nils, and Frank, had pulled up and were listening, taking notes.

"I know just the family back home for him," Bonelli said.

"If he wants to go," Ben cautioned. "Tell the mayor we'll be in his village later on today. Have scouts recon the town and make sure it isn't a trap. Corrie, let's get set up and start receiving field reports."

Bonelli said, "The mayor wants to know what happens to those people who collaborated with the enemy?"

"It's his town," Ben replied. "Do what he thinks has to be done."

Bonelli translated, and the mayor's eyes turned hard. "It will be done," he said in French, for this was mostly a French-speaking part of the country.

Ben did not need a translation for that.

* * *

As Ben worked through the morning, he could clearly hear the sounds of gunshots coming from the small village down the valley. Those who had gotten in bed with the troops of the MEF—sometimes literally—were paying a heavy price for it. Ben did not interfere with the executions. He was here to stabilize the country and help set up a workable government. The citizens knew how best to deal with traitors.

The Rebels of One Batt rested and dried out wet clothing under the warmth of the sun. Supply trucks came through, and everybody got two pairs of fresh, clean, and dry socks. Take care of your feet, and your feet will take care of you.

Ben studied the latest communiques: Denmark had acted, and their troops had thrown up a barrier along their border with Bottger's New Federation, cutting off any escape in that direction. But Norway and Sweden had their hands full. Both countries had troops along the Finnish border, for outlaws from Russian prisons had escaped just after the outbreak of the Great War and now controlled much of that country, threatening to spill over into Sweden and then into Norway. Their numbers had swelled as more and more outlaws poured into the country, either killing or driving out most of the decent folks and enslaving, or attempting to enslave, the rest. There were a number of Finnish resistance groups scattered around the country, but they were vastly outnumbered by the outlaws.

"If we don't get any response out of Russia, I know where we'll probably go next," Ben muttered.

"I can hardly wait," Corrie said. "I have this picture of Cooper on skis. What a sight."

"Oh, boy," Cooper said. "Great big blonde Scandinavian babes!"

Jersey groaned.

And Beth, who almost never entered into the banter, looked up from her paperwork and said, "You mean you've finally outgrown magic fingers, Coop."

Coop left the room with as much dignity as he could muster, doing his best to ignore the laughter.

Bruno Bottger was silent in thought. He had just received word that all the people he had sent into Russia to organize groups had been found—hanging from tree limbs just inside the Polish border with Belarus. Notes found pinned to their coats left no room for doubt about the feelings of the people there toward Bottger's policies and tactics.

He had no place left to run now that his northern borders had been sealed tight by those damnable Danes. Oh, well, he thought with a sigh, who wants to go to that dismal country anyway?

And Bruno, vain though he was, knew at last for a fact that his MEF would never defeat the Rebels. He smiled sadly. It wasn't the end of the world. Just the end of him. But his dream would never die. He reached into a desk drawer and took out a Luger, the same pistol that his grandfather had carried while serving the greatest leader the world had ever known: Adolf Hitler. Bruno Bottger lifted the muzzle to his temple.

* * *

Ben looked at Corrie, speechless for a moment. 'Would you repeat that, Corrie?!'

"I said Bruno Bottger is dead. He killed himself at his castle in Eastern Germany about an hour ago. Some of his generals want to discuss surrender terms."

"One defeat and he kills himself?" Ben questioned. "No way. I don't believe it. *Some* of his generals?"

"Right. A lot of the MEF refuse to surrender."

"It's a trick, Corrie. Bruno Bottger is not the suicide type. They might have a body, but it isn't Bruno."

"I said that, Boss. Their reply was to come to the funeral if you doubted it." She held up a hand. "Just a minute." She listened and then said, "Troops of the MEF are surrendering by the hundreds up and down the line. It's over, Boss. It's really over."

"Get me whoever is in command of the MEF, Corrie."

A moment later, she handed him the mike. "General Max Heinrich, Boss."

"General Heinrich, this is Ben Raines."

"Ah, General Raines! Yes, it is true. Bruno Bottger put a gun to his head and killed himself only hours ago. I have assumed command of the armed forces and have ordered an immediate surrender of all our troops. I beg you to treat the men in a humane manner."

"They will be treated well, General Heinrich."

"Thank you, sir. Now, as to the funeral, I can but assume that you would want to personally view the body and that you think this is some sort of trick. I assure you, it is no trick. However, name the airport and I will have the body flown to that airport for viewing and/or autopsy, if you wish."

"Geneva."

"Very well. When?"

Ben waited on the tarmac for the plane to land. Ike and Georgi had flown in, as had General Matthies, commander of the German Resistance, a man who had known Bruno personally for years.

"An autopsy would prove nothing, Ben," Doctor Chase had said. "We don't have prints of Bottger; we don't have dental records or medical records. We have nothing to compare DNA."

"I will know if the body in the casket is Bottger," Matthies said. "I've known him for years. He has a birthmark on his right forearm, just below the elbow, inside. No way they could fake that."

"Family?" Ben asked.

"He was an only child," Matthies replied.

"This whole thing stinks," Billy Smithson said.

"I agree," Ben responded. "But if the body in the casket is that of Bruno Bottger and his men continue to surrender, then it's over for the most part—except for a lot of mop up."

Ike shook his head. "Something is fishy about this. It just doesn't feel right."

"I am of the same opinion," Georgi said.

Ben said nothing. But like the others, he felt something was wrong. The men of the MEF, from the top general down to the lowest rated enlisted man, were all fanatics. For them to just abruptly quit and lay down their arms, even with Bottger gone, didn't make any sense.

"There's the plane." Ike broke into Ben's thoughts.

They watched the twin-engine plane land and then taxi up and cut its engines. The doors opened, and a man stepped down the ladder.

"General Max Heinrich," Matthies said. "I've known him for years."

Heinrich marched up to the group of men and saluted smartly. General Matthies spat on the tarmac and refused to return the salute or to shake the man's hand.

Heinrich smiled. "We must bury old animosities, now, General Matthies. The conflict is over."

Matthies grunted. "The body?"

"I will have it removed to a hangar. Which one?"

Ben pointed, and Heinrich barked an order.

Inside the hangar, Heinrich said, "We did nothing to the body except wash it. The, ah, odor, might be strong."

"He couldn't stink any worse in death than he did in life," Matthies said.

"No respect for the dead, old friend?" Heinrich asked.

"Not for this son of a bitch. And I am not your friend."

Heinrich smiled and ordered the lid to be opened. The smell was bad, but not intolerable. Ben looked hard at the body. What was left of the face certainly looked like Bruno Bottger. Matthies stepped forward and shoved up the shirt sleeve, exposing a small birthmark on the man's arm. He stepped back.

"That is Bruno Bottger," Matthies said. "There is no doubt of it. The vulture is dead."

"Well, I'll just be goddamned!" Ike said.

"So will he." Matthies pointed to the body. "I hope."

Twelve

General Heinrich signed surrender papers for the men and women under his command and then took the body of Bruno Bottger and returned to Germany for the funeral.

Ben told Vanderhoot of the Free Dutch, René Seaux of the FRF, General Roche of Belgium, General Plaisance of Luxembourg, and General de Saussure of the Swiss Freedom Fighters they could return home and start helping to set up governments; their part in the fight was over . . . except to watch the Rebels' backs.

"According to General Heinrich, we're still facing between fifty thousand and seventy-five thousand of Bottger's troops who refused to surrender. They're scattered over the northern part of Italy, and all over Poland, Germany, Austria, Hungary, and Czechoslovakia. This war is a long way from being over."

"How about Russia?" West asked, sitting beside Ben's daughter, Tina.

"We can't establish firm contact with anyone there," Ben said. "All we're getting is bits and pieces, and that is jumbled and garbled. The same with Slovenia, Croatia, Bosnia and Herzegovina, Albania, Macedonia, Yugoslavia, Bulgaria, Romania, Moldova, the Ukraine, Belarus, Lithuania, Latvia, and Estonia. We don't know what the hell is going on in those countries. But we will. Eventually."

"Then we're pushing on east?" Rebet asked.

"All the way until we're told to stop."

"How are things back home?" Jackie Malone, commander of 12 Batt asked.

"President Blanton is back at work for a few hours each day. He's going to be all right. General Bodison is back as Chairman of the Joint Chiefs." His eyes found Colonel Lee Flanders. "He's sending another full battalion over to beef up your people, Lee, and he asked me to tell you that you have been promoted to general rank. Congratulations. He's sending me your stars, and I'll pin them on you as soon as I receive them. Then you get a salute and you owe me a dollar."

Everyone in the room applauded as an embarrassed Lee Flanders stood up.

Ben picked up a pointer and moved to a large wall map behind him. "General Randazzo, your forces will take the northern half of Italy. General Flanders' men will be working with you. The rest of us will stretch out from Hamburg in the north down to the Italian border and start working east. This is the way we'll do it . . ."

The Rebels would stretch out from the border of Denmark all the way through Austria down to the Italian border. Ben's One Batt would be the furthest north, then the battalions would be in numerical order all the way down to the Italian border, with

Buddy's 8 Batt held in reserve for the dirty jobs and Billy's men positioned just north of the Italian border. Due to the reshuffling of troops and the reorganization after the attempted coup against Ben and Billy, Nick Stafford's battalion had been designated 18 Batt. He would be just north of Billy's troops. General Matthies' men would be driving through the center of their homeland, and Colonel Wajda and his Polish fighters would be just south of the German Resistance Forces.

Just before all the Batt Coms returned to their units, Ben called one last meeting of his own people. "Bruno may or may not be dead. If he is alive, I don't know how he pulled it off. But something is definitely wrong. Bruno had thousands of troops under his command, and hundreds surrendered. The arithmetic just doesn't add up."

"But, dad," Tina said, "General Matthies positively I.D.'d him."

"I know he did. But my gut hunch is still that something is wrong. Mike's got his people working on it, but so far they've turned up nothing. The troops of the Dutch, French, Belgians, Luxembourgs, and Swiss report that all is quiet behind us. They're doing a census as I speak and being very careful about it. We're clear behind us. Bottger's hard-line followers are cut off in three directions. They've got only one way to go, and that way is east." Ben smiled. "It just so happens that's the way we're heading. So let's head east, people."

When the batt coms had shaken hands with each other and filed out heading for their sectors, Mike

Richards walked in through the back door and up to Ben.

"So what do you have for me, Mike?"

"As the saying goes, we're a day late and a dollar short, Ben. Bruno's men had dozens of ships ready to sail out of Wilhelmshaven, Bremerhaven, Cuxhaven—all along the coast. They sailed about a week or ten days ago. Destination unknown."

"Shit!"

"There's more. For about two years now, Bruno has been shipping out men and equipment. Thousands of tons of equipment. Tanks, howitzers, trucks, field rations, small arms, ammunition. Everything he'd need to start a war . . . somewhere."

"Where?"

"I can't get a fix on that. I've run up against a stone wall. People saw the ships being loaded and sail, then return weeks later to repeat the process. Over and over for the past two years. Then, about a week or ten days ago, a mass day-and-night loading and exodus."

"Somebody knows something, Mike."

"Oh, yes. And my people will find them. It's just a matter of time, that's all."

"What kind of resistance are we facing east, Mike?"

"Punks, warlords, the same kind of street crap we hit in France." He held up a hand. "But with one difference: Bottger's men armed them to the teeth."

"Sure they did," Ben said drily. "To buy them time. To hold us up for as long as possible. Those ships will not be returning to any German port."

"Nope. They sure won't. That's my feeling, too. Bottger's men have sailed for a new home."

"Mike, get in touch with General Bodison. See if the satellites have picked up anything on their passes over the North Sea . . . or anywhere else for that matter."

"Will do." The chief of intelligence turned and was gone.

Ben might see the man in two or three hours; he might not see him for two or three weeks or longer. With Mike Richards, you just never knew.

Ben returned to his desk and spread out a map of the world. "Now where in the hell did they go?" he muttered. "And who the hell is running the show now that Bruno is dead?" He shook his head. "God only knows," he finally concluded and folded the map, returning it to its case.

Ben sat down and thought about it for a time. Bruno's factory in Poland was reported to have been shut down and blown up. So that operation had been moved to another location. Had the scientists and their equipment sailed on the ships? Probably. But *where?*

Ben didn't have a clue.

Not yet.

But sooner or later, those men and women of the MEF would show their hand.

Did that damnable serum or vaccine or whatever the hell it was that Bruno's scientists were working on really exist? If so, how close were they to perfecting it?

Ben suddenly sat up in the chair. "Of course," he muttered. "What better place to test it." Now he felt sure he knew where the MEF had gone.

He quickly re-opened his map case and took out

a world map. He began tracing a route and adding up the miles. If they had been gone for ten days . . .

"They could have made it by now," he murmured. And those scientists could well have been sent out weeks ago. "Corrie!" he called. "Find Mike and get him back here, pronto."

"Right, Boss."

Mike had not yet left the area and was tracked down. He smiled when he saw the maps on Ben's desk. "Think you're got it all figured out, huh?"

"You knew, Mike. You knew."

Mike shook his head. "Wrong. I didn't know. I suspected. But I don't have one shred of proof to back it up." He sat down and stared at Ben across the desk. "Ben, don't you see what Bruno's done? Can't you see it?"

Ben stared at the man for a moment. "I'm not following you, Mike. But what I know, what I feel in my gut, is that the MEF is setting up in *Africa!*"

"Sure they are. That's the only logical place. But Bruno knows, or rather, knew, that the majority of the world doesn't give a damn what happens over there. And even if the people did care—which they don't, and that's firm, Ben, firm—no nation has rebuilt itself enough to send any significant number of troops to do any good. So that leaves . . . whom, Ben?"

"The United States and the SUSA. Us. The Rebels."

"That's right. I don't think Bruno ever planned on staying here in Europe. I think: one, he realized very quickly he couldn't defeat us; or, two, he knew all along where he was going and was just throwing up a holding action here to allow his people time to get the hell gone. Bruno knew the people of Europe would never stand for a Hitler clone. Not for long. And he was betting that when America did get involved in reestablishing a world order, they'd send people here first. To Europe, then to South America. Australia. Africa would be low on the priority list. China will take care of itself. So will Southeast Asia. And don't you think for one instant that Son Moon didn't know that. He's a tricky bastard, that one. He's locked you into a deal that you can't get out of."

Ben slowly nodded his head in the affirmative. "All right, Mike, I'll buy that. But give me all of it. Share your hypothesis."

"Bruno tested the waters, so to speak, months ago. Maybe years ago. We know he's got people in America reporting to him. Or he had, that is. If he's dead."

That got Mike a sharp look. "You don't think he's dead?" Ben seized on that immediately.

"No. Just like you, I do not think he's dead. I don't know how he pulled it off, but I believe he did. Anyway, he's betting that when the time comes, you'll call for volunteers to go to Africa, knowing that your African blacks don't really trust whites. With good reason. The best black troops you and Bodison have will step forward, so will hundreds, perhaps thousands of educated and qualified blacks in America. And once they land in Africa, they will never be heard from again."

Ben fell silent. Mike got up and poured a cup of coffee, then sat back down and waited. Ben sighed. "The bastard outfoxed me, didn't he?"

"He outfoxed the whole world, Ben. If what I just laid out has any truth to it."

"By now, the radical white Africans will have been long organized with the MEF."

"That's right."

"And Bottger knows, or knew, or hoped that Billy Smithson's men would take no part in any invasion of Africa."

Mike shrugged. "I personally don't think Billy Smithson will take any part in it. Ben, you were in Africa while working for the Company. You know how big that country is. You could put the United States in the southern half of it. It would take a million plus men to successfully launch an invasion against it. Where are they going to come from? It will take Europe a full decade to just start on the road to recovery. It'll take America at least that long. Or longer. You and I, Ben, we'll be in the grave before the world reaches a point of stabilization and productivity anywhere close to where it was before the Great War."

"The bottom line, Mike?"

"You're not going to like it."

"Probably not."

"The only sensible thing to do with Africa is to write it off."

"Something tells me that is not your opinion alone."

"That's right, Ben. It isn't mine alone."

"Our satellites have never stopped working, have they, Mike?"

"No, Ben. They haven't."

"This is more than just guesswork on your part, isn't it, Mike?"

Mike frowned. "Not really, Ben. I'm not as unfeeling as you think I am. The intelligence communities—and I'm talking about those of the free world,
and we are pitifully small at this juncture—simply and
truthfully does not know what is going on in Africa.
We know that the Jews launched missile strikes at
selected Arab targets when the Great War erupted.
They seized valuable oil fields. We know they've en-
larged their territory quite a bit, but we believe that
not all of it was done without some Arab countries'
approval and cooperation. From the southern border
of Turkey all the way down to Yemen—hell, we don't
know what's going on in there. We do know that Iran
is in total, utter chaos. The Jews kicked the shit of
Iraq and Iran with missiles and air strikes. Casualties
on both sides had to have been terribly high. Russia
is a blank. We have no idea what's going on in that
country. But you are under United Nations orders to
find out, aren't you?"

"Yes."

"Your agreement was to stabilize Europe, right?"

"That's right."

"And was Africa even mentioned?"

"No."

"Don't think for an instant Bottger didn't know
that. And the islands, from the Bahamas all the way
down to Grenada, they weren't mentioned either,
were they?"

"Not to speak of, no."

"The powers that be, Ben, have decided to write
off those countries whose citizens can't pull themselves up by their own bootstraps. We've propped up
too many countries too many times, Ben. The world's

industrialized nations have gone in too many times on too many so-called humanitarian missions only to see those countries fall right back into chaos and savagery and barbarism. They've been written off, Ben. I can't prove that, but I'll bet you it's true."

"The drug that Bottger had his people working on?"

"Hell, Ben, I'll bet you a year's pay there is no drug. There never was. Oh, they were working on something. But not what we were led to believe. Whatever they were working on, it didn't materialize. My guess would be some sort of synthetic fuel. Who the hell knows? Who the hell cares? Not the world, Ben. Not the world."

Mike pushed back his chair and walked out.

Ben remained behind his desk. His team had heard every word of the exchange and remained silent. Mike was right: Ben was locked into an agreement with the U.N. He had affixed his signature to the document, and so had Cecil Jefferys and Homer Blanton and Son Moon. They had all been neatly sandbagged. All but one, and he suspected that was Son Moon.

Ben looked at the world's map and took his pen and drew a big X over the continent of Africa.

There was nothing else he could do.

He threw the pen on the desk.

"Shit!" Ben said.

Thirteen

Ben and his One Batt had driven up to Wilhelmshaven, then over to Bremerhaven, then up to Cuxhaven. In three days, they had not fired a single round nor had they drawn any fire.

Jersey stifled a yawn. "Boring," she said. "Where are all these punks and hotshot street gangs that were supposed to be around?"

"Bremen and Hamburg," Beth said. "Georgi's got Bremen; we've got Hamburg. Population before the Great War, almost two million. It's Germany's second largest city."

"The intell we have says that as soon as Bruno's men pulled out, the punks came right back in," Ben said "And the creepies."

"I wonder what ever happened to Tony Green and Tuba Salami and La Bamba and Richardo," Cooper mused.

"They have teamed up with some character who calls himself Boogie Woogie Bagwamb," Corrie said.

Ben was trying to roll a cigarette and spilled all the tobacco down his shirt at that. "Boogie Woogie Bagwamb?"

"That's what I heard."

"I thought Tuba and Tony and La Bamba and all that bunch of crap were dead," Jersey said.

"So did I," Corrie said. "But they've surfaced now that Bruno is dead and most of his men gone. They're in Hamburg, linked up with some gangs there."

"We'll deal with them," Ben said, rolling another cigarette.

The troops of the MEF had been in such a big hurry to get the hell gone, they had not destroyed any of the port facilities. As the Rebels passed through the towns, the people cheered them and waved both American and German flags.

Just as Bottger had said, he had not abused any of the German people, and their economy was good, and growing. The people looked healthy.

"But now we are happy," one middle-aged man told Ben in a small town between Cuxhaven and Hamburg on route 73. "A hog is fat and healthy, but I've never heard one laugh."

As the column approached Hamburg, after turning onto E22, they began to see signs that the punks were ranging out. Homes were deserted, and fresh graves were in evidence. Stores had been recently looted, and even graves had been dug up and the bodies searched for valuables.

The bodies were lying on the ground, many of them stripped naked and in the most grotesque of positions.

Ben halted the column at each desecrated grave site, and Rebels reburied the bodies.

"Hopefully, we're putting them back under the correct headstone," Ben said.

A roadblock stopped the Rebels just outside the city limits of Hamburg. Scouts had radioed back that the men were friendly, citizens of the city. When Ben pulled up and got out, several men wearing white armbands stepped from behind the barricade and walked toward him.

"General Raines?" one inquired.

"That's me." He noted that the men were all carrying shotguns and knew then why the punks had been able to take over much of the city. The punks were armed and the citizens were not. Same old story: Disarm the law-abiding; and in any type of emergency or civil disorder, the lawless will take over.

"It is embarrassing to have to ask for your help, General," the spokesman said. "But . . ." He shrugged his shoulders.

"I know," Ben told him. "I know only too well. You don't have to explain the situation to me. The same thing happened in America. We'll clean up your city. Are the punks and street crap holding civilian hostages?"

"A few, yes, sir."

"We don't make deals with punks. Some of those hostages are going to get hurt and some are going to be killed."

"Yes."

"Understand something else. When we disarm the street crap, we'll give their guns to you people. Don't ever let yourselves be disarmed again."

"It will not happen again, General."

Ben nodded his head but curbed his tongue. He knew only too well that unless citizens were willing to stand their ground and perhaps kill any authority figure who attempted to disarm them, it would happen again. Unless they were careful whom they put into positions of power in government, it would happen again.

"Night People?" Ben asked.

The man looked embarrassed and then said, "They are here. They are everywhere. Bruno Bottger thought he killed or drove them all out. But he did not."

"And in the short time since the MEF pulled out, the Night People have aligned with the punks?"

"Yes, sir. Unfortunately, that is quite true."

"Here we go again," Jersey muttered.

Ben heard the under-the-breath comment and allowed a small smile to crease his lips. He could well understand the disgust in Jersey's words; every Rebel thought the same way: If you have lawless and Night People, why in the hell didn't you just dispose of them? Why in the hell does it always have to fall on us to do the dirty work?

Ben looked around and spotted what appeared to be an abandoned home. "I'll make my CP there. Check it out."

He swung his gaze back to the civilian. "As soon as I'm set up, we'll talk. Get your community leaders and meet me over there in one hour. I want a briefing."

"Yes, sir. As you wish, General."

Ben walked away. Jersey, keeping pace with him, said, "Our One Batt is going to clear out a city of this size, Boss? How?"

"Those truck-loads of weapons we took from the surrendering MEF people," Cooper said.

"That's good, Coop," Ben said. "Very good. That's right. We are going to arm the citizens and *they* are going to bear most, or at least much, of the brunt of the fighting. Their reaction to that should be interesting."

"What?" a woman blurted when Ben told the gathering of civic leaders what their part was going to be.

It was a warm, quite pleasant, summer's day and the meeting was being held in the side yard.

"It's your city," Ben told her. "I'm here with one battalion of troops. You can't expect us to neutralize a city of this size—unless you want us to destroy it. We can do it that way, if that's what you want."

The same scene was being played out down the battlefront.

Some of the men in the small crowd smiled; most thought Ben Raines' plan was only fair. A few were openly indignant.

"We are not warriors, sir," a man spoke up.

"You will be in a few days," Ben told him. "You people are going to know what it's like to smell the stink of battle, smell your own fear-sweat, and see friends torn to pieces by machine-gun fire. This is not our country; these are not our homes. It's your country and your homes. Fight for them." He let that sink in and then said, "From this moment on, you are freedom fighters. So get ready for it. Get back to your people and tell them what's happening. Be back here with them tomorrow morning at 0600 hours for the beginning of your very brief training cycle. Right now, Sgt. MacNally—that's her over there—will escort you to where you'll draw uniforms and boots. From this point on, you do not wear civilian clothing—"

"Why?" the same woman questioned.

"Yes," the man beside her echoed. "Why?"

Ben smiled. "So you won't accidentally get mistaken for the enemy and get a bullet up your ass. Understood?"

"You don't have to be crude," the man said.

Jersey laughed and Ben cut his eyes to her. A slight nod of his head and Jersey stepped forward and faced the man.

"You want crude, you candy-assed dickhead?" Jersey demanded. "I'll give you crude. I'll put a boot up your cherry ass and show you crude. Now you bow your back and get your big feet movin' and get your civilian ass over to those trucks and draw uniforms, you goddamn sissy-fingered, rear-echelon mother fucker. Move, goddamnit, move!"

"Isn't she sweet?" Cooper whispered.

"Most of the civilians are eager to assist us," Raul Gomez, commander of 13 Batt, told Ben by radio that afternoon. "However, there are a few who became quite upset by the orders. But we quickly showed them the error of that kind of thinking."

Ben did not ask exactly how Raul had accomplished that. He had a pretty good idea. The mental picture of Little Jersey's trotting along behind the two civilians that day, herding them toward the trucks, snapping and growling and cussing as they ran, came immediately to mind. Jersey could be quite persuasive when she put her mind to it.

"How much time are we going to have to train these people?" Mike Post asked.

"Seventy-two hours max," Ben told them all. "Quite a lot of them have had some military training. They can help the others. Each unit will have Rebel leaders, so it's not going to be as bad as it's going to appear the first day out. Don't push them too hard. Just see that they know how to use a weapon and can follow orders. We're not expecting perfection, just some help in dealing with the situation. When we enter the contested areas, we put the civilians at a spot and tell them to hold until they are ordered to move up. We take it house by house, block by block. Just keep shoving the punks and creepies back."

Rolf Staab was the leader of the civilian group attached to Ben's small unit. Rolf had some military experience and was a good, solid, steady, middle-aged man. He was also quite taken by Jersey . . . not in any sexual way, for Rolf was happily married with several children and grandchildren—he was just simply fascinated by her.

"Now that," he told Ben, as Jersey walked by them the next morning, "is a *woman!*"

"Yes, she is," Ben said with a chuckle. "But really, no more so than Beth or Corrie or any other Rebel. But, male or female, we all have years of bloody combat experience behind us and don't have much patience with those who won't fight for freedom. The woman who was appalled at my orders to fight, what political party did she belong to before the Great War?"

Rolf smiled. "In America, I believe it was called the Liberal Democratic Party."

"That figures," Ben said drily. "The man with her?"

"Same party. I, and my entire family, on the other hand, belonged to the party that compared to your Republican Party."

"I knew there was some reason I liked you," Ben said with a grin.

No one knew how many punks made up the gangs who now virtually controlled the sprawling city. When the gangs had descended upon the city, really startling the citizens—for they had experienced a period of relative peace under Bottger's rule—the men and women had been practically powerless to defend hearth and home, for Bottger had, long ago, seized all weapons except for a few shotguns and .22 caliber rifles. The punks were well-armed, thanks to the MEF.

In the few days the civilians were receiving training, Ben had swung Ike's 2 Batt and Dan's 3 Batt around and stretched them out from Hamburg to Lubeck, cutting off any escape except to the north. Troops from Denmark had stretched out along the border, waiting for any fleeing criminals. Ben's plan was simple, for the more complicated the plan, the more chances of screwing it up. Ben planned to drive the punks toward the north, toward the border with Denmark, and box them in. Any who surrendered would be dealt with by the Germans, in any way they saw fit.

On the evening after the third day of intensive

training, Ben told the civilians, "We push off at dawn. Get a good night's sleep and say your prayers, for some of you won't be around this time tomorrow."

"You're such a cheerful soul, General," Rolf said with a grin.

Ben grunted and returned to his CP.

"Ike and Dan are in place," Corrie told him.

Ben nodded and sat down, looking at a map. At dawn, the entire Rebel force would strike at targets stretching for hundreds of miles. In Germany, the cities that would be hit simultaneously were Hamburg and Lubeck in the north, then, working south, Bremen, Hannover, Kassel, Frankfort, Darmstadt, Mannheim, Karlsruhe, Freiburg. Then they would swing down into Switzerland and Italy. If the Rebels could pull it off, they would have very nearly cut Germany in half.

"Ready to see some action, gang?" Ben asked, looking up from the map.

"Hell, we've been ready, Boss," Jersey said.

"We'll see it tomorrow," he assured them. "The city is filled with punks and creeps. The punks are arrogant and stupid, but the creeps know the game is over for them. They will have been in radio contact with fellow creeps over in Lubeck and know we've boxed them in. It'll be a fight to the finish with them."

"I can hardly wait," Beth said, her tone dripping with sarcasm. She spoke for every Rebel, for they hated to tangle with the creepies. They weren't afraid of the creeps; they loathed the stinking cannibalistic Night People.

"If we had the time, I'd throw a net around the city and let the creepies turn on the punks and eat them first, then go in," Ben said, only half-joking. "But as usual, we don't have the time."

"But it was a very nice thought," Corrie said.

And she wasn't kidding a bit.

In the city, the Night People had prepared themselves for their final battle, for they knew the Rebels did not take prisoners of their kind. The punks, being what they were, were confident of victory when the Rebels came at them. Most of them, that is. A few of the punks who had faced the Rebels in France and managed to escape were glum. They knew there was no way in hell they were ever going to defeat the Rebels; but they had no choice except to fight, for they were all wanted on a multitude of charges, including dozens of counts of murder. They faced a death sentence any way they turned.

Sitting in a sacked-and-looted department store, a punk who called himself, when translated into English, Cool Johnny, looked at his Austrian girlfriend, a woman with the street name of Shady. "You believe in God, Shady?"

She cut her eyes to him. "I just right then realized something about you, Johnny."

"Yeah, what?"

"You're a stupid fuck!"

"Where do you get off callin' me stupid, you goddamn road whore?"

She did not take umbrage at his name-calling. "Yeah. Sure. I believe in God. Do you?"

"Sure, I do. You believe in Hell?"

"I guess."

"You think that's where we'll end up?"

She sighed. "To tell you the truth, Johnny, I never

ave it much thought. But yeah, I think we'll both urn in hell." Shady started crying, the tears running ilently down her grimy face.

"What the hell's wrong with you?"

"I wish Ben Raines would give me another chance o surrender," she blubbered.

"Why?" another punk sitting with his back to a ounter asked. "Even if you lived ten days after the rial, which is doubtful, you'd just fuck up again. We ll would. Nobody made us what we are. We chose it."

"Who made you a goddamn expert on anything, Ians?" Johnny asked.

"Nobody. But I know this much: We had a chance o live decent after the Great War. We didn't. We had chance to join Bruno Bottger's bunch and didn't. en Raines has been asking us to surrender for three oddamn days now, and here we sit."

"I wish I'd listened to my mother," Shady said, the ars starting again.

Johnny looked at her as if she'd lost her mind. Jesus, Shady, you stabbed your mother nine times!"

"Ten," Shady blubbered. "I wish I hadn't done hat, either."

"There is no hope for any of us." The voice came om the stairwell off to one side, the smell following he words.

Shady wrinkled her nose. "I wish I'd never gotten wolved with you stinkin' bastards either."

"But you did. You gave us live human flesh to eat nd now you sit and cry and babble about God and sus and Heaven and Hell. Well, I will tell you some-ing. Tomorrow you shall get your chance to meet e devil. His name is Ben Raines."

Fourteen

The Rebels and the civilians moved into the suburbs of Hamburg just at dawn, walking behind the
spearheading tanks and APCs. They knew from experience that many of the punks would be in the
suburbs, the creepies holed up in the city proper.

The civilians soon discovered why the Rebels were
so successful and why they were so feared: The enemy
was offered a chance to surrender—if possible, given
a couple of days to consider it. But if they refused,
the Rebels moved in, careful and ruthless, destroying
everything and everybody in their path.

The Rebels laid down an advancing covering fire
that was a deafening, killing roar; everything from
M-16's to chain guns and sometimes the big guns on
the MBTs. Resistance from the enemy was futile.

Rebel and friendly forces were treated at the
MASH units first, then the wounded enemy was
tended to—if they had not died before the doctors
got to them. If war ever had any niceties to it, Ben
had removed them all.

A punk female came running out of a burning
house, screaming in English and firing an automatic
weapon at the advancing Rebels. "You dirty cocksuck-
ers don't give nobody a chance."

Beth lifted her CAR and stopped the running and silenced the screaming and the cussing. She did so with absolutely no change of expression. She popped a piece of gum into her mouth and kept on walking.

Ben was once more carrying his old Chicago Piano, the .45 caliber-spitter that had become almost as much a legend as the man behind it. Ben saw movement from a house they were passing and turned, firing the Thompson from the hip and fighting the rise of the powerful old weapon. The .45 caliber slugs sang and whined, and two punks by the window danced their way into darkness as the slugs impacted with flesh and bone.

Killing machines, Rolf Staab thought as he watched the Rebels do their deadly work. As finely precisioned as a great watch. A violent ballet with real blood and real pain and suffering. He walked on with the Rebels behind the tanks that were roaring out fire and smoke and death with their main guns. On either side of him, Rebels darted left and right, mopping up anything that might be left alive.

Rolf tried not to think about the fact that the Rebels seldom exited the houses with any prisoners.

As if reading his thoughts, Ben said, during a lull in the battle, "They had their chance, Rolf. They blew it."

Rolf took a drink of tepid water from his canteen. 'No second chance, hey, General?"

"Most of those people have had dozens of chances, Rolf. And you know it. They've been fuck-ups all their lives. They hold society's laws and law-abiding people in contempt. They feel they are above the law, so we put them below the ground."

"And do it quite well, I might add," Rolf said drily.

"We try," Ben said with small smile. "We do try."

By mid-afternoon the Rebels had secured dozens of blocks. Those gang members and street punks who survived the ruthless and seemingly unstoppable advance were sent retreating into the city proper.

"Incredible," Rolf said as he watched Rebel burial crews come in just moments after a block was secured and gather up and toss the bodies of dead punks into the beds of trucks to be hauled off and buried in mass graves which were being scooped out by earth-moving equipment even as the battle raged. "And people talk about Germanic efficiency," he muttered.

"We do it for health purposes," Cooper told the man.

"Indeed," Rolf said.

By late afternoon, when Ben called a halt to the advance, the Rebels controlled all the suburbs and the Rebel line was complete between Lubeck and Hamburg. The punks had nowhere to go except north toward the border of Denmark. Georgi Striganov and his 5 Batt were ripping through their objective and, as soon as that was accomplished, would move toward Hamburg to beef up Ben and his 1 Batt.

"Incredible," Rolf Staab said for about the fifteenth time that day.

"We've had lots of practice at this," Jersey told him. "Once the enemy knows his adversary is not going to cut him one inch of slack, you've got half the battle won. It works." She walked off to join her team.

"I should say so," Rolf said.

Jersey paused and turned around. "But the hard

part comes in the morning. When we meet the creeps. You'll see."

Later that afternoon, Rolf found Ben sitting in a cottage eating field rations and reading an old paperback book he had found. Cooper had found a girlie magazine and was pointing out various attributes of the ladies to a disinterested Jersey, who was trying to take a nap.

"You're not showing me anything new, Coop," she told him. "Now shut up and leave me alone."

Corrie was talking to someone from 8 Batt, and Beth was writing in her journal.

The peaceful scene was warped to Rolf's mind. The smell of gunsmoke and death still hung heavy over the area, yet these people appeared as unconcerned as if they were sitting in their own living rooms relaxing after a day of work at the office.

"Do you really think your General Striganov is going to clear all the criminals out of a city the size of Bremen in two days?" Rolf asked.

"Of course not. Just like we won't clear all the punks out of this city," Ben said as he wiped his mouth with a piece of cloth that looked suspiciously like part of an old BDU shirt. "But we'll cripple them so badly their strength will be broken. After that, it's up to the local people." Ben looked at the man for a moment. "Sorry about that friend of yours. What else can I say?"

Rolf shook his head. "That wasn't why I came over. It's . . . well, a lot of people were shocked at the, ah, brutality of the Rebels."

Ben arched an eyebrow. "What brutality? My people don't torture or brutalize."

"No. I don't mean that. I'm sure that doesn't happen. But, General, the wounded of the enemy were the last to get treated at your mobile hospitals."

"So?" Ben's eyes flashed a clear warning signal—to anyone who knew him—that Rolf was treading on very shaky ground.

Rolf must have caught something in Ben's tone, for he said nothing.

When Ben spoke, his voice was as cold as the grave. "If you think for one instant I would allow a Rebel soldier to suffer one second longer so my doctors can work on some goddamn worthless snakehead, you are badly mistaken, mister."

"I can see why the United Nations picked you for this job, General. You and your people are perfectly suited for it." He offered a slight bow as only the Germans could do. "I bid you a very pleasant *gute nacht,* sir." He left the room.

"Same old song, different jukebox," Cooper said. He picked up his girlie magazine and said, "Great God, Jersey. Would you look at that!"

She looked, reluctantly, then fixed him with a baleful gaze. "Cooper, if you show me another picture of a naked woman, I am going to dropkick your nuts all the way back to Paris!"

Cooper wisely closed the magazine.

The Rebels struck at the city proper at dawn. Ben had called in Buddy's spec ops people, 8 Batt, and they began hammering a path through the waterfront district, slowly working their way in a circling movement on the west side while Ben and his people worked their way on the east side of the city. Now, the advancing was reduced to a crawl for the creeps knew they had no place to run and nothing to do but die.

"Buddy's people found what was left of the hostages," Corrie said. "Looks like the creeps had a snack before they pulled out."

One of the civilians nearby puked all over his boots at Corrie's comment.

Ben looked at Rolf, his eyes hard. "Just remember this, Mr. Staab, the next time you start feeling all warm and gooey toward the punks: It was the punks who *gave* those civilians to the creeps."

Tight-lipped, Rolf nodded his head in understanding.

To Corrie, Ben said, "Mark the building so the dead can be properly buried," then walked away muttering, "what's left of them, anyway."

Only a few blocks of the city were cleared that bloody day, with the Rebels clawing for every inch of it. Georgi reported that Bremen was seventy-five percent clean and the airport in firm Rebel hands; reinforcements and supplies were coming in there and he was sending two full companies, supported by tanks, to assist Ben.

"Corrie, have the reinforcements stretch out on the road between Hamburg and Lubeck. Tell Ike to start his pincer movement up to Kiel. Have the P-51's and gunships ready to start strafing when the punks start running north."

She nodded. "All bridges now under Rebel control," she reported to Ben.

Ben cut his eyes to Rolf. "Pull your people back and

take control of those bridges. Keep them open. We'l
take it from this point on." He turned to Corrie. "Shu
it down for the day. The people need the rest. Bu
we're in boogy country, so maintain a high alert."
Then he spoke firmly to Rolf: "Get the passwords anc
get them right. The only people who will be moving
around this night will be the enemy. If anyone doesn'
know the password, kill them. Is that clear?"

"Yes, General."

"I've arranged transportation for you and some o:
your people to go view what is left of those hostage:
my son found. I want you all, by God, to know what
type of crud we're fighting and to show them nc
mercy. No mercy!"

"Yes, General."

"And take those two bleeding hearts I met with
you. Let's see what explanations the German Libera
Party can come up with to excuse the behavior o:
savages. It should be interesting." Ben smiled. "As :
matter of fact, I think I'll go along. Coop! Let's roll
What was that woman's name, Rolf?"

"Bianka Hodel."

"Yes. By all means, let's find Ms. Hodel."

"She proved to have no stomach for combat. I as
signed her to an aid station."

"That's very sweet and considerate of you. Get her
And that Remington Raider who was with her."

Rolf sighed. "General . . . there are good people
in this world who simply do not and never will have
your capacity for violence. But that does not—"

"Get them!"

"As you wish, General Raines."

The smell from the waterfront warehouse spoke

ilent volumes of what lay inside. Bianka Hodel and
ans Rapp wrinkled their noses at the odor coming
rom the open doors.

"You both said you had friends taken hostage by
he punks," Ben told them. "Some of them are prob-
bly in there. Go take a look and then tell me about
ow we should be more compassionate and under-
tanding toward criminals. Move."

"I really don't think this is necessary, General,"
Bianka said.

"Move your ass, lady," Jersey told her.

"I feel a bit queasy," Jans said.

"You're gonna feel queasier before it's over," Jer-
ey told him. "Move."

The pair moved toward the doors and disappeared
nto the gloom of the cavernous warehouse. Jans let
ut one choking cry and hit the floor in a dead faint.
Bianka came shrieking and wailing and flapping her
rms outside in a dead run, puking down the front
f her shirt. She fell in the middle of the road and
romptly passed out.

Buddy had driven up to stand by his father. Rolf
linked a couple of times at the solid bulk of the
oung man. Buddy looked like he ate howitzers for
reakfast. Ben stood calmly by and rolled a cigarette.

"Proving a point, father?" Buddy asked.

"You might say that, son."

Jans staggered out of the warehouse, his eyes wild.
He took several deep breaths of the more-or-less-
resh air and then wobbled over to Bianka and knelt
eside her, bathing her face with water from his can-
een.

Ben looked at Rolf. "Your turn, Mr. Staab. Go take

a real good look at what the Rebels have been seein
for years. And then come back and tell me abou
compassion and understanding.''

Bianka sat up, crying, and pounded her small fis
on the roadway.

Rolf walked past them and into the warehouse. H
returned a few moments later, his face pale, and ap
proached Ben. "They . . . the Night People . .
they . . . ate parts of the hostages.''

"That's right, Rolf. They like to keep them aliv
while they're dining.''

"You bastard!" Bianka screamed at Ben. "W
didn't know. We didn't know!''

"You're a liar, lady," Ben told her. "European lib
erals and bleeding hearts are no different from you
American counterparts. You both insulate yourselve
from it and pretend it doesn't happen; and when
you're forced to confront it, you make excuses fo
it." He jerked the woman to her feet and shoved he
toward the warehouse. "And bring that son of a bitch
too," he called over his shoulder.

Jans was pulled to his feet and shoved toward th
doors of the warehouse. He tried to run, but Budd
blocked him. Jans took one look at Buddy an
changed his mind.

"This is inhuman!" Bianka screamed.

"No, lady," Ben said, a firm grip on the woman'
arm. "What was done to those people in there wa
inhuman. And those who did it deserve no merc
no pity, no compassion. Now get in there and star
I.D.ing those folks." He looked back at Lt. Bonell
"Find every damn reporter you can round up. Ge
them over here."

"Yes, sir!" Bonelli said with a grin. "A whole shit-ot full of them arrived about an hour ago."

"The more the merrier. Not that it will do any ood," Ben muttered. "They'll just come up with ome excuse—it wasn't the creepies who did it, it was heir knives. People don't kill people, guns do."

Inside the warehouse, a few yards from the pile of aked, half-eaten remains, Beth said, "To quote Lewis Carroll, 'But answer came there none—And this was carcely odd, because they'd eaten every one.' "

"You bitch!" Bianka shouted at her. "You heartless itch!"

Beth shrugged that off.

About a half hour later, the street in front of the eath-house was filled with choking, puking, gasping, nd teary-eyed men and women from the Fourth Es-ate. Ben walked among them.

"It's going to be very interesting to read about his," he said. "What excuses will you come up with or this type of behavior? Let's see. Oh, yes! How bout 'They were spanked as children'? That's always good one. Or 'Their mommies and daddies smoked igarettes and that retarded their brain cells'? Oh! nd let's not forget, 'They were poor.' I've always ked that one."

"Goddamnit, General!" a reporter from a major etwork said.

"Yes, Mr.—ah, whatever your name is? Have you ome up with a new excuse for the behavior of sav-ges? I'd love to hear it. Share it with me, please."

But the reporters were not going to play Ben's ame this time. They were in the country only be-ause there were now so many of them that Ben

couldn't keep track of them all, so he said to he
with it. But they knew they had damn well bette
report the facts and report them accurately withov
slur or innuendo, for Ben Raines had—from the
point of view—a nasty little habit of knowing ever
thing that was reported back home. They also kne
that Ben held most of them in the highest, or lowes
of contempt. What they didn't know was that Ben w:
fully cognizant of the fact that most of them did n
deserve that contempt. But that was Ben's secret.

"A bunch of chickens," Ben said to the grou|
then turned and walked off.

"Asshole," one reporter said, but not loud enoug
for Ben to hear.

There was a new reporter among the bunch, on
who had never encountered Ben Raines before-
Bobby Day. Bobby was young and he was brash an
he was arrogant and he was also not that long out •
what had passed for institutions of higher learnin
during the years after the Great War . . . most of tho
small colleges carefully tucked and hidden away an
staffed by people who felt that if you left the keys i
your car and it was stolen, that was your fault, not th
fault of the thief, and heaven forbid anyone shoul
have the right to shoot the thieving son of a bitch. Th
reporter was also a liberal democrat and with that tit'
comes the awesomeness of thinking—all the tim
without question—that he knew what was best for ev
rybody in the whole wide universe.

"When do you plan on going in and stabilizir
Africa, General?" Bobby called out. "If killing ever
one you encounter can be called stabilizing."

"Oh, shit!" Jersey muttered.

Fifteen

Ben turned around to face his questioner. "Your name?"

"Bobby Day."

"You'll have to take that up with the Secretary General of the United Nations. We work for them. When they tell me to go in, I'll take my people in."

"You're not going to give me a lecture on my questioning your tactics on 'stabilizing a country,' General?"

Ben smiled. "I don't give a damn what you think of my tactics, sonny-boy. Does that answer your last question?"

"It's my understanding, General," Bobby called, "that the U.N. has no plans to go into Africa. Care to comment on that?"

"I don't know what the U.N.'s long-range plans are. Right now, I'm concerned about Europe. I'll worry about Africa when the time comes."

"Have you heard that several senators and representatives back home have gone on hunger strikes protesting the U.N.'s lack of concern about Africa?"

"No, I have heard nothing about that. Who are they?"

"Rita Rivers, former Vice President Harrie
Hooter, Immaculate Crapums, and Wiley Ferret are
among the group."

"They could all stand to lose a few pounds."

A number of the reporters laughed at that, surprising Ben.

"I can quote you on that?"

"Certainly." Ben looked up at the sky. He figured
about one hour before dusk. "Get settled in for the
night, people," he said, only his own Rebels catching
and smiling at the double entendre. "This city is still
crawling with creepies, and they might be hungry."
As Ben walked away, he whispered to Corrie, "Bump
our Intell people. Find out everything you can about
Bobby Day. And find out about that Africa rumor."

Bobby had left the group of reporters and was attempting to get to Ben. He found the way blocked
by Lt. Bonelli's troops. Bobby gave up and returned
to the reporters, who were being herded onto trucks
for the ride back to safe quarters. Ben had finally
relented and assigned troops to guarding the reporters . . . at night; during the daylight hours they were
on their own.

"Smug arrogant bastard," Bobby said, climbing
into the back of a deuce and a half. "I'm going to
bring him down off that high horse."

"Before you do that," a reporter said, "give us the
name and address of your next of kin, will you?"

Bobby thought that was really funny. Looking
around him, he wondered why he was the only one
laughing.

* * *

Conditions back in America were improving dramatically for those who were interested in working toward a common goal. President Blanton had not done a one-eighty in his political leanings, but what he had done was return to the middle of the road and become a moderate. He had begun to realize that with the exception of how justice should be meted out, he and Ben Raines were really not that far apart. They both wanted many of the same things; it was the direction and means taken to achieve them that set them apart.

Blanton ordered a massive rebuilding policy for the nation and set up programs similar to the old WPA and CCC camps of the Depression era; and for a career politician, Blanton had turned uncommonly blunt.

"You want to eat, you go to work," he told the people via his weekly radio broadcast.

Much to the chagrin of the liberal wing of his party, Blanton put the military in charge of overseeing the massive construction projects . . . at least temporarily. A few of the newly reorganized unions set up a howl at that, but the vast majority of union members saw the need for it and went back to work.

Since Ben and the Rebels had destroyed most of the cities in North America, Blanton ordered new cities to be built in close proximity to the old. It was a massive undertaking, and one that would take decades to complete; but it was a start, and a damn good one.

Slowly, slowly, the states that were still in the Union began to shake off the ashes of defeat and despair and climb first to their knees, then to their feet.

A census was underway, and it soon showed that millions had died during and after the Great War the populations of entire towns had simply vanished.

To sort out what belonged to whom, batteries of lawyers emerged from the rubble, briefcases in their hands and mumbo-jumbo in their mouths. Banks that had not been in operation in years began reopening and demanding payment for debts a decade old.

"Oh, no," Blanton said when he heard that news. "No way. We're starting over. Fresh. Anew. Debts owed before the Great War are wiped out. Null and void."

"That's unconstitutional and against the law!" hordes of bankers and lawyers screamed at him.

Blanton smiled and took a line from Ben Raines. "Fuck you!" he told them.

The nation was starting from scratch.

The SUSA was, of course, left strictly alone. And true to his word, President Blanton let Billy Smithson's Free State of Missouri stand. He knew it couldn't survive alone . . . not for long. It was just a matter of time before the people there would ask to join either the USA or the SUSA, and Blanton had a strong hunch which one it would be.

Harriet Hooter and her imitators stopped their hunger strikes, and their new political party began to flounder as its members elected to go back to work. Actually, they didn't have much choice in the matter if they wanted to eat. Blanton had stopped nearly all government giveaway programs. Hooter and those who aligned with her left Charleston, vowing they would be back.

"They will be, too," Blanton said to his advisors. "They still have a lot of followers out there."

One of the fastest growing newspapers in the nation was the paper that Bobby Day worked for, the *Voice of Reason*. The owner, Simon Border, also owned a number of radio and TV stations. Simon was an avowed and unrepentant liberal—or so he said—who hated Ben Raines and everything Ben stood for.

"Simon Border," Ben said, when his intelligence people gave him the report a few days after Ben's questioning by Bobby Day. "I'll be damned. I thought he was dead."

"You know him, Boss?" Jersey asked.

"Oh, yes. We're just about the same age. He was a writer before the Great War—very successful. He sold millions of books and also had a newspaper chain and a broadcasting empire. And he managed to do all that before he was forty years old. Simon also always had political aspirations. Homer Blanton better be on guard, for Simon Border is a force to be reckoned with. And he's coming on strong."

"Is he a threat to us?" Cooper asked. "The SUSA, I mean."

Ben smiled. "Nobody is a real threat to us, Coop. We are the strongest nation with the most stable economy in the world. But Simon would very much like to bring us down."

"Why?" Corrie asked, turning from her radio.

"Oh, a number of reasons, Corrie. Simon was one of those journalists who turned on me before the Great War, accusing me of preaching sedition. He just never could understand that I didn't want violent overthrow of the government, I just wanted change.

I wanted tax relief for the people and a return to a more common-sense approach to government and to law and order. Simon was, and still is, I'm sure, a total gun-control advocate. Not just handguns—all guns. He wanted America disarmed, right down to BB guns. I called him a goddamn nut one time at a writers' conference and invited him to step outside and settle our differences, *mano a mano*. He refused and has hated me ever since. He made a thinly veiled public statement later that he would see to it that I was silenced and put in prison for sedition." Ben smiled.

"Simon was in tight with the administration in Washington at that time and he did cause me some grief, but nothing I couldn't handle. Unlike the Rebel form of government, which believes that each person controls their own destiny, Simon believes the central government should control each person's destiny."

"That's communism," Beth said.

"Sure it is. But Simon and others of his ilk prefer to call it something else. They have a dozen different labels for it. But put them all in a pot and they'll boil down to the same thing; they are socialist to the core."

Ben tapped the folder on his desk. "According to this, Simon opened a small college right after the Great War, tucked away in the mountains of Colorado. Hell, we know now there were dozens of communities and small institutions of learning hidden from us while we were fighting to clear the States of the lawless. But we weren't looking for peaceful settlements; we were hunting gangs of killers and rapists and warlords."

"And this Bobby Day is a graduate of Simon Border's college." Jersey guessed.

"Yeah, he is. Brainwashed right down to his socks."

"What are you going to do about him, Chief?" Corrie asked.

Ben shrugged his shoulders. "Nothing. He has a right to his opinion. That's the great difference in us: I think he has a right to his opinion, but he doesn't believe I have a right to mine."

"Boss," Jersey said, a puzzled look on her face. "This Simon Border and his people, his followers, if you will, they had to have fought off outlaws and gangs and warlords and street crap, just as we did. If they don't believe in owning weapons, how did they do it?"

Ben laughed. "Well, you see, Jersey, that's the rub. People like Simon Border and a great many others who preach about gun control and so forth . . . that doesn't apply to them. They want the masses disarmed." Ben chuckled. "One of the most vocal gun-control advocates shot and wounded an unarmed teenager who was in his back yard . . . and he used an unregistered gun to do it. The old society was full of hypocrisy, gang. Riddled with it. We haven't done away with hypocrisy and injustice completely in the SUSA . . . but by God we've damn sure tried."

"I wonder why President Jefferys didn't pick up on this Simon Border character?" Cooper asked.

"Oh, I'm sure his Intell people did. He just didn't want to worry me with it. Not much gets past Cecil." Ben glanced at his watch. "We'll give Cec a bump in a couple of hours and I'll sound him out about Simon."

The Rebels were slowly pushing the gangs both north and east. They were under no delusions that they had killed all the creepies, for some of their kind always managed to slip through. But Ben's Intell people guesstimated they'd killed over ninety percent of Hamburg's Night People. The bodies had been burned and then the ashes buried. And as always, the Rebels had captured several dozen creepie children. Ben had turned them over to a German relief agency.

"You know what they are and what they are going to turn into," he'd told the relief people.

"We know, General," the head of the Hamburg agency told him, looking at the boy Ben had brought into the office under heavy guard. "But what can we do except take them?"

"Nothing," Ben admitted.

"We have several dozen back home," Doctor Chase said. "They'll be institutionalized until the day they die . . . or kill their guards and escape."

"Oh, please, kind sir," the ten-year-old creepie boy said. "I beg you to take off these handcuffs."

The man smiled grimly at him. "I fell for that several years ago, son. A boy and a girl just about your age. I lost my assistant and my head nurse, and—" He held up his left hand. Three fingers were missing. "—this."

The boy laughed, but it was a laugh that sprang from the bowels of Hell. It chilled Ben, the head of the agency, Lamar Chase, and the three Rebels with Ben. "Someday, I'll tear your heart out and eat it while it still beats," the boy said. "Isn't that something to look forward to? Have sweet dreams now, you old bastard!" He laughed and laughed.

"Get him out of here," Ben told the Rebels. "And for Gods sake, be careful with him."

When the innocent-faced spawn from Hell was gone, the head of the relief agency opened his mouth to speak. Doctor Lamar Chase lifted a hand to cut him off before he asked the question that Chase had heard a thousand times before and did not know the answer to.

"We don't know, Doctor. We have some of the best, if not the best, medical minds in the world living and working in the SUSA. They don't know either. The Night People just . . . are." He looked at Ben. "Is that grammatically correct?"

"Hell, I don't know!"

"Well, you're the writer."

"I had editors, Lamar."

"I bet they loved you," Lamar muttered.

Ben assigned Ike's 2 Batt to chase the remaining punks up to the border with Denmark, and Ben lined up his 1 Batt with the others and they pushed east-ward.

Wismar, Schwerin, Magdeburg, Eisleben, Weimar, Saalfeld, Nurnberg, Ingolst, and Augsburg in Germany were cleared of hoodlums and gangs. Innsbruck, in Austria, fell to the Rebel advance, and a large portion of North Italy was cleared of criminal gangs. Nobody knew about the Mafia since no one would talk about it, except to say it didn't exist.

Ben carefully folded his map and looked at Ike,

who had returned from the Denmark border the day before. "It's going to take a lot of us to clear Berlin. As a matter of fact, it's going to take all of us. Your battalion and mine will clear Rostock and Stralsund, and then start working our way south. Dan, West, and Georgi will advance to a line running north to south from Neurappin to Brandenburg. You and I will be stretched out west to east from Neurappin to Finow. We'll be stretched thin, but I'm going to double our usual complement of tanks. General Randazzo and Smithson's people will remain in Italy. Colonel Wajda and General Matthies will remain to the south of us, with General Flanders' people along the borders of Austria and Czechoslovakia. All battalions south of us will, when their sectors are clear, start advancing north to Berlin. Buddy's 8 Batt and Nick's 18 Batt will act as the stopper in the bottle to the east of the city. The rest of us are going into Berlin." Ben leaned back, rolling a smoke, then tossing the makings to Ike. "If you can see a flaw in it, Ike, or have a better plan, let me know now."

"Looks good to me, Ben. Before the war, it was a city of nearly four million. It shore ain't gonna be no piece of cake, brother," the Mississippi-born Ike drawled.

Ben smiled at Ike's grammar. Ike was a highly educated man, but as the ex-SEAL liked to phrase it, "My neck do still get red ever' now and then."

"What about Norway, Sweden, and Finland?"

"I'm waiting for word from the U.N. But I have a hunch they're going to tell us to keep up the eastward push instead of turning north at this point."

"Ben—"

"I know, Ike. I know. We get past Poland, Czechoslovakia, Hungary, we could be in a world of hurt. Don't think I'm not aware of that. From Estonia all the way down to the Black Sea is unknown territory. And now Cecil tells me that Simon Border is raising an army of some sort back home. He's calling it the Christian Front, and fanatics are running over each other to join the ranks. It seems that after the Great War, Simon found the Lord, or so he says. Personally, I think he's running a scam. Anyone who opposes Simon's beliefs is the enemy. And guess who is the Great Satan?"

"Has to be you, Ben."

"You got it. Ben Raines. The Great Satan. Simon Border is another Jim Jones, Ike. But a hell of a lot smarter and totally sane. He's going to make a run for the Presidency the next time around, and he might get it."

"You talked with Blanton?"

"Yeah. He's worried about Simon. With damn good reason, I might add. The man is dangerous."

"The SUSA?"

"Oh, he won't attack us. Not at first. He'll take the USA and then make his move against the SUSA."

"While we're ten thousand miles away."

"Yeah. Cecil says he's pushing hard for us to leave Europe and to quote/unquote 'go help the starving millions in Africa.' "

"You think he's tied in with Bruno Bottger's movement?"

"That thought has crossed my mind."

"What does Cecil think about Africa?"

"Stay away from there."

"He spent a couple of years there, didn't he?"

"Yes. A long time ago. Cecil says it's always five minutes to high noon in Africa."

"What the hell does he mean by that?"

"When I ask him, he just smiles. But I think he means that somewhere in Africa, one is always five minutes away from a showdown with somebody. I guess. I don't really know. I've heard the saying before."

"Ben, I have people in my batt who don't want to go to Africa, both whites and blacks. They just feel if we go, we'll get bogged down in a hopeless situation. It's the same up and down the line. They'll go if you give the orders, but they won't like it."

"I know. I feel the same way about going into Bosnia and Herzegovina. If I can possibly skip those places, I will."

"That would suit me just fine," Ike said drily. "Talk about gettin' bogged down."

"Well, I told Son Moon that if the majority of citizens in a country want their government stabilized, we'll go in. If they don't, we'll stay out. He accepted the deal and I'm going to hold him to it."

Ike nodded and stood up. "I'll see you on the road to Berlin, Ben." He smiled. "I seem to recall from history books that this same scenario was played out back in '45."

"Hopefully, this will be the last time."

"It will be for you and me, ol' buddy," Ike said somberly, then left the room.

"Yeah," Ben whispered. "You're right about that."

Book Two

Talk sense to a fool and he calls you foolish.
Euripides

One

Before the war, Rostock had been a city of about a quarter of a million, a port, industrial city, and home of a fine university. Now, it appeared very nearly a ghost town.

"What the hell?" Ike asked, walking up to Ben, who stood in the middle of the highway.

"The punks and creeps cleared out, Ike. But what they left behind is not going to be pleasant viewing."

"You think they killed the people?"

"As many as they could, yeah. That's what fly-bys tell us. The creeps took the rest of them as a food source."

"And went to Berlin."

"Yeah. I'm waiting on a report from scouts now."

"Fly-bys over Stralsund show it a dead city," Corrie called. "Absolutely no signs of life. The streets are littered with bodies."

"So we bury bodies instead of fighting," Jersey said.

"That's about it, I guess," Ben said.

"Scouts report a dead city, Boss," Corrie said. "And real unpleasant in this heat."

Ben sighed. "Get into gas masks," Ben ordered. "This is not going to be any fun at all."

The streets and sidewalks were covered with the bloated and stinking bodies of men, women, and children. Some had been shot in the front, but many more had been shot in the back as they were trying to get away from the horror. Mothers had flung themselves over children in an attempt to shield them from the bullets, and men had flung themselves in front of women to protect them. But nothing had worked. The Rebels could not find a single living person amid the carnage.

"Let the reporters in," Ben said wearily as he stood among the hundreds of bodies in the street, his voice muffled behind the protective mask.

"Get them buried quickly, Ben," Doctor Chase said. "There is no time for formalities or niceties. This is a real health hazard."

The bodies were buried in mass graves and the locations carefully marked. The Rebels moved on, leaving the dead city behind them. Since Stralsund had suffered the same fate as Rostock, Ben sent burial parties on to that city and he and Ike cut south toward Berlin. Ben took his battalion and cut over toward Gustrow and highway E55 while Ike traveled on and cut south toward Neubrandenburg. From there, he would take his 2 Batt over to Prenzlau, then down to Finow, where he would wait for Ben to arrive at Neurappin.

As Ben and Ike traveled south, they witnessed the wanton and mindless destruction and killing by the gangs of punks as they traveled toward Berlin.

"They know they're rapidly reaching the end of the road," Ben said. "It will soon be all over for them, so they've gone on an orgy of killing. It's mindless and obscene. They're telling us this will be a fight to the death. No surrender. And I don't plan on offering them any."

"The press is going to love to hear that," Beth said. Then she smiled, knowing exactly what Ben's response was going to be.

He didn't disappoint her.

"The citizens themselves cleaned out Frankfurt," Corrie told Ben, after receiving several reports from scouts. "With the exception of a very few small towns, and of course, Berlin, Germany is clear."

Frankfurt wasn't the only place where the citizens had taken all they were going to take of punks and street trash and turned on them. The people of Leipzig had done the same thing; and when they had finished dealing with the criminal element, they buried the bodies quite unceremoniously and got on with the business of living.

"For some strange reason," Corrie continued, "only a few of the punks crossed the borders for safety in other countries. They've all congregated in Berlin."

"One last battle," Ben said. "I will never understand the criminal mind. They can't win and they know they can't. They've never defeated us in all the years we've been fighting them. Each time we offer them a chance to start all over, all sins forgiven, they turn it down cold. When will all the battalions be in place?"

"Three more days. Everybody is running on schedule. We will be completely resupplied and ready to go, and the supply lines open and running, by that time."

"How many punks in the city, Corrie?" Cooper asked.

"Thousands. Every punk and creepie we didn't kill in six countries have gathered there."

"So Berlin is gonna be a real piss-cutter and bitch-kitty?"

"How eloquently put," Jersey said, looking up from cleaning her M-16. "I don't believe I have ever heard of an objective referred to with such verbal brevity."

Cooper gave her the finger.

Jersey gave him two in reply.

"All right, children," Doctor Chase said, walking into the room. "Mind your manners, now." He walked to the coffeepot and poured a cup. "Bruno Bottger was a monster, Ben, no one would argue that, but he certainly cared for the citizens of this country. My people are complaining about the lack of something to do. Once Berlin is cleared, this country will be off and running with a strong industrial base and a solid economy."

"All that ends at the border," Ben replied.

"Then the rumors are true?"

"Yes. Bottger gutted Poland, Austria, Czechoslovakia, and Hungary. We're finally getting some intell out of those areas. They're a mess. In the few weeks since Bottger's MEF pulled out, hundreds of armed gangs have either surfaced or come in from other countries . . . probably a combination of the two. There isn't anything that even resembles a stable government anywhere. Anarchy reigns. There haven't been proper medical facilities in those countries in years. Tell your people to enjoy the rest while they can."

"What's the news from back home, Ben? The real news, not that crap in the papers."

Ben leaned back in his chair. "Simon Border's political party is growing and so is his militia, the Christian Front. Blanton is holding on, but not gaining in popularity with the great unwashed. They seem to feel he is treating them unfairly by making them work. And many of them are *refusing* to work. But the armed forces and the police are solidly on Blanton's side and so is the SUSA. Cecil has sent troops to beef up Blanton in certain areas. The sight of Rebels seems to have an almost immediate calming effect on the malcontents."

"I wonder why," Chase said sarcastically. "Taking into consideration that your people are such a gentle, caring, and compassionate bunch."

Ben ignored that.

"The civil liberties bunch is challenging Blanton's policies of forcing people to work and cutting off benefits if they refuse," Ben said. "Harriet Hooter's flagging political party suddenly began picking up steam and she is now considered a dark horse in any election. I suggested Blanton suspend any upcoming elections and the Constitution until he get things going."

"His reply?"

"He said he has suspended all the civil liberties he is going to. No more. Let the chips fall."

"His ass," Chase said bluntly. "How will this ding-dong, Simon Border, affect us, Ben?"

"He won't bother us at all. Not if he has any sense. The SUSA has an excellent relationship with Mexico, Central America, and those countries in South America that are up and running. Much of Canada is aligned solidly with us, and much of Europe will swing our way in the coming months. Simon Border knows I won't hesitate to have him killed if he gets too big for his britches and starts making trouble for the SUSA."

Doctor Chase laughed. "Democracy at work, Rebel-style."

Ben chuckled. "It's called live and let live, Lamar. That's something that Simon Border and Harriet Hooter and others of their ilk have never understood and will never understand."

"Billy Smithson and his Free State of Missouri?" Lamar asked, taking a seat.

"They'll be part of the SUSA in a matter of weeks. I'm sure of it. Billy knows they can't stand alone." Ben stood up and moved to the wall map behind him. He tapped it with a fist. "Berlin. Approximately three hundred and forty square miles of real estate that is filled with thousands of well-armed thugs and creepies. Get your people geared up to move, Lamar. Berlin is going to be one tough nut to crack."

"A piss-cutter," Cooper said, winking at Ben.

"Yeah, Coop," Jersey said, surprising him. "A bitch-kitty. Is it kick-ass time, Boss?"

"It's kick-ass time, Jersey," Ben said.

Within the city of Berlin, the punks and street crap partied and had a high ol' time. The Night People huddled in their lairs and made plans for the Rebels' final assault on German soil. Unlike the fools above them on street level, the creeps knew that, for most of them, it was all over. They were surrounded and the noose was tightening.

The creepies also knew that, thanks to the mindless barbarism of the punks in dealing with civilians on the way to the city, Ben Raines would not be offering his usual surrender terms to the street trash. The Rebels would be coming in for the cold kill.

"Take the children, the fresh women, the virile males, and leave," the judges said. "Use the tunnels. Go. There is little time left. There is no point in stopping in Poland, for that country is next on that devil Ben Raines' list. Our friends in America say that there is a good chance the Rebels will be ordered out of Europe before they reach the Ukraine. So you have a chance if you keep moving east. Go now, quickly!"

It was near the end of the second day since the Rebels had first begun circling the city, and the creeps knew their time was nearly up. Their patrols had seen the Rebels completely encircle the city. But there were only two battalions of Rebels to the east of the city, so those escaping in that direction might have a chance.

The judges issued the orders: Take your positions and prepare to fight to the death.

Buddy's 8 Batt and Nick Stafford's 18 Batt were stretched out along highway E55, two battalions to cover almost forty miles of highway. But they were backed up by double their usual number of tanks and had the assistance of scouts who were on constant roving patrol up and down the highway.

The evening before the push-off, Ben gathered his Batt Coms and told them, "We'll try to save as much of the city as possible. But I made no guarantees for Berlin. It's much too large for that and we're up against at least our number of punks and creeps. I want everybody in body armor—with no exceptions. Tanks will spearhead the drive. That's it. We shove off at dawn tomorrow."

There were now several hundred reporters in the country, at least that many, and Ben had given up trying to control them. Fifty or more had gathered at Ben's jump-off spot waiting for the push to begin. He ignored most of them.

Ben had not seen Cassie for several days, but that in itself was not unusual for she had been doing human-interest stories and was spending a lot of time talking with the German people. About an hour before the push-off, she found him standing in the darkness beside his Hummer, drinking coffee. Ben offered her his mug and she sipped from it.

"Things are beginning to heat up back home, Ben," she said finally, breaking the silence.

"Simon Border?"

"Among others."

"He's an asshole."

She smiled in the darkness. "I assure you, he feels the same about you."

"He's going to run for President, hey?"

She exhaled in exasperation. Ben was always about two jumps ahead of her. Even as close as they were, Cassie had no idea just how massive the Rebels' intelligence network was. Ben had operatives all over the world, but especially in America, for he knew that was where the greatest threat to the future of the SUSA lay. "Do you have spies sitting on his inner council, Ben?"

"I wish."

"Well, you're right. He is going to run for President, but that's only a part of it."

Ben waited. Around them, the machinery of war was cranking up in the warm, humid air of pre-dawn.

"Harriet Hooter will be the dark horse in the upcoming elections, and no one will get a clear majority."

"Harriet is a fool and so is Simon Border. Neither one is a threat to the SUSA."

"Have you heard that Simon's Christian Front is making talk about invading Smithson's Free State of Missouri?"

"Yes. I spoke with Billy about that." What Cassie didn't know and Ben was not yet ready to tell her was that Billy and his men were on their way back to the States. They had been flying out daily from an old military base in Italy since before Ben had arrived at the dead city of Rostock, days earlier. The huge planes that carried them back to America brought back supplies,

"America is going to be divided, Ben, torn apart in war."

"When Simon invades the Free State of Missouri, President Blanton will have no choice but to send troops in to assist Billy Smithson. He gave his word on that."

"The people of America will not support a racist state, Ben."

Ben smiled. "The Free State of Missouri no longer

exists, Cassie. Billy signed papers days ago. Missouri is now part of the SUSA."

"What?"

"If Simon Border wants trouble, just let him invade a member state of the SUSA. I'll kill that son of a bitch before he has time to blink."

Cassie stared at Ben for a moment. She experienced a chill at his words, knowing that Ben did not make idle threats. "Are you giving me this story, Ben?"

"Yes. I was planning to wait a couple more days. But you can broadcast it now if you'd like. It should be interesting to hear Simon's reaction."

"Does Blanton know about this?"

"Yes. It came as no surprise to him."

"Ben, are you planning on someday ruling all of America?"

He looked at her as if she had taken leave of her senses. "No. Hell, no! I've told you that before. Cassie, I don't personally *rule* anything. It's a philosophy, a way of life. People of like mind gathered together. I have no desire whatsoever to have to listen to a bunch of sobbing, whining, hanky-stomping liberals pissing and moaning every time a punk is caught breaking the law and gets his or her ass shot off by a law-abiding citizen. That's why I will support and help defend Homer Blanton and his party. I want him in power. He can put up with the liberals. They are American citizens; they have as much right to their views as I do to mine. I just don't want them around me." He shook his head. "Why is the Rebel philosophy so difficult for people to grasp?"

"Ben, people outside the SUSA understand the

Rebel philosophy. They just don't want to live under it."

"But they don't *have* to live under it. That's my point, Cassie. That's what the Rebels fought and died for all those hard years—the right of a people to work and play and live under a government of *their* choosing, not one that is forced on them. You can't argue that the Rebel form of government doesn't work. You know it does—for those who choose to live under it. People who don't want it can live under your so-called democratic form of government. Which was fine until people started tinkering with the Constitution and fucked it all up."

As always happened, Rebels began gathering around Ben, walking up to stand silently in the waning moments of pre-dawn, listening to Ben Raines defend the philosophy they would all willingly die for. And several dozen reporters were among the silent group.

"Cassie, we don't try to run people's lives in the SUSA. We let the individual control his or her own destiny. The SUSA runs like a well-engineered and well-oiled piece of machinery. It just chugs right along without a hitch. Why in the hell can't others just leave us alone? And why am I bumping my gums explaining this? You understand it perfectly. Why can't your viewers and listeners and readers accept it?"

"Because, General Raines—" Bobby Day's voice came out of the crowd. "—those living outside the SUSA feel your form of government is barbaric."

Bobby Day suddenly found himself very much

alone as other reporters quickly put some distance between Bobby and themselves.

"Barbaric," Ben repeated softly. "Well, now. That is most interesting. The SUSA has the strongest economy in the world. We have zero unemployment. We have practically no crime. We have the finest schools and the finest medical facilities in the world. No one is denied medical care. There hasn't been a racial incident within our borders in so long I can't remember the last one. We have no slums. We pay the highest wages and have the lowest income tax, sales tax and property tax in North America. Most people don't lock their doors or take the keys out of their cars or trucks. The streets are safe to walk anytime of the day or night. We've set aside thousands and thousands of acres for wildlife to live free and safe. Yet you say we have a barbaric form of government. Now just how in the hell did you arrive at that conclusion? And make it brief, please, we have a war to fight."

Bobby Day looked around him at the faces of the Rebels, visible now in the first gray light of dawning. Black, white, oriental, Spanish, Native American, Catholic, Protestant, Jew, Hindu, Buddhist, Moslem, atheist, agnostic—all races, all creeds, all colors. Bobby Day had never been inside the borders of the SUSA. He knew only what he had been force-fed from the mouths of college professors, many of whom lived in such an insulated world they really didn't know horse shit from hog jowls about reality.

Bobby Day turned around without replying and walked off.

The dawning was complete, gray light turning to colors of all hues.

"Kick-ass time, Boss," Jersey said.

"Let's do it," Ben said.

Two

The American military knew, of course, that Billy Smithson's people were returning from Europe, and they informed the President, who kept that bit of news to himself. More and more, Homer was taking cues from Ben Raines and holding back more and more from the press.

The planes carrying Billy's people were angling south and landing at airports in the SUSA, refueling, and then taking off and landing in Missouri after flying through SUSA territory. Simon Border didn't have a clue. But when he heard—reported over satellite by Cassie—that Smithson had dissolved his Free State of Missouri, opened his borders as much as the SUSA did (which wasn't all that wide), and joined the SUSA, Simon threw himself into a towering snit. After he calmed down, he ordered a nationwide hook-up on his television stations and denounced the SUSA as the twenty-first century's equivalent of Sodom and Gomorrah. "They even have *whorehouses* down there!" he thundered, waving a Bible.

They sure did. Ben had legalized prostitution and regulated and taxed it. The "ladies of the evening" saw a doctor every week and practiced safe sex with their customers. Consequently, sexually transmitted diseases were practically nonexistent in the SUSA. Some of the preachers in the SUSA didn't really approve of such things, but they kept their mouths shut about it and their opinions to themselves since the men who frequented the houses were not likely to show up in church anyway. Or so the preachers thought.

Those who listened regularly to Simon Border's daily harangues hung on every word from his sanctimonious mouth and agreed that, yes, indeed, Ben Raines was the Great Satan and his nasty filthy whore-ridden empire had to be destroyed before Ben Raines corrupted the entire world. Just how that was going to be accomplished was somewhat of a mystery since the residents of the SUSA were all armed to the teeth with the most modern of weapons and everyone between the ages of sixteen and sixty was in the Army. The followers of Simon Border also knew that troublemakers didn't last long in the SUSA and that violent criminals had a life expectancy of about a minute and a half—or less.

"God will show us the way!" Simon Border promised his listeners. "God will answer my prayers, and I will personally lead the armies of the Christian Front into battle and defeat the Great Satan, Ben Raines."

"That guy," Cecil Jefferys said after viewing a tape of Simon Border's broadcast, "is a nut!"

"You'll get no argument from me on that," a battalion commander replied. "But a nut that we're going to have to deal with sooner or later."

"True," Cecil said.

"Have you heard from General Raines?"

"The Rebels entered the outskirts of Berlin yesterday morning."

The punks and street gangs who had occupied Berlin slowly fell back under the slow and relentless advance of the Rebels. This time, there had been no
offer of surrender and it didn't take the punks long
to realize that playtime was over and they were facing
the end.

European street gangs and their leaders were much
the same as their American counterparts: cruel and
arrogant, believing they were invincible. The Rebels
quickly changed their minds.

The creeps took no part in the first few days of
fighting, staying in the central part of the city and
letting the street crap get bloodied and very dead.

Those citizens of Berlin who had managed to get
out when the hordes of punks descended upon the
city had returned with the Rebel advance. Using the
weapons taken from the dead street trash, Ben, after
his own people had carefully interviewed them on
their political views, armed the Berliners and formed
them into rear guards. Any Bottger supporters
among the citizens were dealt with by the citizens of
Berlin in final fashion, with the Rebels not interfer-
ing as quick justice was meted out.

West and his 4 Batt took the airport on the northwest side of the city, and supplies began flying in and
carrying the badly wounded out. The airport on the
southeast side of the city fell under the Rebel advance, and the noose began tightening on the punks
in the city.

Punks, male and female, began staggering out of the smoke and fire, hands in the air, begging to be allowed to surrender. They were taken into custody and handed over to the German authorities. After they were ID'd and their criminal records checked, most of them were either shot or hanged, the rest given long prison sentences.

General Matthies and his people were pulled up from the south, and Ben handed over the remainder of the retaking of Berlin to them, pulling his Rebels out. With the exception of a few small pockets of criminal defiance in the countryside, Germany was clear. It had taken the Rebels and the resistance forces about nine months to retake most or all of seven European countries.

Now, seven more countries were added to the growing list of countries that made up the United Nations.

Ben stood his people down and waited for orders from the United Nations.

The orders weren't long in coming: Stabilize Poland, Czechoslovakia, Austria, and Hungary.

"We're gonna get caught in Eastern Europe right smack in the dead of winter," Ike groused. "And winters there will freeze the balls off a brass monkey."

"Oh, it isn't that bad, my friend," Colonel Wajda teased. "Wait until you get to Russia."

Ben looked up from a map. "Ike, you take your 2 Batt and battalions 10 through 18 and go into Austria and Slovenia and work east. I'll take my 1 Batt, 3 through 9, and General Wajda's people and go into Poland and Czechoslovakia. Generals Flanders and Randazzo have their hands full trying to get some order into Italy. Lee Flanders says it's the biggest mess he's ever seen. Lee says there are about a hundred and fifteen political parties surfacing and everybody is talking at once. Lamar, make sure he gets plenty of aspirin. Lee says headaches are the most common ailments among his people."

After the laughter had faded, Ben said, "Ike, you're going into unknown territory in Slovenia and Croatia. We've made contact with some resistance groups, and they've agreed to meet you at the border and offer you as much assistance as possible; but if you feel yourself getting bogged down and over your head, back out. The resistance leaders assure me that you'll be welcomed in there, but that's iffy. Play it safe and cautious. Now then, I want as much intell as you can gather about the countries between Hungary and Greece. Serbia, Albania, Macedonia—if those countries still exist. But I'm afraid that intell is going to be precious little. All we know right now is that those countries are supposedly locked in civil war. And if that proves out, we don't go in. Not without a hell of a lot more people than we have now. Cooper managed to round up a lot of maps and we've made plenty of copies. They're over on that table by the far wall.

"Colonel Wajda, you'll take Rebel battalions 4 through 7 and neutralize your home country."

The Polish Colonel nodded his head in approval.

"Battalions 3, 8, and 9 will go with me into Czechoslovakia. Therm, Colonel Wajda has said the roads in Poland are in bad shape, so we can figure the roads where the rest of us are going are just as bad or worse. Logistically, this might be a real nightmare."

"Where will I be, Ben?" Thermopolis, the ex-hippie, asked.

Ben smiled. "You've been bitching for months about wanting front-line duty, so all right, you've got it. I'm placing your wife, Rosebud, in charge of the detail work and creating a new battalion, 19, with you in charge."

"Ben, if you leave Emil Hite with my wife, she'll kill him within two days. Bet on it."

"No, she won't, because Emil and his band of warriors will be with you."

"Oh, shit!" Thermopolis said.

"You're the only one who can control him, Therm. What do you say?"

"Where will Rosebud be?"

"With us. Each of the battle groups—excuse me, stabilization groups—will have their own company to handle details."

"Fine. Sounds good. She's been saying—quite frequently of late—that I'm getting underfoot, and I know that is my cue to make an exit."

"Well, that's it, then. Start gearing up to spread out and start the push."

The batt coms began trooping out, but Thermopolis caught Ben's eye. "Who gets to tell Emil he's back on the front lines?" he asked.

"I thought I'd leave that honor up to you," Ben said with a wink.

"Gee, thanks. You're just too nice to me."

"Think nothing of it, Therm. Glad to have you back with us on the line."

Therm turned to go, hesitated, then said, "Ben, you remember the first time we met?"

Ben laughed. "Sure. I have to say that we've both come a long way since then."

"In more ways than one, for a fact. Ben, rumor has it that Bruno Bottger is still alive."

"I think he is. I don't know how he pulled it off, but I believe he did."

"Any ideas where he might be?"

"Just one. Africa."

"You know, Ben, I've always wanted to go to Africa. Rosebud, too."

Ben stared at the man for a moment—ponytail and all. "If you think I'm going to send you to Africa, put it out of your mind, ol' buddy."

Therm waved that off. "No, no, I didn't mean that. What I meant was, it will be interesting when we *all* go."

Again, Ben stared at him. "You seem damn certain we'll get there, Therm."

"Eventually, Ben. Yeah. I think we will." Therm smiled and walked out of the room.

Ben looked over at Jersey, sitting with her M-16 across her knees. "When the betting started, Boss," she said, "it was about fifty to one against our going to Africa. Now it's pretty much even money."

"What is the consensus, Little Bit?"

She shrugged her shoulders. "The majority will go without bitching too much. Some people think we should stay out, but color doesn't have a thing to do with it."

"Not since the attempted coup, you mean."

"Right."

"If we go to Africa, Jersey, it will be only after we've

completed our objective here in Europe. And that's going to take a few years, the way we're going."

"And by then, you know what we'll have to do?"

"Stabilize North America all over again," Cooper said.

Ben looked at him. Cooper had spoken with a grim look on his face. "You sound pretty sure of yourself, Coop."

"Yes, sir, I am. A certain type of American just can't leave things alone. The majority gets a good thing going, then somebody else comes along and wants to screw it all up. Take the SUSA, for instance. We've got the best government in the whole world, with more than ninety-five percent of the people who live there in agreement with it. Yet we're the most hated in all of North America. Why? Because people like Simon Border and Harriet Hooter and those mealymouthed ass-wipes who follow them just can't stand it when they're not in total control of people's lives. If they're opposed to someone's smoking a cigarette, then the whole nation should be smokeless because *they* think it should be . . . and to hell with the rest of the constituency. If they're opposed to the ownership of pistols, then all the pistols in the nation should be gathered up; again, to hell with what other people think. In the SUSA, we've got a near-perfect balance, and they can't stand it. If President Jefferys lets his guard down for one second, those bastards will be all over him. They're just waiting for the slightest crack in our security. And it will happen. No nation can be totally, one hundred percent vigilant all the time. And then we'll have to do it all over again."

Ben looked at the faces of his team and saw only serious sober eyes looking back at him. "That's a . . . depressing thought, Coop. What do you think should be done about it? Get rid of those who are opposed to our form of government?"

Cooper shook his head. "No. That's where we're different from those who oppose us. We believe that nations-within-a-nation is the best way. They don't. We want them to have their government, but they won't want us to have ours. That makes us a cut above them."

"For a long time now, Chief," Corrie said, "we've been having study groups. In every battalion. We thought you knew and wouldn't object."

"I don't object. I think it's a good thing."

"Well, we find boxes of old magazines and books and study them and then discuss what we've read. For instance, just before the Great War, the term racist was slung around pretty damn loosely—"

"I'll certainly agree with that. I was accused of being a racist."

"But you're not," Beth said. "None of us here are racist. You can't be a Rebel and be a racist. It's impossible. Thing is, and this just came up a few nights ago, there was this article about this man who bought some land up in the northwest part of America and took his family there. He wanted to be left alone and raise his kids and teach them himself, and he and his wife were qualified to do that. He called himself a separatist, but many of the press called him a racist."

"And the federal government staked him out," Ben noted, "set him up, and eventually killed his wife and one of his sons and put him in prison for a time. I know the case."

"What was he doing wrong to deserve that kind of treatment?" Corrie asked.

"Nothing. But the government was out of control by that time, and getting worse. Soon it was spinning completely out of control. The feds were sticking their noses into everybody's business. Congress was passing legislation that, in effect, stated we must all love everybody. One racial group could cast aspersions against another group, but the group who could be prosecuted for casting aspersions could not, under the law, cast racial aspersions against the first group."

"We read about that, too. But none of us could figure it out," Jersey said.

"Well," Ben said with a laugh, "don't feel alone. None of us could either."

"Boss," Cooper asked, "what in the hell was sensitivity training?"

"Police officers, for instance, had to take classes in order to better understand the criminals they might have to arrest."

Jersey's dark eyes darkened even more. "Would you repeat that, Boss? I mean, that sounds like a bag of shit to me."

"It was. And is. Which is why we don't have such nonsense in the SUSA."

Corrie had turned to her radio and was listening. She spoke a few soft words and then looked at Ben. "That was a report from our scouts. The thugs and gang leaders in Prague have warned that if the Rebels enter the city, they will die there." She shook her head. "Some things never change, do they?"

"Sure looks that way." He glanced at Jersey.

She smiled and said, "Should we take sensitivity training before we go into Prague, Chief?"

"I don't think so, Jersey."

"Kick-ass time!"

Three

"It says here," Beth said, reading from an old tourist guidebook, "that Prague is a city of one-and-a-half-million people. It has warm rainy summers and long dry winters. And if you get in trouble, contact your country's consulate for assistance."

"Why don't we leave Emil Hite in Prague and he can be the ambassador from the US?" Jersey suggested.

"We want to help these people, Jersey," Ben said. "Not plunge them into depths of depression. What's the latest from Prague, Corrie?"

"There is a sizable number of punks waiting for us. Exact numbers unavailable, but they appear to be well armed. Scouts report no sign of creepies. The city has been trashed and looted. Residents have fled into the countryside. We should be coming up on the first refugee camps in about an hour. That'll be just across the border at Teplice. That town is secure."

"The roads have turned to shit," Cooper bitched.

"They're going to get worse," Corrie warned him.

"Any word from Ike?" Ben asked.

"Not a peep."

The town of Teplice was overflowing with refugees

from in and around Prague. At first they were stunned into silence to see the Rebel army rolling in. Communications had become so bad, most had little or no knowledge of what was going on fifty miles away. It had become a matter of day-to-day survival.

Ben was standing outside his Hummer when Doctor Chase walked up. "I know, Lamar. I know. Don't start. We'll be here for a few days."

"These people haven't had proper medical attention in years. The children need basic inoculations." He handed Corrie a list. "I need those medicines. Yesterday. Arrange for a drop, please." He turned and walked away.

"Well, he's happy now," Ben said. "His people are finally getting something to do. Come on. Let's see the town and talk to some people from Prague."

The people were shabbily dressed and weary-eyed. They stared in disbelief at the healthy, well-fed Rebels. But there was no sense of defeat about them; they were simply tired and hungry and confused.

The Rebels had begun to realize that the massive resistance they had first faced in every town and village was over for a time. Since landing in France, some months back, the Rebels had killed, wounded, or—in a few cases—taken prisoner thousands of criminals. They had no firm numbers as to how many punks and gangs they had driven eastward, but there is a limit to how many thugs one country can produce. Behind the Rebels, mass graves lay in silent testimony to what happens to those who resist the stabilizing of a country.

"I wonder how many of these people were in gangs

just a few weeks ago, or even a few days ago?" Thermopolis asked, falling in step with Ben.

"Quite a few, I would imagine. And there is a good possibility some of them will return to a life of crime once we pull out. But if these citizens adopt the form of government I hope they do, criminals won't stand much of a chance once we leave."

"They've got to get their economy cranked up."

"That isn't our job. There are so-called political experts from the U.N. coming in right behind us to help the people do that." He grimaced. "The world is getting smaller again, Therm."

Thermopolis knew what he meant and nodded his head in agreement. "I just hope it's for the better."

"It will be for a time. Then it will revert back to the same ol' have and have-nots it was before the Great War."

"That's a dismal thought, Ben."

"Human nature, Therm. You know that as well as I do. That's why you and your group dropped out."

"Then the world learned nothing from all the wars and the following years of suffering and tragedy, did it, Ben?"

"Not much, Therm, I am sorry to say. Not much."

The Rebels pushed deeper into the Czech Republic. So far, not a shot had been fired since they had crossed the border. They stopped at every town, every village, spending anywhere from a few hours to a few days, treating the people and giving kids childhood shots. The Rebel medical and political people were happy at work, healing and teaching; the Rebel combat teams were bored. They had been primed and cocked for action . . . and none had come for weeks. But all that was about to change.

"We're about five miles away from combat," Ben told his team after looking at and then folding and putting away his map. "Order the convoy halted here, Corrie."

Batts 3, 9, and Therm's short battalion had cut off from the convoy and would attack the city on the Slany Highway, first taking the airport, while Ben's 1 Batt and Buddy's 8 Batt would hit the city from E55.

Scouts who had been roaming around the outskirts of the city for days joined up with the two columns.

"It's going to be house to house and block by block," they reported to Ben.

"How are they outfitted?"

"Small arms and machine guns. Some mortars and rocket launchers. Nothing heavier that we've seen." The young Rebel grinned. "And we've been in close enough to hear them fart."

"They're a pretty motley bunch, General," another scout said. "Not much in the way of discipline. But they're hard-core criminals and they're not going to give it up without a fight."

"Then that's what we'll give them," Ben said. "At dawn tomorrow."

The Rebels had become the world's leading experts in the taking and clearing of cities, suburbs, airports, and just about anything else one might care to name. As one reporter wrote in his column: *Watching the Rebel Army work is something like viewing a very brutal and violent ballet, and, as in ballet, you know who is going to win.*

The Rebels, with tanks spearheading, struck the city just after dawn and, by noon, had taken the airport and hammered their way well into the suburbs. Grateful citizens, quickly organized by Rebel political teams, moved in right behind the combat teams—oftentimes working while the fighting raged around them—and immediately began clearing away the debris and putting some order back into neighborhoods.

It really came as no surprise to anyone that at noon the second day of fighting, groups of punks and thugs and street crap started appearing with white flags, their hands in the air. The criminals simply were not prepared for the Rebels' methods of clearing and cleaning out cities. They were used to dealing with police, who were under strict codes of conduct on how to cope with the lawless. The Rebels went straight for the jugular and didn't give a damn for the feelings of thugs and punks.

Ben, as usual, was leading the assault very deep in a hot sector and came upon what appeared to be a badly frightened, shocked, and shaken group of men and women. They were sitting in the middle of an old cobblestone street, their hands in the air.

Ben and his team stopped at the corner and quickly scanned the area for a possible ambush. He didn't like what he saw or what he felt. The street was narrow and lined with old vehicles on both sides.

"It's no trick!" a woman called out in heavily accented English. "We give up! Don't shoot us. Please, God, don't kill us!"

"Stand up and move toward us," Ben called. "No tricks or you're dead."

The group struggled to their feet, which is no easy task with your hands in the air, and stood, their eyes shifting from left to right.

"Move toward us," Ben called. "Slow and easy." To his team, he said, "They're going to pull something. Watch it."

"There's something strapped onto that big guy's back," Beth observed.

"I saw an old movie during R&R," Coop whispered. "About the second world war. One Japanese fellow who offered to surrender had a small machine gun strapped to his back. You know what happened next."

"You may be right," Jersey said. "Although it pains me to admit it."

"Now!" the woman screamed, falling forward to land on the cobblestones, her group with her.

Cooper had pegged it: The man had what appeared to be a German MG-3 strapped onto his back. Another of the group jerked it up just as men and women began firing from behind the old cars and trucks parked along the street.

Ben flattened out on the sidewalk and let his old Thompson sing its .45 caliber song, the fat slugs tearing into flesh and whining off the cobblestones.

Coop was carrying his SAW, and he quickly ducked into the building and started firing out of a broken window, letting the .223 rounds from the two hundred round box magazine fly. Jersey, Corrie, and Beth leveled their M-16's and added to the death songs in the old street.

A Bradley Fighting Vehicle rolled up and cut loose with its 25mm cannon, quickly turning the narrow street into an avenue of death for the gang members.

Automatic weapons' fire began coming from the second-story windows on both sides of the street. The M3 Bradley began swiveling its two-man power turret and opening up with both cannon and machine gun fire while Ben and his team let the lead fly from ground level. The Bradley turned, and the Rebels inside opened gun ports and added more fire-power to the narrow street fight.

The Rebels poured on the fire for a full sixty seconds until Ben signaled Corrie to call for a cease fire. The six Rebels inside the Bradley exited through the ramp in the rear and took up positions on both sides of the street. But no returning fire from the gang members greeted them.

This brief firefight was over. Or so Ben and the others thought.

"We may have a slight problem, Boss," Corrie said after listening to her headset for a moment. "We're cut off from the main group. This area was controlled by a warlord named Viktor Sima. I think I pronounced that right. He had the largest gang and vowed to fight to the death. I just got that word from intell, who got it moments ago from captured punks." She held up a hand and listened for a couple of seconds. "That's ten-four. We'll sit tight." To Ben she said, "We are most definitely cut off. Some of the street gangs formed up and found some reserve of courage and counter attacked."

"Screwed their courage to the sticking place, hey?" Ben said with a smile.

"Screwed their *what?*" Cooper asked.

"That's Shakespeare, Coop," Beth said.

"How about ammo?" Ben called.

"Everybody's all right," Corrie said after checking with the others. "About six hundred rounds of 25mm for the cannon left."

"Anybody hit?"

"Nobody got a scratch."

Ben looked around him and spotted an old garage across and down the street. "Back up to that building," he ordered. "Now! Go. Go. Go!"

Everyone safe in the garage smelling of old grease and gasoline, Coop unfolded a map and studied it for a moment. "Where the hell are we?" he asked. "All the street signs have been torn down and I can't get my bearings."

"That's why I ordered the Hummer parked," Ben said. "In these old cities you can get turned around very quickly." He indicated a location on the map. "I think we're right there—give or take a block or two."

"Deserters from Bottger's MEF are fighting with this Sima guy," Corrie called from across the room. "Intell underestimated the strength and firepower of the street gangs."

Ben prowled both floors of the old building and found it well built and in pretty good shape. There were two back doors that led into a very narrow, by American standards, alley. Too narrow for the Bradley, he guessed.

He motioned for two Rebels who had arrived in the Bradley. "Check out that building there," he said, pointing across the alley, "and keep going to the end of the block. When you reach the end of the block, report by radio."

They nodded and were gone.

Ben returned to the front of the building and looked up the street. The bodies of the men and women were still sprawled in pools of blood on the cobblestones. The Bradley had been pulled back into the depths of the old garage and was parked in the gloom, impossible to see from the street. Above them, the sky was dark and leaden, the clouds threatening a downpour.

Corrie held up a hand for a few seconds, then said, "That's a roger." To Ben she added, "The end of this block opens into a wide park. If we tried to go that way, we'd be exposed to enemy fire."

"All right," Ben responded, "get those two back here." When she had recalled the men, Ben asked, "How hard cut off are we, Corrie?"

"It isn't good, Boss. The street gangs have rallied and are holding. It's going to take a couple of hours, at least, to punch through to us. But they're not real sure of our location."

Ben nodded his understanding. He pointed to two Rebels. "Get that machine gun the punks were about to use on us and that can of ammo. That'll give us extra firepower, and we're going to need it. We're going to be here for a while."

When the men had returned, carrying the MG3 and a bi-podded RPK and several boxes of ammo they'd found, Ben assigned positions. "Maintain noise discipline," he directed. "Leave the garage doors open just as we found them. Get back into the shadows and stay put and I think . . ."

The sounds of mortar rounds exploding cut him off in mid-sentence. "I can't tell if those are ours or theirs. I suspect theirs. This is going to be a tougher piece of cake than we were led to believe." As he stood, he sniffed the air. "Who shaved this morning and used after-shave?"

"Me, sir," a young Rebel said.

"Goddamnit." Cooper swore at the mistake.

"Smear grease on your face and kill that odor, boy," Ben told him. "As a matter of fact, all of us will smear grease on our faces to help conceal the paleness. If you can't find enough grease, use your cammo paint. Do it."

The Rebel on the second floor radioed to Corrie, "We've got company. Heads up."

"Company coming, Boss," she told Ben.

"Fade back and hold your positions. Do not fire unless we're spotted. Stand easy."

The sky darkened further, then opened up and began to rain over the city, turning midday into near-dusk. The Rebels trapped inside the old garage waited, weapons at the ready. They breathed through their mouths to cut down on even that slight noise. They heard the sounds of running boots, then silence as the men flattened against the outside of the building. Muffled voices over the sounds of rain drifted to them. The Rebels saw the fast-moving shapes of men and women dart across the open doors of the garage and slip on past, working their way up the street.

So far, so good, Ben thought.

Then Lady Luck lifted her slightly soiled skirts and crapped all over the Rebels as they heard the sounds of the two back doors opening and the sounds of voices speaking in a language none of them understood.

Ben shifted his eyes and looked at Jersey, who stood close to him. She arched an eyebrow.

The men drew closer. They were dressed in a mishmash of clothing that clearly ID'd them as street punks. The weapons they carried were all different, and they handled them carelessly. They stopped in a group, talked briefly in low tones, then spread out across the rear of the building, unzipped their pants, and took a piss on the floor.

Jersey rolled her eyes in disgust, and Ben struggled to keep a straight face.

The punks spotted the Bradley and lifted their weapons.

"Shit!" Ben muttered, then stepped out of the shadows and blew the men into eternal darkness.

"Talk about gettin' caught with your dick hangin' out," Cooper quipped.

"Wonderful, Cooper," Jersey said. "You certainly have a way with words."

Then there was no more time for talk as the men and women in the rain-slicked street doubled back. The fight was on, but not for long.

Sima's people ran right into a classic Rebel ambush, and those that remained alive were forced to retreat across the street.

"We can't hold here," Ben said. He motioned his forces toward the back door. "Out into the alley," he said. "Move it."

"The Bradley—"

"Leave it." He took a grenade from his battle harness and said, "Move, goddamnit! Out the back."

Ben was the last to leave the building. He popped the pin and tossed the grenade into the belly of the Bradley and then stepped over the bodies of the gang members and out into the rain, following his team up the alley at a dead run.

The grenade did exactly what Ben had hoped it would. It set off the 25mm rounds in the vehicle; and when *they* started blowing, they set off all the spare 7.62 ammo for the vehicle's machine gun. After the grenade's muffled explosion, it sounded like a major battle was taking place.

"The open park is just over there," one of the Rebels who had checked out the block panted, pointing, when Ben had caught up.

"Then we'll go the other way," Ben said.

"That's bogy country, sir!"

"That's right, son. It sure is. And the last place Sima's people would think to look for us. Let's get going, people. We don't have much time to find a hidey-hole."

They jogged two blocks up the narrow alley and then cut to their right and ran for two more blocks. They were becoming hopelessly lost as they ran from alley to street.

"What happened to all the goddamn street signs?" Jersey cussed as they ran. "I'm lost as a goose."

"Join the club," Beth told her. "The map is useless. I have no idea where we are."

When they finally paused to catch their breath, they flopped down on the dirty, rat-chewed, paper-littered floor, and Cooper said, "What's that I smell?"

"The river," Ben told him. "It's got to be. We can't be more than a few blocks from it. Damn, we're deeper into bogy country than I'd thought. But there is no way we made the city proper." Ben opened a map and studied it in the dim light coming through a dirty window. "I think we're right here." He shook his head. "No. We might have turned onto this street initially and gone too far. Those short blocks were our undoing. I have good news and bad news, people. Our guys don't have the vaguest idea where we are."

"If our people don't know where we are, what's the bad news?" Jersey asked.

"Neither do I," Ben admitted.

Four

"I suppose we could ask the first person who wanders by," Coop said with a smile.

"Great idea, Coop," Jersey said. "We'll elect you to do that."

"Ho ho," Coop said.

"Bump somebody, Corrie," Ben said. "And tell them we're all right. Just lost." He shook his head. "I hope Ike never learns of this."

"He will," Jersey said as Corrie reported in.

She finished her brief report and looked at Ben. "Needless to say, a lot of people are highly irritated at us."

"Especially at me."

"Right."

"They'll get over it."

"Buddy suggests that we stay on the air long enough for him to get a fix on our position."

"Negative."

"That's what I told him. He's very unhappy about our getting cut off."

Before Ben could reply, a Rebel by a window called in a hoarse whisper. "We've got company. Coming up from the south. At least I think it's south."

"How many?"

"Hard to tell in this rain. Maybe ten to fifteen. Nope. Here comes some more around the corner."

"We're all right from the front," Ben whispered. "But anyone approaching from the rear will see the boot tracks."

Without being told, Cooper took his SAW and left to cover the back room. Anyone opening the door would step into a death trap.

Several of the gang members paused at the front of the building to peer through the dirty windows. No one attempted to enter through the rear, and they walked past, on through the driving rain.

"We're so far in front of our lines, we can't even hear the gunfire," Beth commented.

"The rain is helping to muffle the noise," Ben said. "But I thought I heard shots just a few seconds ago. I don't understand how we got so far ahead."

The Rebels fell silent, enveloped in the sounds of the hard-driving rain and a couple of drip-drops splattering on the floor from a leak in the roof. Ben looked at his watch. Four o'clock. They needed to get back to their lines, but Ben had no idea where their lines were.

If they weren't back among friendlies by dark, they would have to sit it out, for moving around at night was a sure way to get dead in a hurry. On the other side of the coin, they wouldn't go hungry or thirsty, for they each carried emergency rations and two canteens of water.

Ben glanced at Jersey just as she chanced a peek out the dirty window. She looked right into the eyes of an outlaw. Ben shot him in the center of his face just as the man was lifting his AK to cream Jersey. The .45 slugs took half the man's head off.

"Where the hell did he come from?" Beth asked as bullets began whining off the outside stone on the front of the building and smashing through windows.

"Doesn't make any difference," Jersey said. "They're here."

From the rear of the building, Cooper's SAW barked and men screamed in pain.

"Three to the rear to help Cooper," Ben called, and Rebels from the Bradley crawled out of the room, staying low to the floor.

Within seconds, all the front windows were gone, smashed by unfriendly fire.

"Bloop those across the street!" Ben called.

They loaded 40-mm grenades into the bloop tubes of the M-16's and fired. The explosives did their work; the fire from across the street suddenly stopped and was replaced by moaning and crying from the badly wounded.

A woman zigzagged up the street, carrying what looked like a satchel-charge. Ben cut the legs from under her with a burst from his Thompson, and she went screaming and sprawling and cursing facedown on the rain-slick cobblestones, sliding a few yards before coming to a halt on the sidewalk in front of a building where unfriendly fire was coming hot and heavy. The charge she was carrying blew, and the woman disappeared in a sickening splash and slop of color. The charge must have been massive, for it took out the entire front of the building and silenced the gunfire.

"The back is clear," Cooper called.

"Let's get out of here!" Ben said, lunging to his boots and heading for the rear door.

Ben took the lead and led his people up the alley for half a block. He turned left and ducked into the back of a building, leading them through a dark maze of litter and then out the front. He turned right and ran up the street to the corner, his eyes searching for some remnant of a street sign.

Nothing.

"Shit!" Ben cussed and ran across the street, the heavy rain partly obscuring the Rebels as they sought safety and a way out of bogy country.

Suddenly, the short blocks and narrow twisting streets ended, spilling into a wide boulevard. A block away, a half-a-dozen main battle tanks flying the flag of the SUSA rumbled in their direction. A dozen or more Hummers and Bradley's were right behind them. Ben recognized Buddy's personal Hummer.

"It's been an interesting afternoon," Ben said, leaning back against the building under what remained of an awning and rolling a cigarette. "Now I guess my son will chew me out."

"Goddamnit, father!" Buddy hollered a few seconds later. "Where in the hell have you been?"

"Everything is back to normal," Ben muttered.

The Rebels seized the bridges the next day and crossed the river Vltava—also known as the Moldau. Ben (as he had accurately foreseen) found himself surrounded by Rebels and unable to leave his new CP, an old castle, without bodyguards watching his every move.

"Don't you trust me, son?" Ben asked.

"You have to be joking!" Buddy replied.

Doctor Chase chuckled at the tanks surrounding the palace and the guards in the halls and in front of Ben's office. "Buddy sure clipped your wings, didn't he?"

"Very funny, Lamar. I'm amused. What do you want?"

Taking his time, Lamar poured coffee and sat down. "Look, Ben, you're not yet ready for a cane or wheelchair, but you have no business getting into combat situations. You are the commanding general of the largest standing army on the face of the earth—as far as we know. It's about damn time you acted accordingly."

"Oh, I will, Lamar. I will."

"Until the next time you find a window of opportunity to sneak off and get into trouble."

"That's probably true, but I've got enough paperwork to keep me occupied for about a week, at least. So stop worrying."

"What's the word from Mike?"

"I haven't seen him in weeks. No telling where he is. But I did speak with Homer Blanton a few hours ago and he's back to work full time and doing well. Simon Border is still waging a war of words over his radio and TV stations. And Harriet Hooter and her followers are marching and waving placards. Homer finally wised up and nationwide elections have been postponed indefinitely in the USA."

"And the SUSA?"

"Running as smooth as can be."

Lamar nodded. "I am surprised that we managed to save as much of Prague as we did."

"I think in the final analysis we'll save about ninety-five percent of the city. But the museums and art galleries have long been looted. Somebody is sitting on millions and millions of dollars worth of valuable paintings and artifacts."

"They'll surface, eventually."

"Yeah, on the black market."

Corrie entered the huge room. "It's just about over, Boss," she said. "The punks are giving it up in droves."

"Viktor Sima?"

"Looks like he took what was left of his bunch and headed east."

"Well, we'll meet him again. Does anybody know what happened to those idiot gang leaders? Boogie Woogie Slam Bam, or whatever that fool called himself?"

Corrie laughed. "Boogie Woogie Bagwamb?"

"That's him."

She shook her head. "Those people dropped out of sight. Intell thinks they'll eventually surface back in the States."

"They better keep their asses out of the SUSA."

"I don't think they'll get within five hundred miles of our territory," Jersey said from her spot across the room. "They're stupid, not crazy."

Ben stood up. "Come on. Let's take a look at the city."

"You just don't want to deal with all that paperwork," Lamar said.

"You damn sure got that right," Ben replied.

Seventy-five percent of the city had been cleared, and those gang members who still fought were now surrounded. Encircled by a host of Rebels, Ben began a tour of Prague.

After about fifteen minutes, Ben said to his body-guard, "You know, Sergeant, I could just order you to leave me the hell alone, you know that?"

The sergeant did not reply.

Ben stared at him. "Who the hell are you? I don't know you."

The man smiled. "Sgt. Matt Andrews, sir. From 2 Batt. I take my orders from General McGowan. He said to blanket you; we're going to blanket you."

"Ike," Ben said, then grew thoughtful. "That tubby, Air Force fly-boy. I might have known it." Ben looked around him. There was a main battle tank in front of the short convoy and another MBT in the rear. In between, two Bradley Fighting Vehicles and one APC with twin .50-caliber machine guns filled with Rebels.

"All right," Ben said cheerfully. "Come on. Let's get this circus on the road."

In the Hummer, Jersey gave him a questioning look. "You're happy about all this protection, Boss?"

"In a way, Little Bit. You see, those guys are not Rebels and Ike didn't send them. I just called Ike a tubby, Air Force fly-boy and that so-called sergeant didn't bat an eye. Everybody in the Rebel Army knows Ike was a Navy SEAL. If they'd just done a little bit more research they might have pulled this thing off."

"The punks we've been fighting aren't that smart, Chief," Cooper said.

"No. These impostors were either sent in here by someone else or have been close by waiting for us to show up. And I'll bet on the latter."

"Bottger's MEF people?" Beth asked.

"Probably. Just another reason for me to think he's not dead."

"Ah, Boss," Cooper said, "we're getting further away from the good guys and closer to the still-hot zone. What do you want me to do?"

"The next time we come up on an alley, cut down it and floorboard this Hummer. Those APC's might be able to follow us, but the tanks won't. They're twelve-feet wide."

"Then what do we do?" Cooper asked, glancing in the side mirror.

Ben smiled. "You been to church lately, Coop?"

"No. Why?"

"Because once we cut into the alley—we pray for divine intervention."

"Oh, Lord!" Coop said.

"That's a pretty good start, Coop," Jersey said. "But always remember, don't pray for yourself, pray for *me!*"

Cooper muttered something under his breath.

"Are you praying already, Coop?" Jersey asked.

"No. I was suggesting some places for you to go."

"You asked for that one, Jersey," Ben said.

"Every now and then he will get one on me," she admitted.

"Turn right up here, Coop," Ben said. "Now. Pour it on."

Cooper whipped into the alley and floorboarded the pedal. Ben noted that the narrow street was plenty wide enough for the Hummer and probably for the APC's as well.

"You want me to lay some grenades down?" Jersey yelled, crawling into the back-space and loading up her bloop tube.

"Not yet. Let's see what they do."

That didn't take long.

The M2 turned into the alley and cut loose with its 25-mm chain gun just as Coop roared out of the thoroughfare and onto a narrow, cobblestone street. The 25-mm rounds tore off bricks and hammered the buildings but miraculously missed the Hummer.

"Down this way, Coop!" Ben said.

Just as Cooper turned, the lead MBT rounded the corner and cut loose with a machine gun, the .50-caliber rounds hitting the left rear tire of the Hummer.

"We've had it, Boss!" Cooper yelled, fighting the wheel.

"Grab what you can and follow me!" Ben said. "Let's go!"

Ben and his team exited the Hummer and ran up the street, straight into the uncleared hot zone. The MBT turned into the alley, and the big .50 hammered again, one of the rounds ricochetting off the bricks and punching right through Corrie's radio, the impact almost knocking her off her feet. Beth steadied her and helped her struggle out of the smashed radio, and then they were off and running again.

"You all right?" Jersey yelled over her shoulder.

"I'm O.K.," Corrie said. "I hope somebody grabbed a walkie-talkie."

"I've got mine," Ben said. A second later he kicked open a door and yelled, "In here. Quickly."

His team inside and unhurt, Ben secured the door with a broken chair. His would-be assassins were at the far end of the alley and would not know for sure which door they had entered; they would have to try them all.

"Out the front, gang," Ben said. "Move it."

They ran through the ground floor of the building. A quick eye-sweep of the street, left and right, and they were across it unseen—they hoped—and into another building.

Ben pulled his walkie-talkie from his harness and keyed it. Nothing. He tried again. Nothing. He opened the battery compartment and checked. Everything seemed to be all right.

"Batteries are gone," Corrie said. She looked around. "Anybody else got one?"

No one did.

"Maybe Jersey remembers how to use talking smoke," Cooper suggested with a smile.

"I wish," Jersey said, "but my tribe was corrupted by the white man's telephone."

"What now, Boss?" Beth asked Ben.

"We stay alive," he said simply.

Five

"They can't take the time to go block by block, searching every floor of every building," Ben said. "They don't even have a general idea where we are. So if they find us, it'll be pure luck on their part. We stay put and hope for the best."

"And pray," Coop added.

"That, too," Ben agreed.

"Here, Jersey," Cooper said with a grin, moving close to her. "Let me put my arms around you and we'll pray together."

"Which arm do you want broken, Coop?" Jersey asked him.

Cooper tried his best to look hurt. He really didn' pull it off. "Jersey, that is no way to talk to a man who has just found salvation."

"You want to try for a hospital bed?"

"Tank," Beth called. "Coming up on our left."

Ben looked. The tank was buttoned up tight. Ben and the others carried bandoleers of 40-mm gre nades for their bloop tubes, but while the M-433 round could penetrate up to two inches of armor, i would not penetrate the new armor of the Rebe tanks.

The tank slowly rumbled past.

"I sure would like to have an Armbrust," Coop muttered.

"I'd like to have a glass of cold milk and a piece of apple pie," Ben whispered just as his eyes caught troop movement slowly working up the street. "Back," he whispered. "Out the back door. They're checking every building."

At HQ, Rosebud was frantically trying to reach the Eagle. She hit the panic button, and Thermopolis was the first to respond.

"The Eagle has dropped out of sight. No response from him or his guards."

"Who were those guys?" Buddy radioed from just about a mile away.

"Ike sent them."

"Bump Ike and confirm that. I have a funny feeling about all this."

Less than a minute later, Therm and Buddy got the news. "Ike sent no one."

"Shit!" Therm said.

"Which way did they go?" Buddy radioed.

"East."

"Straight into a free-fire zone," Lt. Bonelli said. "Jesus, I never suspected anything bogus about those people. Hell, neither did the general. They just fit right in."

"From now on we confirm all new troops," Rosebud radioed. "With no exceptions."

"Yes, dear," Thermopolis said.

"Someday I must get married," Buddy said. "It surely must be a unique arrangement."

Therm looked at him and said nothing.

* * *

The first few doors they tried were locked, and Ben didn't want to kick his way in for that would be a dead giveaway. They moved on cautiously until they found a building that was unlocked and quickly ducked inside, careful not to disturb the litter. Ben closed the door.

They didn't dare set up to make a stand, not against tanks; they wouldn't have a chance against the big guns. To stand and fight would get them killed.

"If the bastards would just unbutton," Coop said, "we could drop a grenade down the hatch."

"If your aunt had balls, she'd be your uncle," Jersey popped right back.

"Screw you, Jersey!"

"I have a headache, Coop. Sorry."

"The back door leads into another alley," Beth said. "And we've got people coming up the alley—this way."

"From which end?" Ben asked.

Beth pointed.

Ben handed Corrie his Thompson and clip pouch and picked up her M-16 and took her spare magazines. He hung a bandoleer of 40-mm grenades around his neck. "This is pissing me off. I'm tired of it. You get ready to make a break for it."

"Which way?" Corrie asked.

"Right out the way we came," Ben replied. "And don't wait for me. As soon as I open up, you go. And that is an order. You all understand? I'll be all right. Just get back to our lines."

They all nodded. "This is personal now," Ben said. "Get ready."

He walked to the back door and opened it a crack. Half-a-dozen men from the "sergeant" 's team were about fifty feet away, walking abreast up the street. Ben stepped out and said, "You bastards looking for me?" Then he pulled the trigger and held it back, spraying the thoroughfare from left to right until the magazine was empty, and then he fired a grenade for good measure.

Ben took off running up the alley until he came to an open doorway and stepped inside. He fitted a full mag into the belly of the M-16, then slid the tube forward, loading the launcher with a HEAT round (high-explosive antitank). Ben ran up the stairs to the roof and waited.

Cooper had given him an idea when he wished for the tank's hatch to be open. He was taking a chance, but Ben liked to take chances and he liked to operate as a lone wolf. He just didn't get much opportunity any more.

He'd had the time of his life a few years back after he'd escaped from a kidnapping along the Arkansas-Missouri border and spent a few weeks operating as a lone wolf against a bunch of outlaws.

He smiled in remembrance of those few weeks of intense guerilla warfare.

Then his attentions were pulled back to the present as the sound of a tank came to him. The tank commander was doing exactly what Ben had hoped he would do. The alley was wide enough for him to make it, but he had popped his hatch for a better look.

"Come on, you bastards," Ben muttered. "Come to daddy, now. I have a nice little surprise for you."

Ben slipped his fingers around the 30-round mag, using it as a hand-grip, and laid his finger along the side of the trigger guard of the M203.

"Come on, come on," Ben whispered. "I want you closer."

The round he was using, M-433, was both an anti-armor and fragmentation grenade; shrapnel from the fragmentation liner would turn the inside of that tank into a slaughter house . . . if he could get it down the hatch.

Ben had run past the dead men in the alley, knowing that when, or if, a tank showed up, it would not run over the bodies. The tank stopped a few feet from the sprawled bodies and the commander looked around carefully . . . but not carefully enough. The driver popped his head out of the hatch and Ben fired the grenade, then sprayed the commander and hit the deck as the tank exploded. Fire shot out of the open hatches and turned the interior into an inferno.

Ben was up and running, staying low, until he came to a rusted fire escape on the far side of the building. Before he went down, he loaded up the bloop tube with a buckshot round and smiled as he did.

Just as his boots touched the stones of the alley, three MEF men came charging out of the building. Ben emptied his bloop tube and the three men went down, mangled from the buckshot. One was kicking and screaming, both hands to his ruined face. "Your mama should have told you there would be days like this," Ben muttered, loading up again.

Ben ducked across the alley and into an old store. He didn't realize it, but he was still smiling.

The stench of burning flesh from the tank was strong in the late summer air. It was nothing new or different; Ben had smelled it before. He sat on the floor of the shop and ate a vitamin-packed chocolate bar from his emergency ration pack and sipped water from his canteen.

Those stalking him would be very cautious now. But they would also have to get the job done quickly, for they would know they were running out of time.

"Come on," Ben muttered. "Let's do it, boys."

He waited a couple more minutes and then moved slowly toward the front of the building. He stopped when he saw shadows on the sunlit sidewalk. He heard a murmur of voices speaking in a language he did not understand. Ben moved to his left, stepping deeper into the gloom and giving himself a better angle of the area just outside the smashed show window.

He took a fire-frag grenade from his harness and slipped the pin, edging closer to the open front just as the men on the sidewalk started to move. Ben released the spoon and underarmed the fire-frag, hitting the floor just a second before it exploded about waist-high among the men. The mini-bomb spread three people over the street and sidewalk in bloody blobs of meat.

Ben had already located the steps leading upward and took them two at a time, slipping onto the roof of the two-story building just as an APC rolled up and the men started out. Ben blooped them and burned a full magazine after the 40-mm grenade had done its work.

The street and sidewalk below him was getting awfully messy.

Ben started building-jumping. When he had reached the far end of the block, he looked down. No fire escape.

"Well, crap!" he muttered. He tried a roof door. Locked. He tried another one, and it swung open. He peered into the darkness and could see that some of the steps leading downward were missing. "Wonderful." He decided to try the stairs anyway.

Ben almost broke his neck twice on the rotting steps as they gave way under his weight. He managed to make it to ground level in one piece and moved toward the front of the building. It had, at one time, been a clothing store; mannequins were all over the place. One wore nothing but a wide-brimmed lady's hat. Ben patted the stationary model on her cold unresponsive butt and moved toward what remained of the smashed window-front, briefly studying the street.

The APC was still burning, but the smoke and the dead had drawn no one to the scene.

Ben sat down on a high stool and waited in the deep gloom of the store.

Suddenly he heard a shout in accented English. "The dirty bastards have broken through! Rebels are all over the goddamn place. Fall back, fall back!"

"Fall back where?" another voice responded. "We're completely surrounded, you idiot!"

A third voice added, "I hate Ben Raines and his Rebels."

The group moved to the sidewalk in front of the store. Ben lifted his M-16 and listened as the punks spewed their verbal garbage.

"I'd like to take this M-16 and stick it up Ben Raines ass and pull the trigger," one said.

"I wouldn't like that." Ben spoke from the darkness of the store.

The group of career criminals whirled around, and Ben eased the trigger back and held it until the thirty-round mag was empty. Most of the Rebels had reworked their M-16's, eliminating the three-round-burst pattern and making the weapons fully automatic. Five punks did a macabre dance for a moment and then lay in sprawled death in front of the store.

"Pricks," Ben muttered, slipping a full mag into the M-16.

Ben heard the main guns of several MBT's boom and decided to stay put until his people smashed through to his position. He wisely concluded that now would not be a good time to step out onto the street.

A few minutes passed before Ben heard familiar voices speaking in English.

"In here, boys and girls!" Ben called. "Don't get itchy trigger-fingers."

"General?" an anxious voice called.

"In the flesh. Coming out." Ben stepped out onto the bloody sidewalk and looked into the concerned faces of a squad of Rebels.

"You boys and girls missed all the fun," Ben said with a grin.

* * *

"Fun!" Buddy and Tina both yelled at their father.

Ben had taken a bath to wash away the smell of death and sweat and was sitting behind his desk in the old palace.

Doctor Chase stormed into the office. "Goddamnit, Ben!" Lamar roared.

Batt Coms from all over the place had been on the blower, raising hell about how Ben had been duped into a near-fatal tour of the city.

Ben drank a cup of coffee and ate a thick sandwich, remaining silent, letting everyone else vent their spleens.

Emil Hite came rushing in, sputtering and stuttering, all in a flap. His boots slipped on the marble floor, and he went spinning and sliding across the room.

"Oh, no," Ben said, grabbing his sandwich and keeping it out of harm's way.

Emil came to an abrupt halt on top of Ben's desk, his nose about two inches from Ben's face. "Are you all right, my General?" Emil said.

"I was until this moment, Emil. Now will you kindly get your ass off my desk and your fingers out of my coffee cup?"

Buddy lifted the little man off the desk and set him upright. Then he thought better of it, picked him up, and placed him in a chair, away from Ben.

"Thank you," Emil said.

"Think nothing of it," Buddy replied.

Ox! Emil thought.

Idiot! Buddy thought, although in a way he did like the little con artist.

Corrie brought Ben's old Thompson back to him

and retrieved her M-16. "That is one hell of a weapon, Boss," she said.

"You're right. I heard you had to use it."

She smiled. "As I said, that's a hell of a weapon."

"All right," Ben said. "All of you. Get the hell out. I have a lot of work to do. Move! Go. Go. Go!"

Doctor Lamar Chase remained seated, watching Ben with traces of amusement in his eyes. When everyone had left, except for Ben's personal team, who were always near, Lamar said, "You just can't give it up, can you, Ben?"

Ben met his old friend's eyes and shook his head. "No, to be honest, I can't."

"You're a step slower than you were ten years ago, Ben."

"I know that better than you, Lamar."

"*You* set the age rules for a cut-off for combat, Ben."

Ben smiled. "That's the nice thing about being the boss, Lamar. Nobody can fire me."

"The field is going to kill you, Ben," Lamar said seriously. "I know I just had this conversation with you a short time ago, but it's worth repeating."

"Lamar," Ben said, leaning forward and putting his elbows on the desk, "I've been in and out of combat since I was just a kid. I've spent the last ten years in combat. I'll quit when somebody zips up the body bag containing what's left of me. Now, I'll do the paperwork and all the rest of this happy bullshit that lands on my desk. But if I get a chance to mix it up, I'll take it, and nobody is going to stop me."

Lamar smiled and stood up. "Oh, I know it, Ben. But I have to keep bitching at you about it from time to time. If I didn't, you'd think I was sick." He walked to the door and turned around. "I'm not sick, Ben. But I am right. And you'd better give that some thought." He grinned and tossed Ben a deliberately sloppy salute and left the room.

Ben poured a fresh cup of coffee and returned to his desk, a real desk this time. He stared down at the papers for a time, but his mind was not on them. Lamar was right, of course. Ben couldn't deny it. He realized he was middle-aged, but he also knew he was still a strong and virile man. There was gray in his hair, yes. And he was a step slower than men younger than himself. Maybe two steps, he acknowledged. But there was something that Lamar did not realize: When the time came that Ben felt he was endangering others by his being in the field, he'd quit. Right then, with no hesitation and damn few regrets.

He also knew that that time was still a few years away. And he would know when it had arrived. He would not kid himself.

He looked over at Corrie. "Corrie, has anyone figured out how those bogus Rebels got so close?"

"Pure luck and a lot of brass on their ass, Boss. They just walked right in and no one questioned them. Rosebud says that from now on, everybody will have verifiable orders and they will, by God, be checked."

"All right. Beth, make that a standing order." Ben sighed and leaned back in his chair. The Rebels had always operated loosely; now it was time—way past time, really—for that to change. They had become too large a force.

Ben could vividly—and longingly—recall the days

when he knew everybody in the Rebel Army and could call them by name. But, he sighed, many, if not most, of those men and women were gone—either retired from combat or dead.

Corrie broke into his thoughts. "Replacements are coming in at the airport, Boss."

Ben rose. "Let's go greet them personally."

"We're going to have lots of company," Jersey said, standing up. "Buddy and Tina threw a security blanket around you. And it's a tight one. Bonelli is under orders not to let you out of his sight for a second."

"My kids the only ones who gave those orders, Corrie?"

"No. President Jefferys did."

"Who bumped him?"

Corrie shrugged her shoulders.

"Shit!" Ben said, and sat back down. Somebody was always trying to rain on his parade.

Six

Two days after Ben's little adventure, as Lamar called it, Prague was declared clean, with many of the former residents returning, and the Rebels prepared to move on eastward. Ben planned on heading toward Brno, in Moravia, as it was called before the Great War. Not much was coming out of that part of the old Czech Republic and Ben did not know what sort of reception the Rebels were going to receive.

And he still had heard nothing from Mike Richards. It had been weeks since he'd seen the man. He had no firm idea where he was, but Ben was making silent bets with himself as to Mike's location. And if he were there, when he returned, he would bitch nonstop about it.

Ben split up his forces, sending Buddy and Dan toward Hradec Kralove, while Tina and Therm's batts went with him.

To the north, Colonel Wajda had pushed into Central Poland, meeting little resistance. The Polish people had taken quite enough from punks and street gangs and roaming bands of criminals and had begun to deal with them quite effectively before General Wajda and his forces arrived.

To the south, Ike and his forces weren't meeting

with much resistance, but he reported that many of the people were sullen and not at all cooperative.

"They want our medicines and arms, but then want us to leave" Ike reported.

"Then do just that," Ben said shortly. "I'll be god-damned if I'll put up with uncooperative people we're only trying to help. Piss on it. Back off and head for the Austrian border and sit tight until I work something out."

"That's ten-four, Ben. More than happy to do it."

"Ike? What about this 'ethnic cleansing' that was going on before the Great War?"

"I think that's why they want us out, Ben. I believe the cleansing process has been successful and the victors don't want us to find the mass graves. The few people who will talk to us say it was really bad down in Bosnia and Herzegovina."

"What about all those resistance groups who agreed to work with us?"

"I guess they changed their minds."

"I'll see what Son Moon has to say about it and get back to you."

"Shark out."

"It's going to get rougher and rougher from here on," Ben muttered.

"What happens when we hit Russia?" Coop asked.

Ben shook his head. "God only knows, Coop."

The people of Moravia welcomed the Rebels warmly, with open and seemingly genuine hospitality. The Rebels quickly discovered that the crime wave that had erupted all over the world had not occurred in this part of the Czech Republic. At Jihlava, they found the town virtually untouched. Ben set up a CP, and Lamar and his medical people met with the town's doctors and went to work.

With nothing to do, Ben and many of the Rebels went exploring Jihlava, once an important silver-mining town. Something was nagging at Ben, but he couldn't put a finger on it, so he put it out of his mind.

"How come the punks and street shit didn't hit this region?" Jersey asked.

"I was told they tried more than once," Ben said. "But the people rose up and put them down. Very hard and brutally. The word spread quickly, and gangs stayed the hell out of this area."

They were standing in front of the *Kostel Svateho Jakuba*—St. James Church—on the east side of the main square of the town.

"Says here," Beth said, reading from an old tourist guidebook, "there used to be a wall around the town, with five gates. I wonder what happened to it?"

"Time," Ben said softly. "It eventually erases almost everything." He looked around him, and the nagging inside his brain began again.

"Even the pyramids?" Coop asked.

"Given enough time and enough wind and sand, yeah, even the pyramids, Coop."

"Are we going to see the pyramids this time around?"

Ben sighed. "We probably will, Beth. I don't imagine we'll see home for several years. Only the badly wounded will get to return home."

"And our dead that we can find," Jersey added softly.

"Yeah. And the dead."

They roamed throughout Moravia, and not one shot was fired at or by the Rebels. What few airports could be found were in deplorable shape, and supplies had to be dropped in. The further east the Rebels went, the worse the roads became and useable airports were nonexistent.

Ben halted the eastward push of all his columns except for those with Colonel Wajda and began preparations for his 1 Batt to move down to meet with Ike in Vienna, or as it is spelled on European maps, Wien.

Early fall had settled over the land, and the mornings were crisp. What concerned Ben now was being caught in unknown and, while not necessarily hostile, often just downright unfriendly territory in the dead of winter.

There was another reason that Ben called for a meeting with Ike and his other Batt Coms: Mike Richards had returned, and all he would say over the air was that the news he had was not good.

Vienna, or Wien, was another city that had fared well since the Great War, remaining virtually untouched by gangs of criminals.

"It's weird, Ben," Ike told him on the ride to quarters. "Some cities were torn to pieces and controlled by punks and street shit, while others . . . it's like the war never happened."

Parts of the city were deserted, however, as many residents had fled in panic when the Great War struck, years back, and never returned. Ben lowered the window and sniffed the early fall air.

"Creeps," he said.

"We know they're here," Ike confirmed. "But we just can't find the bastards."

"You may have been talking with them every day," Ben said softly. "And so have I," he added sourly, as what had been nagging him for days finally fell into place.

"What do you mean, Ben."

"That's why the city has remained so seemingly untouched."

"You mean . . ."

"Yeah. I mean." Ben scribbled on a notepad. "Pull over here," he told the driver. Ben got out and walked back to his team's vehicle. "Corrie, hard scramble this transmission." He handed her the note. She read it and her eyes widened.

"Holy shit!" Corrie said.

"Yeah. At least that." He walked back to Ike's vehicle and spoke to the driver. "Get out and raise the hood; pretend there is something the matter with the engine." Then he turned to General McGowan. "Ike, get on the blower and tell your people to fall back toward the airport. Do it slow and easy, now. Let's don't spook the creeps until we've got some more people on the ground."

"Are you sure about this, Ben?" Ike asked.

"No. I've just got a hunch about it, that's all."

"That's good enough for me." Ike shuddered. "I suddenly have this sinking feeling that we're being watched, ol' buddy."

"We are."

"What happened to the regular folks of this city?" a Rebel escort standing outside the rear of the vehicle asked.

"The creeps ate them over the years," Ben said. He looked out the window. "If we can get your full battalion, with armor, back to the airport, we stand a chance, Ike." Ben shook his head. "Son of a bitch, but I've been had and had proper."

"What do you mean?"

"All the nice, friendly people we've been meeting in certain sections of Moravia."

"What about them?"

"They're all creeps. Every goddamn one of them. We pushed a lot of them east, where they joined up with others of their kind who've been in place for years."

"Oh, shit!" Ike muttered.

"Let's make a big production of stepping out of the vehicle, looking under the hood, and then kicking a tire or two before we turn around and head back toward the airport at a very leisurely pace."

"And once we're there?"

"We're going to have to hold for hours. Maybe all night. Our battalions are spread out all over Eastern Europe. Come on, let's put on a show for the creeps."

The men stood around the vehicle and cussed and waved their arms and kicked tires and looked under the hood and then got back in the vehicle and turned around, heading slowly back to the airport, about 20 kilometers southeast of the city, at Schwechat.

A few miles up the road, Ike's radio operator said, "Two and Ten batts clear of the city and rolling toward the airport."

"All right!" Ike said.

"And 12 batt is in place ringing the airport," Ike said. "We did that yesterday."

"Good," Ben said. "We've got a chance." Ben lifted a walkie-talkie. "Corrie, where are the nearest P-51's?"

"Prague."

"Easy trip for them. Get them up."

"The creeps just overwhelmed headquarters company," the radio operator said. "Last transmission said good luck to us."

"Son of a bitch!" Ike said.

Ben's thoughts turned dark and ugly. They could not turn around; to do so would be a suicide-run.

"Chief?" the word sprang out of Ben's walkie-talkie.

"Go."

"All battalions advised and on full alert. Colonel Wajda is cutting south now and moving as fast as he can toward the Czech Republic. Meteorology says it'll be pouring down rain here in a few hours. Big front heading our way."

"Wonderful," Ike muttered.

"Roadblock up ahead, sir," Ike's radio operator said. "About fifty people manning it."

"Advise the lead tank to blow it," Ike said tersely. "Clear us a way through."

"Yes, sir."

The booming of an MBT's main gun came seconds later, then again and again.

"Roadblock neutralized, sir."

"Thank you," Ike replied.

The short convoy rolled past what was left of the burning and smoking roadblock. Bodies and body parts littered both sides of the highway. They didn't get a second look from the passing Rebels.

The airport soon came into view.

"We used to drive creepies out of airports," Ike said. "Now here we are taking refuge in one." He shook his head.

Ike's XO met them outside a terminal. "We had a little trouble a few minutes ago," he said matter-of-factly. "We handled it. We're doing a search of the terminal buildings right now to see if any creepie tunnels are under us, and I suspect they have several of them."

"No doubt," Ben said, climbing out of the vehicle. "You can bet on that. More than several, I would think." Ben didn't have to tell the man what to do with the tunnels once they were found. That was fully understood S.O.P. with the Rebels.

"Here we go," Corrie said. "Hundreds of creeps leaving the city. Fanning over the countryside in a rough half-circle. They're coming this way."

"The first wave of planes should be here in about forty-five minutes," Ben said, glancing at his watch. "Or less. They'll be pouring on the juice to get to us. I figure approximately two hundred and fifty air-miles from Prague to here. Tell the pilots to do their stuff and give us some relief. Right now, let's get set up. It won't be long before it'll be show time. We want to be sure to get a good seat." He looked around and pointed at a young Rebel. "You."

"Sir!"

"Go to my Hummer and get me my old M-14 and that clip pouch."

"Yes, sir!"

"You and your goddamned old relics," Ike said.

Ben smiled and held out his Thompson to another Rebel.

But the young woman would not touch it.

Ben didn't push the issue. He knew that many of the younger Rebels, and more than a few of the older Rebels, viewed Ben and the old Thompson with more than a touch of mysticism. He knew there were clans of people who lived in the forests of North America who carved statues of him and viewed him as a god. He had, many times over the years, tried to dispel those myths. He had never been entirely successful.

"Take the weapon and stow it in a safe place, Christy!" Ike barked out the order.

"It's all right, Ike," Ben said. "I understand." Ben cut his eyes at Cassie Phillips, Nils Wilson, and Frank Service, standing several yards away. The three of them wore puzzled looks.

Cooper took the Thompson and walked off with it.

Ben patted Christy on the shoulder. "It's all right," he assured her. "Get back to your unit now."

"Yes, sir. Thank you, General." She turned and left quickly at a trot.

"What the hell was all that about?" Nils asked, his words reaching Ben.

"Some things don't need to be talked about," Jersey said, shifting her boots to face the man. "Not now, not ever. Not at all."

Nils arched an eyebrow and wisely did not pursue the subject.

Jersey had that effect on people.

"The creeps are pouring out of the city, Boss,"

Corrie said. "Not hundreds of them. Thousands of them."

"It's going to get real interesting around here in a few minutes," Ben said, taking his M-14 and thanking Cooper for fetching it. He looked at Jersey and smiled.

"Kick-ass time!" she said.

Seven

Ben sensed someone standing at his elbow. He turned to face Mike Richards. "How was Africa, Mike?" Ben asked.

Mike shook his head. "Where do you keep your crystal ball, Ben?" He waved that off. "Never mind. Africa was just as it was the last time I was there. It stinks. And I'll tell you something else that stinks even worse: Bruno Bottger is still alive."

"I figured he was, Mike. How'd he pull the switch?"

"I've got to keep this short. We do have something of a major engagement to fight in a few minutes. Bruno had a twin brother. An identical twin. Right down to the birthmark. Both he and Bruno were born at home, so there were no hospital records. The twin brother was an idiot. Hopelessly so. The parents confined him to a home when he was about two years old and then, later, spread the story that he had died. They even had a closed-casket funeral for the kid, so all the neighbors naturally assumed the retard had croaked." Mike could turn such a delicate phrase when he put his mind to it. "Anyway, when Bruno wanted us to think he had committed suicide, he went to the nut farm where his brother was being held, sprung him, and killed him."

"Such a loving brother," Ben said.

"Oh, yeah. Just delightful. So doting and all that. But that's it in a nutshell, Ben."

"And Bruno is setting up shop in Africa?"

"You got it. He's transplanted thousands and thousands of whites over there in the past five years. From all over the world, Ben, including America."

Ben nodded slowly. "How many black Africans have they killed, Mike?"

"Twenty-five million to fifty million, give or take a million either way." He said it without changing expression. "And sent another ten or fifteen million fleeing for their lives. Bruno and his people control the entire southern part of Africa. And I mean *control* it. They went in as friends, with food, medicines, the whole ball of wax. Then they subtly turned one tribe against another. The whites sat back and watched the blacks kill each other. By the time the blacks got some order restored and began talking sense to one another, it was too late. Bruno killed any white who opposed his methods. A few got out. I talked with some of them."

"What countries do Bottger's people control, Mike?"

"Namibia, Zambia, Zimbabwe, Mozambique, Botswana, and South Africa."

Ben was skeptical. "That's a hell of a lot of territory."

"Yes. But you've got to understand that by the time Bottger's people arrived—four or five years ago, maybe more—millions and millions of black Africans had already died. Africa literally exploded along with the Great War. Old tribal hatreds surfaced; racial hatreds sprang to the fore. Blacks began killing whites, and whites began killing blacks. Crops were ignored and food ran out—then there were food riots, until disease struck. Without proper medicines, millions died; whole tribes were wiped out. I doubt that anyone will ever really know how many native Africans died in the years just after the Great War . . . white and black."

"Nuclear capabilities?"

Mike shook his head. "No. Moments after the Great War began, a group of South African scientists destroyed their nuclear arsenal. They died in the process, but they did it."

Jersey walked up carrying Ben's body armor. "We're going to have company in a few minutes, Boss."

Ben struggled into his protective gear. "We'll talk more when this little venture is over, Mike."

"Oh, yeah," Mike agreed. " 'deed we shall."

"Our P-51Es are five minutes away and screaming in, Chief," Corrie said when Ben walked out of the terminal to take his position. "The battalions we left in Moravia are under attack. You hit it right on the head. Those were creepies that greeted us there."

"They came close to fooling us. Too close. They must have been keeping their food sources in basements and tunnels."

Coop shuddered at the image and Jersey didn't kid him about that; she felt the same way.

Beth pointed and handed Ben binoculars. "Look."

Rebel eyes shifted, lifted binoculars, and took in

the almost-unbelievable scene. Thousands of people, men and women and children, all armed, were massing around the airport. The creepies were still over a mile away, but the scene was chilling.

"Tank commanders want to know if they can open fire," Corrie noted.

"No," Ben said. "I want the creeps massed the way they are when the planes come in for their first strafing and bombing runs." He glanced at his watch. "They should be here in about two minutes."

"I'm in contact with the squadron leaders," Corrie informed him. "Ninety seconds from target."

"Some of them will be dropping napalm," Ben said. "Get ready for fried creepie."

Cooper pointed at faint specks in the sky. "There they are."

The souped-up and modified P-51Es began peeling off and screaming in. Suddenly, the land in front and on both sides of the airport blossomed in fire as the napalm was dropped. The flames licked across the ground at amazing speed, moving as if it had a mind of its own, incinerating hundreds of creepies within seconds. Those standing on the fringes of the fire zone ran screaming, balls of fire sticking to their clothing and flesh like giant, glowing leeches.

The second wave of planes opened up with cannon and machine-gun fire, knocking the creepies spinning and sending bloody chunks and torn-off arms and legs of the cannibalistic clan flying in all directions.

The creeps charged the airport, screaming and cursing and howling as they ran. It was a fearful sound.

"Commence firing," Ben said, and Corrie calmly relayed the orders.

The main guns of the MBTs and heavy machine guns opened up, followed by the thunk of mortars. The tanks were firing anti-personnel rounds called FRAGs. Each round contained either fragments of steel or small grenades that exploded on contact. The land around the airport was rapidly turning into a killing field.

Shoulder-fired ground-to-air missiles were useless against the low-flying, high-speed planes; some of the P-51s were no more than a hundred feet off the deck.

Creepies died by the hundreds that afternoon. They crawled over their comrades' bodies and continued their mad charge against the defenders of the airport. The stench of charred bodies was thick and oppressive in the moistening air; the approaching storm was not far away.

"That's it, Big Chick," the flight leaders radioed to ground. "We'll head back, reload, and return. Can you mark targets at night?"

"That's affirmative," Corrie said. "Many thanks."

"Think nothing of it, Big Chick. Is the Eagle all right?"

"Fine and dandy."

"See you in about an hour."

"I wouldn't count on night attacks from the air," Ben said after Corrie had relayed the messages. "It's going to be storming in about two hours. That will make it impossible."

"Supply planes want to come in for a drop," Corrie told him.

"Negative. We know the creeps have Stingers. The

planes would have to drop at three-and-a-half miles up. Supplies would be all over the goddamn place with most of them going to the creeps. We'll have to be resupplied by the ground. How far away are Buddy and Dan?"

"They left two hours ago," Corrie replied. "They should be breaking through by 0800."

"Then we've got to hold out for sixteen hours. Probably longer than that if the weather turns rotten."

Corrie nodded, listening to both Ben and to the reports coming in. "The creeps are falling back to regroup."

"They'll wait until night to attack. They've tested us and they flunked the exam. They won't try a daylight charge again. They have no way of knowing whether or not we have more planes circling just out of sight. We'll use the time to fortify our positions. Let's get busy."

The Rebels began tearing down and ripping up and hauling off anything they could use as a barricade.

"We've found the tunnels," Corrie said, "and they are being booby trapped."

"It's a safe bet we haven't found them all. Get the engineer platoon busy welding all basement doors to their steel frames. Weld all manhole covers tight. Any basement door that can't be welded shut, booby trap it."

Ben prowled the terminals, talking with Rebels as he walked. He wasn't particularly worried; their position was good, and they had plenty of food and water and ammo. They were five-battalions strong with plenty of heavy armor. But he knew the creeps had mortars and they would begin using them very soon. How many? he wondered.

"Get spotters up onto the roof and into the tower," Ben said. "Make sure they have night-vision equipment. The creeps are going to be dropping mortars on us P.D.Q., and I want their positions spotted . . if at all possible."

"Beginning to rain," Corrie said.

"At least it will stifle some of the stink from those dead bodies. It's going to be dark soon. Heads up."

Buddy and Dan just made it out of their area before the creeps attacked. The other battalions, including Colonel Wajda's were locked in combat with the Night People. The attacks stopped their advance toward Ben's position, and stopped it cold.

All over Eastern Europe, creepies by the thousands were rising up, throwing off their disguises, and attacking Rebel columns.

But the creepies had chosen a bad time to attack for—with the exception of Ben's 1 Batt—all the other battalions were traveling heavily supplied. Even without any additional supplies, the Rebels at the airport could hold out for days.

"Creeps setting up mortar positions in the low hills west of the airport," Corrie reported to Ben. "Spotters have several locations pinpointed."

"Order artillery to start giving them a mix of willie peter and anti-personnel rounds," Ben said.

The 105s and 155s started booming and the low hills began lighting up as the white phosphorus ex

ploded, burning into flesh and bone. The anti-
personnel rounds, each projectile carrying anywhere from sixty to ninety grenades, impacted and
sent deadly shards of steel flying everywhere.

The creepies retaliated, and their mortar crews
started dropping in rounds. While the first few
rounds fell far short, the Rebels dug in at the airport
knew that would not be the case for long.

"Tell our mortar crews to commence firing," Ben
said.

Rebel 81-mm mortars thunked out high-explosive
rounds, laying down a devastating field of fire while
a light rain continued to fall.

"Planes coming back for one more pass before the
storm hits," Corrie said.

"Drop in smoke to mark the targets," Ben told her.
"Tell the pilots I want a wall of fire in those hills."

"That's a roger," squadron leaders acknowledged.
"Y'all just sit back and enjoy the show."

"Cheerful bastard, isn't he?" Cooper muttered.

And as has been observed since the first airplane
flew wobbly support for ground troops nearly a century back, a Rebel said, "He's got a right to be cheerful. He's up there, and we're down here!"

Ben smiled. How many times had he heard those
same remarks over the long and bloody years?

The P-51Es came in low with everything they had
roaring and booming. By the time they had pulled
up and banked, the area behind them was a searing
inferno. Every fighter at Ben's command was in on
this raid, and the napalm they dropped turned the
land into a burning, smoking hell for the creeps.

Wave after wave came in, dropping every conceivable weapon at their disposal.

Finally, the squadron leader radioed, "That's it, Eagle."

Ben said, "Thanks. We'll see you when the storm breaks."

"Roger."

The planes disappeared into the darkening clouds, and the area around the airport grew quiet.

"I believe that run sort-of discouraged the creepies," Cooper said.

"Yes," Ben agreed. "All their mortars weren't put out of action, but enough of them were knocked out to reduce their effectiveness."

Cooper looked confused. "Didn't I just say that?" he whispered to Jersey.

"In a manner of speaking, Coop. Loosely speaking."

"Oh."

Ike joined Ben outside under the terminal overhang. "We're all set," he said. "I don't think the creeps can overrun us, but it's going to be an interesting night."

Ben pointed to the low and darkening clouds. "We're about to have one hell of a storm."

"Yeah," his longtime friend replied. "Up there and on the ground."

"Corrie," Ben said, looking around for her. "Have all mortar crews keep IB rounds close at hand." Illumination bombs could be fired to a height of approximately 600 yards at ranges of over 3300 yards. They could light up an area of over 1200 yards for 60 seconds.

The concrete under their boots trembled as the muffled sounds of heavy explosions reached them.

"Some of the creepies trying their tunnels," Ike said as the rumbling stopped and smoke and dust began leaking out of exhaust vents set just off the road. "It's gonna be messy as hell beneath us in a few minutes."

"Yeah, but some of them are sure to break through," Ben said. "Alert the guards at all basement entrances. And, let's all try to get some rest while we can. Post enough EF's (eyes forward) to maintain vigilance out here, and the rest knock off for a time. Get something to eat and drink." Ben's eyes lingered on the outside vents for a moment. "Keep an eye on those vents. Even though they're all welded closed, the creeps could easily chunk grenades out of them. We don't have this fight won by a long shot."

"Every battalion except Batts 3 and 8 are engaged in heavy firefights with the creeps," Corrie said, seconds after receiving another report. "Batts 3 and 8 making good time, and their ETA is several hours sooner than first anticipated."

"Any word from Tina?"

"9 Batt holding their own. No K.I.A.'s and only a few hits. None serious so far."

Thunder rumbled in the distance. "The creeps are going to get wet this night," Coop said.

"Good," Ben muttered. "I never encountered one yet who didn't need a bath."

Eight

The skies sprinkled showers until an hour after full dark, and then the storm roared in with a fury of lightning and thunder and drenching rain, rain that reduced visibility to no more than a few yards. With the darkness and the storm, every Rebel was up and at his or her post, for everyone knew the creeps would be coming at them under the cover of the storm.

"Tell all tank commanders to load up with FRAG rounds and tell our mortar crews to get ready to light up the sky at my orders," Ben told Corrie.

"You see something I don't?" Jersey asked.

"Just a hunch, Little Bit. I just had a chill crawl up and down my spine."

"Jersey has that every time I look at her," Cooper said with a wide grin.

"Accompanied by nausea," she popped right back at him.

"Spotters see something moving out there," Corrie said.

"How close?"

"Fifteen hundred meters in the front. Nothing happening on either side of us. They're creeping slowly. No play on words intended."

"Let them get closer." Ben checked his watch and waited for three minutes. "Bump the spotters, Corrie."

"Still coming, Boss. About eleven hundred meters out."

"Count to thirty and light up the sky."

Thirty seconds later, the IB rounds were dropped down the tubes and the night became day and the creepies were caught flat-footed out in the open.

"Open fire," Ben said.

The Rebels around the airport threw everything they had at the night crawlers, and the rain-soaked ground became slicker still with creepie blood. But still the creeps came on, climbing over the bodies of their dead.

Some were close enough to the terminal buildings for rifle fire to reach them, and Ben started chopping at them with his old M-14. Using the NATO 7.62 round, Ben reached out and touched a dozen creeps before the night crawlers broke off the attack and dropped to the ground, scurrying behind whatever cover they could find in the stormy night.

The firing gradually ceased as no more targets presented themselves.

Corrie was busy checking each platoon by radio. Anticipating Ben's question, she said, "No dead, no wounded."

"How many IB rounds do we have left?"

She had checked that, too, and her reply was brief. "Not enough." Ben looked at her and she added, "Firing two rounds every ten minutes, we'll be out of IB's at 0300."

"Use one round every ten minutes, staggering the illuminated area."

Sniper fire began coming at the Rebels from Night People hidden among their own dead. The entire airport complex was dark, so the snipers could not really see any targets; they were simply harassing the Rebels.

"When is this rain supposed to stop?" Ben asked.

Over the years, Corrie and Beth had learned that Ben asked the most impossible of questions, and they were able to anticipate many of them.

"Sometime tomorrow," Beth replied, having checked with meteorology back in Paris. "During the early afternoon."

Ben nodded in the gloom of the terminal. "Even if we stagger the pattern of illumination, it won't take long for the creeps to figure out we're low on IB's." He looked at his watch. "They'll be coming at us again about ten o'clock."

The savage air-attacks from the modified P-51Es had taken out many of the creep's mortars, but they still had a few left. Rounds began dropping in, and this time they were on target. They were answered by the Rebel's 81-mm mortars and by main guns from the tanks parked around the terminal and on the tarmac. It was an astonishingly unequal artillery duel and, before long, the mortars of the creeps fell silent.

No Rebel there had any doubts about their ability to hold and to beat back any creepie attack—this was just a nuisance, that was all. The Rebels didn't like being on the defensive; it was a situation they were unaccustomed to facing. And it was highly irritating to them.

The battlefield fell silent under the onslaught of the storm. Lightning helped illuminate the grounds, but the creeps were not moving. Ten o'clock came and went with no creepie attack. Eleven o'clock crawled by, and then it was after midnight.

Ike made his way through the darkened buildings to Ben's side. "What the hell, Ben?"

"I don't know, Ike. If I had to take a guess, I'd say they were gone."

Ike stared at him for a moment. "Gone . . . where? Back to the city?"

"No. Just gone. Fanned out into the countryside to hide until we've left." He smiled in the darkness, his teeth flashing white against his tanned face. "But then again, maybe that's what they want us to think."

"Yeah. That crossed my mind, too."

"Therm on the horn, Boss," Corrie said.

"Go, Therm."

"The creepies here have vanished, Ben. We had one hell of a firefight for hours, then nothing for the past four hours. I'm getting the same reports from other batts."

"It's all quiet here, too, Therm. So let's sit tight until dawn."

The pre-dawn hours crept by slowly. No unfriendly fire came at the Rebels. During that time, Ben made contact with every batt com. Each one of them reported the same thing: quiet, except for the fury of the as-yet unabating storm that was lashing the countryside.

"One hell of a storm front," Ben said to no one in particular. "It's all over Europe. Damn thing must stretch for three hundred miles."

Gray dawn broke through the rain and clouds, and the scene in front of the Rebels was unbelievable: hundreds and hundreds of bodies littered the land, beginning to stiffen now after hours of cold death. They lay in twisted and grotesque shapes.

"Buddy and Dan are a few miles out," Corrie told him. "They've met no resistance for hours. Fighters are about fifteen minutes away. Squadron leaders say it's nice and sunshiny where they are."

"Yeah," Ben said. "Thirty-five thousand feet up. Tell them to come in and make a few passes and see what they can spot, if anything. Advise them of the location of the Rebel columns and tell Buddy and Dan to come on in."

The P-51Es made recon pass after pass over the city and the suburbs and the area around the airport. "There is nothing down there, Eagle. Nothing living, that is," the pilots reported. "Absolutely no signs of life. The creeps have either gone underground beneath the city or have pulled out."

"All right," Ben radioed. "Hang around for a few minutes until we can inspect the runways."

"That's a roger."

In an attempt to fool the Rebels into thinking the city was populated by normal human beings, the creeps had kept the airport terminals and the hangers clean and the runways clear. Within ten minutes, the fighters began landing and taxiing up.

Ben shook hands with a squadron leader. "Your son and his convoy are about two miles out, General," the flyer said. "You needn't have worried; we knew who they were. What's the story here, the creeps just quit?"

"Looks that way. We'll check the city, but I think we'll find them gone. They've scattered in order to survive."

The flyer shook his head. "I don't get it, General. What was all this about? These . . . crazy suicide charges by the creeps, all over Europe?"

"One wild, last-ditch attempt to kill us, I guess. It was a well-thought-out plan. And all I had to go on was a last-minute hunch."

"Thank God for hunches," the pilot said.

"Oh, they've pulled this several times before, but never on so grand a scale. And they're likely to pull it again. Creepies are not very original."

The pilot grinned and gave Ben a salute—of sorts—and left to check his plane.

"Get the battalion together, Corrie. We're going into the city at noon."

Ben stowed his M-14 and retrieved his old Thompson and clip pouch. Then he waited for Buddy and Dan's convoy.

They were a tired-looking bunch, having been on the road for many hours, pushing their vehicles as fast as they dared through terrible weather.

"Tell your people to get a few hours sleep," Ben said after shaking hands with Buddy and Dan. "We're going into the city this afternoon."

Dan and Buddy both smiled. They knew that Ben had been up all night, with the exception of perhaps a few catnaps. Ben didn't push his people any harder than he pushed himself.

Back in the terminal building, Ben found Ike. "I saw some earth-moving equipment on the drive into the city. When the troops have had a few hours rest, send the engineers in, with heavy guard, to see if that equipment runs. If so, get it out here and start burying those creeps before they present a real health problem."

"Right, Ben."

"And be careful. The retreating creeps do booby-trap their dead." Ben stepped back and looked at Ike. "And get some rest, Ike. You're beat."

Before Ike could retort, probably to remind him that he was younger than Ben—although not by much—Ben had walked off. Ike sputtered for a few seconds, then hollered at Ben's back, *"You* get some rest!"

Ben kept walking . . . with a smile on his lips.

Ben stood on the outskirts of the city, scanning the area in front of him through binoculars. The city appeared to be deserted. And indeed, Ben felt reasonably sure that it was. But he'd been fighting creepies for a long time, and knew that, while they were not terribly original when it came to tactics, they were fearless in combat. Ben lowered the binoculars and hopped down off the hood of the HumVee.

"Ike, what was the last reported position of your headquarters company?"

Ike spread a map out on the hood and pointed. "Right there, Ben."

"We find them first," Ben said, a grim note to his words. "Or what's left of them."

The Rebels started a slow advance into the suburbs of the city toward the last known position of Ike's headquarters company. They met no resistance. It was an eerie advance, for they encountered not one, single, living thing. Not a cat, dog, squirrel, or bird. The silence spooked them all.

"This place is giving me the heebie-jeebies," Cooper said.

"We agree on something else," Jersey replied. "That's twice in a week, Cooper. Either you're improving or I'm slipping."

"Surely the former," Cooper said.

"Scouts have found where our people made their last stand," Corrie informed them in a soft voice. She looked at a map. "Turn right at the next intersection. It's about halfway down the block."

"Tell Ike to take the lead. They were his people."

Ike's Hummer pulled around Ben and turned just ahead of them. Cooper parked behind Ike's Hummer, and Ben and his team got out and waited by the curb. Rebel trucks and Hummers were parked around the three-story building. They had all been burned.

Ike came out of the building, his face ashen and his big hands clenched into fists of rage. Ben strode past him and entered the building. The scene that greeted him was worse than he had imagined. A dozen or more Rebels had been taken alive and tortured to death . . . tortured in the most hideous of ways.

"Body-bag them all," Ben said in a gentle tone. "Get them to the airport for transport back home."

Ben returned to the clean, fresh air and breathed deeply, then joined Ike.

"I have a lot of letters to write," Ike murmured.

"It's never easy," Ben acknowledged.

"No. It isn't."

"You want to stay here and ride back to the airport with your people, Ike?"

Ike shook his head. "No. No, let's get busy clearing this city, Ben. That's what we came to do."

"Are you sure?"

"Yeah. I just want to find some creepies alive so I can have the satisfaction of shooting them."

"Believe me, Ike, I do know the feeling."

Nine

It was a dead city—literally.

Drawn by the smell, the Rebels found dozens of underground passages where the creepies had kept their human food sources alive and fattening. It was the most disgusting, horrifying, and mind-numbing two-week period any of the Rebels could ever remember enduring. The sight and smell of rotting human flesh is not something easily pushed aside. Before pulling out, the creepies had killed those captives they could not take with them—machine gunning them—and left the bodies to rot and be fed upon by the city's thousands and thousands of rats.

The Rebels approached and entered the underground caches cautiously for, more often than not, the piles of human bodies would be completely covered with huge rats in a monstrous, wriggling, brown-and-gray mound of snake-like tails, flea-infested fur, large yellow teeth, and savage eyes.

Once Doctor Chase had flown in, he took one look at the moving mounds of rats and ordered the Rebels out of the tunnels and sewers and basements.

"You know what has to be done, Ben," Lamar said. "This is a monumental health hazard. As distasteful as it is, you have no choice."

"Yeah," Ben said with about as much enthusiasm as a man facing a visit to his proctologist. But he did not hesitate. "Flame throwers," he ordered. "Burn the bodies down to char and the rats with them. I don't see any other way." *God have mercy on their souls and ours,* he added silently. *I just don't know what else to do.*

Fried rats and charred bodies and bones were buried together in mass graves. There was no way the Rebels could separate them or ID the victims of the Night People's atrocities. It was just another crappy job that had fallen to the American Rebels who made up the World Stabilization Forces.

A few days after the battle at the airport, people trickled back into Vienna, silent watchers as the Rebels cleared the city—and the Rebels could not understand why they did not offer to help. They were examined by Rebel doctors and many were found to be in mild shock. For years they had been living in small groups in the woods, without adequate arms, fearful each day of their lives of being captured and eaten alive by the creeps.

Austrian medical people began surfacing shortly after their dazed countrymen arrived, and they pitched in to help the Rebel doctors.

"When did the Night People begin their campaign of terror?" Ben asked a group of Austrian citizens who seemed to be more or less in control of their facilities.

"Right after the Great War. Those of us who saw what was going on tried to tell those in other countries. But they wouldn't believe us. They thought we were all insane—a condition that soon gripped many of our people shortly afterward," he added grimly.

"What lies east of us?" Ben asked a former Austrian government official.

The man shook his head. "With the exception of Hungary and the west part of Romania, the *unknown* is all I can tell you, General. Hungary is filled with roaming gangs of thugs and hoodlums and cannibals. Romania is . . ." He shrugged his shoulders. "Romania. What can I tell you? A land of beauty and mystery and superstition. We have been living hand to mouth for years, lucky to have some scrap of news of what is happening in the next valley. Now, with your help, perhaps we can pick up the pieces of our lives and start anew."

Ben stared at the official and the men and women with him. He stared at them for so long, they grew edgy under his hard gaze.

"What is wrong, General?" the official asked.

"I have a lot of questions and damn few answers," Ben replied. "That's what is wrong. What happened to the Austrian Army?"

"I would imagine the same thing that happened to most armies of the world. We felt the world was ending. We were told that the world had exploded in nuclear warfare. We were told that America had been destroyed. We were told—"

"Who told you?" Ben interrupted.

The man again shrugged his shoulders. "Why . . . voices on shortwave radios. Knowledgeable officials. Many in the armed forces rushed back to their homes to see about their loved ones. Others just . . . disappeared."

"So the creeps took over without a fight?" Ben questioned. "Weren't any of you armed? Why didn't you stand and fight? Why didn't you kill the bastards?"

"With what, General? Small-caliber rifles and shotguns filled with bird shot? Against machine guns and mortars and organized forces?"

Same old story, Ben thought, studying the men and women seated around him. Big government promised they'd take care of their people and then disarmed the law-abiding, tax-paying citizens. Big government lied here just as they had lied in America and England and everywhere else.

Ben didn't dislike politicians: He hated them.

"We'll help you set up a police force and arm the citizens with the weapons we took from the creeps and punks on our push through Europe," Ben told the delegation. "The rest is up to you."

Fall was beginning to brown the leaves and turn the winds cold as the Rebels wrapped up their work in Vienna and prepared to move east. Ben had straightened out his lines, north to south. They now ran from Sopot in the north of Poland, down to Nagykanizsa in the southwest part of Hungary.

Batt coms flew into Vienna for one more meeting before winter shut down the Rebels' eastward push.

Vienna lay peacefully under the thin rays of late-fall sunshine as the batt coms gathered in a meeting hall. The smell of death that had lingered over the city for so long was gone as the people begin anew.

"We're going to move eastward about a hundred

and fifty miles before we shut everything down for the winter," Ben told the gathering. "That's going to put us on a line running north to south from the southern tip of Lithuania down to Warsaw, Krakow, through the eastern tip of Czechoslovakia, over to Budapest, down to Szeged in the south of Hungary. When those lines are established, shut it down for the winter, but make damn sure you're near a useable airport that will handle our supply planes. If not, we'll have to resort to airdrops."

"What do you hear from Colonel Flanders in Italy?" Pat O'Shea from 10 batt asked.

"Well, Flanders and Randazzo have managed to bring the fighting to a halt," Ben replied. "Actual combat, that is. Right now they're trying to help the Italians form up some sort of workable government. Flanders says he'd rather be in open combat—he understands that."

After the laughter had died down, Ben added, "General Randazzo threatened to shoot a half-dozen or more Italian politicians unless they reached an agreement and did it damn quick. As soon as the words left his mouth, the entire parliament walked out en masse, with many of them making obscene gestures in General Randazzo's direction. Flanders is using his people to keep order and letting Randazzo handle the political end of the operation. Personally, I think they're all having a good time."

"What about creepies, Dad?" Tina asked.

"An *Italian* creepie?" Ben responded. "Not likely. Italy is the only country thus far that has reported absolutely no sign of Night People."

"They'd have to have a side order of fettuccine

with a little glass of grappa," Lt. Bonelli said with dark humor, and again the meeting hall reverberated with laughter.

"Italy is Italy," Ben said after order was restored. "And I don't plan on trying to change it. That would be an impossible task."

"What are we facing on this eastward push?" Buck Taylor, commander of 15 Batt, asked.

"Hundreds of gangs of thugs and hardened criminals and street crap and warlords roaming the countryside. And let us not forget about the creepies; don't discount their popping up when you least expect them. We certainly haven't seen the last of the Night People. I just don't know how much hard and sustained combat we'll meet on this push. Intell says the gangs we'll engage are poorly armed and poorly organized. What we'll be doing mostly, I think, is bringing medicines and food and hope to the law-abiding people of these countries. But be ready for anything. The U.N.'s political teams will be going in with us to do their thing." He paused, then added, "And I know you will all be glad to hear this: The reporters have finally caught up with us, so we'll have them to contend with."

His final announcement was greeted with catcalls and boos and hissing, and Ben let it run its course.

"Any more questions?" he asked.

There were none.

"Let's do it," Ben said.

When the room had cleared, Ben joined Mike Richards, who had stood on the sidelines throughout the briefing.

"Billy Smithson's men—the turncoats who staged the coup," Mike began.

"What about them?"

"It's as we suspected. They left Germany with Bottger and his men. They're in Africa."

"Setting up their own little Reich." Ben pressed his lips together in a hard, firm line.

"That's about it."

"So, you finally got people in." It was not phrased as a question.

"Reluctantly, Ben. Very reluctantly."

Ben did not have to ask how far in they were. He had worked for the Company, and he knew they were in deep . . . or they had damn well better be.

"And?—"

"Bottger is waiting for you to show up, Ben. Just patiently waiting for you."

"He's that certain?"

"Well, not really. But it's going to take two or three years to wrap up things in Europe. By that time, perhaps the good citizens of America and the other predominately white countries in the world will have recovered sufficiently to start worrying about Africa and we'll be ordered in to stabilize that continent. When that happens, Bruno and his army will be ready."

"And when, or if, that time comes, you think I should do what, Mike?"

"Refuse to go. Once Europe is stabilized, let's go back home and live out the remainder of our years in peace in the SUSA."

"Mike, somebody, someday, will have to deal with

Bruno Bottger. The longer the world waits, the stronger he gets."

Mike shook his head and then said, "Why am I not surprised at your response?"

"Cheer up, Mike. Africa, if it comes, is a couple of years away. Probably longer than that. And who knows, maybe by that time Bruno will self-destruct."

Mike stared at him for a moment. "Don't bet on it, ol' buddy. Don't bet on it." Mike turned and walked away. At the door, he paused and looked back. "The Rebels will follow you there if you lead, Ben. They'll do it without question. But there will be a lot of Rebel lives lost on the dark continent, Ben. And it isn't worth one Rebel life. It just isn't worth it." Then he hurried away without another word.

Ben remained in the big hall, conscious of the eyes of his team on him. He met them, one by one.

"Oh, what the hell, Boss." Jersey broke the silence. "I always wanted to meet Tarzan."

The long Rebel line, over four hundred miles long, straightened out north to south and moved on slowly toward the east. Over the long and bloody months since the Rebels had landed on the beaches of France, their reputation had grown, just as it had grown back in the States. Very few of the smaller gangs really wanted to mix it up with the Rebels. . . . The price they would have to pay—in lives and blood—was just too damn high. But they really had no place to go to escape the ever-advancing Rebel army, except east toward Russia, and they did not wish to head in that direction for Russia was an unknown. Very little in the way of news had come from Russia since the Great War, and the news that had filtered out was anything but good.

Ben's command, his own 1 Batt and Dan's 3 Batt, were just inside the Hungarian border when the first of the gangs began surrendering. Like nearly every gang the Rebels had ever encountered, both in Europe and Stateside, they were a sorry-looking bunch of crap when compared to the well-fed, well-trained, well-equipped, and highly motivated and disciplined Rebel soldiers.

This gang numbered fifty men and women ranging in age from fifteen to twenty-five. And to a person, they were scared and made no attempt to hide that fear.

They especially showed that fear when the whispering started among them that they had been captured by Ben Raines himself—the Devil, as Ben was called by criminals in this part of Eastern Europe.

Ben slowly walked in front of the line of prisoners, a representative of the Hungarian resistance with him.

"This particular band of hoodlums is one of the milder gangs," the interpreter told him. "They steal, but we've never heard of any of them killing or raping."

"Well," Ben said, winking at the resistance fighter. He had been told that most of the line-up understood and spoke some English. "Maybe we won't have to shoot all of them."

At that, one gang member promptly fainted dead away and another evacuated his bowels.

"Raines," Doctor Chase said, disgust in his tone, "your sense of humor is grotesque."

"Oh, hell, get them out of here and clean them up," Ben rejoined. "After that, turn them over to the interrogation teams and see what we can get out of them."

"Are you really going to shoot us, General?" a young girl of perhaps fifteen or sixteen asked.

Ben stared down at her. A pretty girl with blond hair and pale blue eyes . . . and a very scruffy young lady, too, badly in need of a long, hot, soapy bath.

"We've really harmed no one," the girl said. "We steal in order to live. And we are in a war with the cannibals. All of us have been a prisoner of the creepers at one time or another. We all escaped from the cannibals in the city."

That got everyone's attention.

"The Night People?"

"Yes, General. Those that creep about at night."

"What city?" Ben asked her.

"Budapest, General."

"Get them cleaned up and then bring this girl to my CP," Ben ordered. He looked at the resistance fighter. "And get me a female translator to stay with us while I talk with her."

The gang members were separated by sex and herded off. Ben turned to Dan Gray. "If she really did escape from the creeps, she's got a head filled with valuable information."

"If she isn't a creep herself," Dan said.

"Yes." Ben sighed. "There is that to consider, isn't there?"

Ten

"Did she seem repulsed at the thought of taking a bath?" Ben asked Jersey.

"No. Not at all. We practically had to drag her out of the shower. She washed her hair three times. Now she's on her second plate of food at the mess tent. If she's a creepie, I'm Joan of Arc."

"Who is with her?"

"Cooper. He says he's in love with her," Beth said.

"Cooper is in heat," Ben said. "Cooper is always in heat. What's the girl's name?"

"Anna," Jersey replied. "I can't pronounce her last name. What the hell language do these people speak?"

"Magyar. I'm told it's difficult."

"They told you right."

Anna was brought in, along with a female interpreter—which proved to be unnecessary since the girl spoke excellent English.

She stared at Ben through eyes that were much older than her years. "You want to know about the creeps, right, sir?"

"As much as you can tell me."

"And what do I get if I do tell you?"

Ben started to tell the girl she wouldn't get spanked,

then decided she was a bit too old for that threat to work. "What do you want, girl?"

"Anna."

"All right, Anna. What do you want?"

"To be safe. I want to be a Rebel."

Ben smiled. "Anna, being with the Rebel Army is not the safest place to be. We fight wars."

"What do you think I've been doing since I was old enough to remember? Sir."

Ben figured the girl had, at best, just started school when the Great War had toppled every government in the world. "How did you survive, Anna?" Ben asked softly. "You couldn't have been more than five- or six-years-old."

The girl's face screwed up in a storm of emotions. "I fought dogs for rotten meat in the streets. I ate grubs I found under logs. I made me a slingshot and learned how to knock squirrels out of trees and hit rabbits on the run. I teamed up with other kids my age, and we had us a gang. One of them was the son of someone who worked at the U. S. Embassy in Budapest. We learned English from him. He died two years ago." She grimaced. "Well, in a way. The creeps ate him when we were captured over in Gyor. That's a town just down the road. We held the gang together for a long time. Years. The creeps used to live in the old U. S. Embassy in Budapest. They may still be there. That's the last place they held me."

"How did you escape?"

"I killed one of them with a knife, put on her robe, and just walked out unnoticed. I made up my mind right then that they would never take me again. I heard they were offering rewards for me. They'll torture me to death if they get the chance." Sudden tears sprang into her eyes. "You've got to let me be a Rebel. The creeps will catch me if you don't . . . and . . . I've seen what they do to people."

Ben handed her a clean handkerchief and a cup of coffee and brought sugar and artificial creamer to her, setting it on the table. "You drink that and compose yourself. I'll be back in a minute."

He went into another room where an operator was running a state of the art P.S.E. machine. Psychological Stress Evaluator. Anna was being given a lie-detector test without her knowledge—which is the best way to give one; the subject is much more relaxed that way.

"She's telling the truth, General," the operator said. "Truthful all the way across." He glanced up at Ben. "Why so much interest in this kid, General?"

"I don't know, Mark. Something about the girl got to me, I guess. Stay with it."

"You got it, sir."

Ben talked with Anna for over an hour, then let her relax for a few minutes while, once again, he checked with the P.S.E. expert.

"I haven't caught a lie yet, General. She's shooting straight."

Ben nodded his agreement. "All right, Mark, that's it. Pack it in. Thanks."

Jersey, Beth, Corrie, and Cooper had watched Ben chat with the girl, so it came as no surprise when Ben said, "Beth, take Anna down to the quartermaster vehicles and get her fitted out with BDUs, will you?"

"Sure, Boss."

"Then take her over to Chase's MASH tent. I'll meet you over there."

The girl's eyes brightened. "Does this mean I'm a Rebel, now?"

"It's a start in that direction," Ben told her. "Now go along with Beth."

Ben walked over to the MASH tent and up to Lamar, who was sitting at a portable desk. Chase looked at him. "Are you sick?"

"No." Ben squatted on the ground. "Beth is bringing a girl over here sometime within the hour. Check her out and shoot her up, will you?"

"Sure. Something special about this woman, hey?"

"She's not a woman, Lamar. I figure the kid is about fifteen, tops."

Lamar smiled. "Well, I'll be damned. Did the old parental urge strike you, Ben?"

"You might say that. She's a good kid who needs a break, that's all."

"Over the years, we've met thousands of good kids who needed a break, Ben. What's so special about this one?"

"How the hell do I know?" Ben retorted sharply, then stood up and walked away.

Lamar chuckled and returned to his paperwork. Ben had a soft spot for kids and animals, and everybody in the Rebel Army knew about it.

Ben pulled a mug of coffee and wandered over to a stand of trees and sat on the ground near Jersey, Corrie, and Cooper. About fifty meters away, part of Lt. Bonelli's command threw up a loose circle around Ben.

Ben rolled a cigarette and drank his coffee and waited for Anna and Beth. Ben figured Anna to be about five feet, three inches, for she was about two inches taller than Jersey and Ben towered over her.

"You like this kid, huh, Boss?" Jersey broke into his thoughts.

"Yeah, I do, Jersey."

"We had a meeting while you were in the other room talking to Mark. Me, Cooper, Beth, and Corrie. We decided Anna was a keeper and not to throw her back."

Their way of telling Ben that they approved of Anna and that whatever Ben decided to do, they were solidly behind him.

"I'm real glad to hear that, Jersey."

"I'll keep a good eye on her, Boss," Cooper said.

"I'm sure you will," Ben said drily. "And knowing she's fifteen-years-old, I would advise you to keep statutory rape in mind while you're keeping a good eye on her."

Cooper pulled a worn paperback book out of his jacket and busied himself reading a Fred Bean western.

"Has anybody seen Cassie lately?" Ben asked, field stripping his cigarette butt. Cassie was a career reporter and Ben was a career warrior. Their affair had burned brightly for a time, and then the light had begun to flicker until it had finally gone out as the two realized that, while they genuinely liked each other, as a pair, they were not meant to be.

"She hooked up with Ike's 2 Batt," Jersey said. "Frank Service is with Colonel Wajda's bunch. And Nils Wilson is down in Italy with General Flanders. We still have Bobby Day."

"How wonderful for us," Ben said.

"You realize, of course," Corrie said, "that Bobby Day will try to make something dirty out of your taking Anna in."

"When he does I'll kill him," Ben said quietly. He saw Beth and Anna approaching and left to greet them at the MASH tent.

"How do I look?" Anna asked excitedly, doing a rather clumsy pirouette in her stiff combat boots.

"You look just fine," Ben told her.

"I'm really a Rebel, aren't I?"

"You're getting there," Ben said as Lamar and a female doctor walked over to them. "Lamar, this is Anna."

"Prettiest soldier I ever did see," Chase said. "Anna, this is Dr. Judy McMasters. She's going to check you out and then we'll bring you up-to-date on some shots. You go with her, now."

Anna looked at Ben with anxious eyes.

"I'll be right here," Ben assured her. "You go with Dr. McMasters."

When Anna was out of earshot, Lamar said, "What the hell are you going to do with her, Ben? Keep her with you? What kind of home is that?"

"A hell of a lot better than what she's had for ten or so years, Lamar. The subject is closed. Have a nice day. Go back to sticking people with square needles."

Lamar stared at Ben. "You know what, Raines? You're turning into a goddamn grouch."

"Maybe I've been around you, too long," Ben returned.

Chase threw his hands into the air and stalked off, muttering under his breath.

"What are you going to do with her, Boss?" Corrie asked.

"Well . . . that's a damn good question."

There were no shots fired as the scouts entered the suburbs of Gyor, which back before the Great War had been a thriving city of nearly a hundred and fifty thousand. Scouts radioed back that there were perhaps five thousand people left in the city and they were in sad shape. Anna laughed strangely at that.

Ben's Hummer had blown an engine just inside the Hungarian border and, at Ben's request, Dan had set about procuring a van for him. Dan's scroungers had found the big van hidden in a barn and had pulled it out and gone over it. It was plush, seated six comfortably in captain's chairs, and had enough room for all their gear . . . once the small refrigerator and stove were removed. Papers in the glove box showed that it had belonged to a government official before the Great War. When they got to Gyor, the Rebels would cut a hole in the top for a machine gun mount and bullet-proof the van.

To absolutely no one's surprise, Anna rode with Ben and his team in the van.

What did come as a surprise was Anna's proficiency with a number of weapons, including the M-16 and the AK-47.

"I'm also real good at making and tossing Molotov cocktails," she told them. "I've fried about a hundred and fifty creepers with them over the years. At least that many."

"We use grenades, Anna," Ben said.

"I prefer gas bombs," she said stubbornly. "I like to hear those sorry bastards and bitches scream."

Beth arched an eyebrow but said nothing.

"You really hate them, don't you?" Cooper asked.

"They ate my mother and father," Anna said softly. "Yes, I hate them."

Nobody had anything to reply to that.

"Gyor is an old town," Anna went on. "It's the capital of Gyor-Sporon *megye*. That means county. Like most of the old towns in my country, the streets are narrow and winding. And there are still creepers there, too. So watch it. They're underground."

"Scouts reported nothing," Jersey said.

"As I told you a few miles back, your Scouts are wrong," Anna said flatly. "I know. Don't trust the people you meet, either. The creepers have them terrified. Besides that, they're cowards." She cut loose with a long string of words that Ben and the others could not understand, but knew perfectly well what she meant. She was giving both the creepers and the locals a sound cussing.

"Whatever you said," Beth told her, "if it was about the creepies, I agree with you."

"It was about the people left there, too. They're stooges for the creepers. All the good people either fought the creepers and died or left to live in the hills and fight a guerrilla war against them."

"All of them, Anna?" Ben asked.

"Why else would a good person stay?"

"Scouts now reporting the smell is getting tough to take," Corrie said.

"Tell them to back out and wait for us at the edge

of the city," Ben told her. "Here we go again," he muttered.

Anna heard him. "What do you mean, General Ben?"

Ben had insisted the girl call him Ben, but she couldn't bring herself to be that informal—at least not yet.

"We bring the gangs under control, and the creeps pop up. We bring the creeps under control, and the gangs pop up. It just never seems to end."

"No more gangs, General Ben," Anna said solemnly. "At least not in this part of what used to be my country. The gangs are all in Budapest and east and south of there. Everything else is all creeper controlled."

"What a cheerful thought," Jersey said. "You just made our day, Anna."

The girl's smile was thin and her pale blue eyes glittered with a bright hardness. When she spoke, her voice was flat and cold. "I'm looking forward to it."

The others in the gang had verified Anna's story. The girl had been on her own since she was five-years-old, and she was one tough girl.

"You're not going into combat, Anna," Jersey said. "You've had no training."

"I'm a Rebel now. This uniform says I am. You can't keep me out of combat. Besides, I've been fighting the creepers since I was five. I started fighting them with rocks. You think this is something new to me? Bah!"

"She meant . . ." Cooper opened his mouth.

"I know what she meant." Anna shut him up. "You think you can't depend on me. You're wrong. My life is fighting creepers. I hate them. Once, when I was captured, there was this big creeper who took off his robe and stood naked in front of me. He was filthy and stank like sheep shit. I was, oh, ten-years-old, I think. He told me if I would become his personal slave and suck him off he would let me live. I said, Oh, sure, I would. He got himself hard and stuck it in my face. He didn't know I had a knife. I cut his dick off and ran. The next time I was captured, about six months later, in a little town called Olet, there was this creeper woman who wanted to love me . . . in a perverted way. I beat her head in with a club. You want to hear more?"

"I think we get the picture, Anna," Beth said.

"Then don't tell me I can't fight. I will fight."

Ben cut his eyes to Jersey.

"Yeah," Jersey said. "Kick-ass time!"

Eleven

Anna preferred the chopped-off version of the M-16, the M16A1; and when Ben said he wouldn't get her one, she got one of her own. As soon as the convoy reached the edge of Gyor and pulled over for the night, it took Anna about fifteen minutes to either steal one or charm some Rebel armorer out of it. Ben's team was amused; Ben was not. At least not that he would show.

"I will fight," Anna told Ben. "You cannot stop me from fighting the creepers."

"All right, all right." Ben gave in. "Then fight, goddamnit."

"Thank you," Anna replied with more than a trace of humor in her eyes. "You want creeper prisoners to question?"

"The scouts haven't been able to find any."

"They don't know where to look. I will show them."

Before Ben could protest, Anna was off and running. "Well, hell!" he said.

"We've never been able to get much information out of the creepies," Cooper said.

"Maybe we should turn Anna loose on one," Jersey

suggested with a mean smile. "I think she might be more persuasive than we've been."

Ben shook his head. "I wouldn't want to be any where close should that happen. Anna harbors a real hatred toward the creeps. With good reason," he added.

Anna and the scouts were back in less than an hour with half-a-dozen creepies. "The kid took us through an old tunnel, General," the team leader said. "I have to admit, it spooked me at first. I tell you what, General. Anna can move like a ghost and cut a throat with the best of us. She can be on my team anytime she wants to."

Ben nodded and looked at Anna. "You think you're pretty smart, don't you, young lady?"

"Yeah. I do, General Ben. Now give me my reward."

"Reward?"

Anna put a finger on one cheek and grinned impishly. "A little kiss, right here, General Ben."

Embarrassed, Ben shuffled his boots and cleared his throat. "Oh, all right!" he harrumphed. He bent down awkwardly and gave the kid a peck on the cheek amid cheering and applauding from the Rebels gathered around.

The creeps stood by and glared their hatred at the Rebels, especially at Anna.

"I don't think they like you very much, Anna," Ben said when the shouting and laughing had died down.

"Oh, they *hate* me, General Ben," the girl corrected. "I've killed a lot of creepers over the years." She spat in the direction of the captives, and the creeps finally broke their silence and cursed the girl. She laughed at them.

"Take them to the interrogation teams," Ben told the scouts. "Give them the works; see what we can get out of them."

Anna pulled a double-edged dagger from her jacket. "I can get information from them."

The creeps hissed at the sight of the knife. It was obvious to all present that they not only hated Anna, but were more than a little afraid of the girl.

"Put it away, Anna," Ben told her. "We have drugs that work much better."

Anna reluctantly sheathed the razor-sharp blade, and the creepies were led away. They seemed glad to go.

Anna shouted at them in her native tongue. One of the creeps turned and shook his head and replied in the same language.

"What did you ask him, Anna?"

"Where the men are who killed my friend Robert. The son of the employee of your embassy."

"And his reply?"

"The same as always. I will never find them. But I will. And when I do, they will die very slowly and painfully. Just like Bobby. They raped him over and over. I had to listen to his screaming and watch while they used him. I will find them. Someday. Sooner or later." She cut her pale eyes to Ben. "My ancestors came to Hungary from Romania. They were gypsies from the Transylvania Mountains. We Rumanians can be . . . inventive when it comes to pain." She smiled . . . sort of. "Just study the life of Vlad the

Impaler. I am hungry now. I will eat if you don't mind."

"Go on," Ben said softly.

Ben watched her walk to the mess tent. Dan had strolled up. "You have yourself quite a handful there," he said.

"Yes, I sure do."

"But to her credit, Ben, everybody likes her. After only a few days, she's won the hearts of us all. She's a bonny lass, she is."

Behind Dan's words he heard the unspoken questions. *But Ben, what in the hell are you going to do with her? Adopt her? Send her back to the States?*

Ben didn't know. "We'll find a place for her, Dan," he said lamely.

"She needs proper schooling, Ben."

"Beth has already started with that. The older kids in the gang taught her to read and write. And she is amazingly well read. When she isn't concentrating on killing creeps, she's got her nose stuck in a book."

Reading was something that was heavily stressed in all Rebel schools, and most Rebels carried books in their gear.

"How about the other kids Anna's age that were in that gang?"

"We found families to take in some of the younger children. The older ones are helping to rebuild and restore order. None of them went to jail. That particular gang was lucky."

Dan studied the general's face. "Ben, old friend—" Dan put a hand on Ben's shoulder. "—I have to say this, and you're not going to like it."

"Go ahead."

"Anna is a human killing-machine. You know it; I know it. She's quite lovely and very personable. But she was made homeless at a tender age. She grew up like a wild animal. She admitted she fought packs of dogs for scraps of meat. How she got as far as she did is nothing short of a miracle. She's only a cut above a feral child."

"I know all that, Dan."

"Do you even know her last name?"

"She says it's Hunyadi, which may or may not be true. That is a famous name in Hungarian history. There was a Hunyadi king in the 14th century, but the truth is, Dan, I don't think she knows for sure. She may have just taken the name out of history. But one thing is firm: Anna Hunyadi is one orphan kid who is going to have a chance."

"End of discussion?"

"End of discussion."

Dan clasped Ben's shoulder briefly, then left him alone.

Ben walked to the mess tent, pulled a cup of coffee, and sat down beside Anna, who had a huge plate of food in front of her. The girl was sitting off by herself, as if she had anticipated Ben's arrival.

"While you eat, we're going to talk about your future, Anna."

"I fight," she said.

"I'm sure that's true. But when you're not fighting, you're going to get some schooling."

"Okeydokey. That's cool, General Ben."

Ben sighed. Dealing with teenage kids was not his strongest suit.

She looked at him with a mischievous twinkle in

her eyes. "You going to tell me about the birds and the bees, General Ben?"

"I . . . don't think so, Anna."

"That's good. I already know all about fucking and stuff like that."

Ben's sigh was definitely heavier and longer than the first exhalation. He looked down at his cup and wished he had some bourbon to add to it.

"Anna, proper young ladies do not use words like the ones you just used."

"Are you going to teach me to be a proper young lady, General Ben?"

"I am going to try, yes."

"That's awesome, man."

Ben rubbed his temples with his fingertips. "I think I'm going to need some help in this," he muttered. His eyes reached Thermopolis, who had just entered the tent. Therm spotted Ben sitting with Anna and noticed that Ben had a strange smile on his lips. Therm recognized that smile and beat a hasty retreat out of the mess tent.

"I raised my kids!" Therm called over his shoulder, hastening to 3 Batt's mess area. "You're on your own."

"Chicken!" Ben called.

"You'd better believe it," Therm returned and kept on walking.

"Therm is funny," Anna said.

"Yeah, he's a real riot," Ben muttered. "Have you met Rosebud?"

"Oh, yes. She's nice. Emil Hite?" She waggled one hand from side to side.

"We agree on that. I'll see you around."

"That's cool."

Ben walked over to Corrie, Beth, and Jersey. Cooper was with the mechanics, working on the van. Ben paused at their table. "You three teach her to be a proper young lady," he said, and beat a fast retreat.

One of the women smiled and the other two frowned as they exchanged glances. Jersey held out one hand and Beth and Corrie each dug in their BDU's and dropped a five spot into the out-stretched palm. "Told you," Jersey said.

Gyor lay quiet under the fall sun as the Rebels began tightening the noose around the town. The small city looked peaceful enough; but the captured creepies had, before they died, confirmed there were several thousand of their kind in the city.

The locals had begun coming out at first light, their hands held in the air. To a person, their eyes narrowed and their faces paled at the sight of Anna, standing beside Ben, a faint smile on her lips.

"Believe nothing that she-devil says!" a man cried out, pointing at Anna. "She lies. We were forced to serve the Night People."

Anna spat on the ground in contempt and fired off a verbal round in Hungarian; loathing dripped from her words and the man trembled.

The Hungarian Freedom Fighters gave Anna a wide berth whenever possible. The leader of one HFF group had told Ben that Anna lived to kill creepers . . . and for several years had done a bang-up job of it.

Anna pointed to a man. "That one gave his own

daughter to the creepers. They used her horribly until she went insane, and then they ate her. And that is the truth."

The man leaped at Anna, screaming curses at her, a knife flashing in one hand. Anna raised her CAR and stitched him. The collaborator died in a heap on the cracked concrete of the old highway.

"Pig!" Anna spat the words at his bloody body.

The group of locals began talking at once, pleading for their lives. Ben ordered them taken away for interrogation.

"Why waste the time?" Anna questioned as the men and women were led away. "Put them all up against that stone wall over there—" She pointed. "—and shoot them."

"We had to comply!" a man screamed at her. "We had to!"

"No, you didn't," Anna said. "I didn't. I fought. So did Jaroslav and Herbert, Stephen and Sigismund, Bobby and Elizabeth, Jagiello and Tadeusz . . . and dozens of others who fought and died. We were still fighting when the Rebels came, and some of us surrendered and joined them so we could continue to fight." She spat in the man's face, and the spittle ran down his cheek. "Some of you pointed your finger at Bobby and Jan. And some of you were witness to Jan's torture. I know that for the truth. And I will find out which ones were there. And when I do, I will kill you! I swear it."

"You damn dirty gypsy!" a woman screamed at Anna. "You thieving whore-slut!"

"Get them out of here," Ben ordered. "Who was Jan, Anna?"

Anna had tears in her eyes. "A friend of mine. We'd been together since I was about eight-years-old. Bobby and Jan and I were all that was left of our original gang of fighters. Some of those people turned us in to the creepers."

"They'll be dealt with. I promise you that. Corrie, get the tanks moving. Let's take this city."

The suburbs appeared deserted, but the eerie silence fooled no one. The creeps they'd captured had told them that much of the city was honeycombed with tunnels and the Rebels could expect a savage fight in Gyor.

Ben laid it out bluntly to Anna. "You do exactly what you are told to do, Anna. If I say stay put, you stay put. If I say move, you move—without hesitation or questions. Do you understand?"

"I understand."

"We work as a team. The only person who lone-wolfs it is me. And that isn't often." *Not nearly as often as I would like,* Ben added silently. "Do you understand that?"

"I understand."

Anna had been dressed out in body armor, right up to the newest helmet—made of laminated kevlar, even stronger than the ones used by the U. S. Army before the Great War.

"This throat-collar is uncomfortable," Anna bitched, tugging at the collar.

"You'll get used to it," Ben told her. "Now leave it alone."

"Tanks in position," Corrie said.

"Let's go."

"What are we doing?" Anna asked, moving awkwardly in the unaccustomed body armor.

"We go in behind the tanks. It's comforting to have nearly sixty-five tons of steel in front of you."

"I would think it would be more comforting to be inside one," she countered.

Ben muttered under his breath. *Smart ass!*

Anna looked at him and grinned. "Why is the commanding general of such a great army going into combat like a common soldier, General Ben?"

"Because I like it."

"I can dig it!"

They continued on for two blocks and saw nothing. "Where the hell are they?" Ben muttered.

"They're here," Anna said. "Believe that if you believe nothing at all."

At the end of the third block, silent warning bells began ringing in Ben's head. "Hold it! Corrie, have everyone halt where they are and set up battle lines."

"What's wrong?" Anna asked.

Ben squatted down and looked around him. "Every other tank swivel their turret," he said softly. "The creeps are going to be popping up all around us any second now."

"How do you know that?" Anna whispered.

"Because they've tried everything else, that's why." Ben looked around him at the silent houses on both sides of the street. "I wish I had not brought you along, Anna."

"You couldn't have stopped me from coming, General Ben," she reminded him.

Ben grunted. "Yeah. I know that, too."

"Listen up, everybody. What the hell is that sound?"

Jersey asked, squatting beside Ben on the old street. "It's gone. No! There it is. Hear it?"

Ben listened. "Sounds like . . . yelling. Sort of. But where in the hell is it coming from?"

"It's muffled," Beth said.

"The sound is coming from under us!" Lt. Bonelli called. "They're under us. They'll be coming up out of the tunnels."

The roaring increased in volume.

"They must have spent years honeycombing this city with tunnels," Ben said. "But to pop up out of manholes would be suicide. Not enough of them could get through to be effective. So they have to have tunnels leading to the homes and businesses."

"Dan reporting creepies pouring out of houses and businesses," Corrie called.

"Here we go," Ben said.

Then the Rebels were surrounded by hundreds of robed figures running at them at nearly point-blank range.

"Fire!" Ben yelled.

Twelve

Those first creepies who charged Ben and his team died in a storm of bullets, their closeness actually building a protective wall of bodies around the Rebels. The creeps were forced to slow their assault in order to climb over their dead kind.

The main guns of the tanks began howling; at this range, the impacting artillery rounds literally blew houses apart, the stones and bricks raining down on the charging Night People. Fifty-caliber rounds at a range of a hundred feet or less were awesome, tearing human bodies apart and literally stopping the charging creeps in mid-stride and flinging their torn bodies backward in a bloody macabre dance.

But on the dark side of the coin, Ben and the Rebels were trapped within the circle of torn and bloody and stinking dead, unable to break free.

A huge creepie leaped over the ever-growing pile of bodies and hurled himself straight at Ben, screaming curses as he sailed through the air, his bare hands outstretched in anticipation of closing around Ben's throat and choking the hated life from him. Ben lifted the muzzle of his Thompson and blew the man's hooded face into a thousand pieces of blood, bone, and tissue. Ben sidestepped, and the nearly headless body flopped, lifeless, on the stones of the street.

One creep leaped onto the tank where Ben and his team crouched and tried to wrest the fifty-caliber gun from a Rebel. Corrie shot the sub-human being in the head.

"Start tossing gas!" Ben yelled. "Tear gas and pepper. Everyone into masks."

"Button up," Corrie radioed to the tanks crews. "We're using gas."

The tank crews quickly screwed it down tight and switched to their chemical protection systems as the Rebels started throwing tear gas and pepper gas grenades over the wall of dead and badly wounded creepies, with the occasional Fire-Frag tossed in just for kicks.

Ben's mask was equipped with mike and receiver so he could both hear and communicate with Corrie, squad and platoon leaders, and company commanders. "We're getting out of here," he radioed. "Tanks, clear us a hole through the bodies."

The sixty-three- and fifty-seven-ton MBT's rolled right over the mounds of dead and dying creeps, the treads squashing the bodies and making a great big sloppy mess in the road.

The Rebels ran through the gore and out of the swirling clouds of tear and pepper gas. The tanks swiveled their turrets and fired grenade-filled rounds into the mass of choking and near-blinded creepies, many of whom had hit the street and grounds on their hands and knees and were scurrying like big bugs back to what was left of the buildings they had exited only moments before.

A block and a half away, Ben halted the retreat and threw up defensive lines. Anna had not gotten her mask seated properly and was nearly blinded, as well as coughing and choking. At Ben's wave, a medic took her off to treat her eyes.

Like Ben, Dan had been caught off guard by the creepie's attack and was furious.

"Calm down, Dan," Ben said after the Englishman had exhausted his repertoire of cuss words. "We made a mistake by underestimating the creeps. We've done it before and we probably will again. Considering that this could have been a real disaster, our casualties are very low. We'll just flush them out with chemicals."

"Bobby Day is going to love that," Jersey said after Ben had told her what they planned to do.

"Who is Bobby Day?" Anna said. Her eyes were bloodshot and red-rimmed from the gas and her voice husky from coughing.

"He's a reporter who hates me. And he is also a person I don't want you talking to," Ben told her.

"Why not?"

"Because he'll twist everything you say before he reports it. He'll try to get you to say things that can be used to hurt me."

Anna nodded slowly. "So your enemies are not just the people we meet on the battlefield, hey, General Ben?"

"You're catching on, Anna. Very quickly. I just don't want the lessons to be learned the hard way."

Anna's eyes turned cold behind the redness caused by the gas. "If he is a threat to you, why not get rid of this Bobby Day person?"

"Because it isn't done that way if one is to have

any kind of a democracy, Anna. The first amendment of our Constitution protects the freedom of speech."

Anna thought about that for a moment. "Even if it's used wrongly?"

"Even then, Anna."

"Why?"

"Because what is wrong to you might be right to somebody else."

"Right is right and wrong is wrong," the girl replied stubbornly. "Everybody knows the difference between right and wrong."

"It's all a matter of interpretation, Anna," Ben explained. "Now, go sit over there with the medics until your eyes are totally clear. And that's an order, young lady."

She grinned. "O.K., General Ben. Whatever you say."

She headed off toward the medic's tent. "Tell the medics to watch her," Ben told Corrie. "She gave in entirely too easily."

"I got the transports," Corrie said. "They'll be bringing in canisters of chemicals. First planes should be touching down late this afternoon."

"We should be ready to start pouring in the gas by midmorning tomorrow. It's skin-irritation gas. Not fatal."

"Good, maybe that will appease Bobby Day."

"I wouldn't count on it."

Ben smiled. "Oh, I'm not. Not at all. We just won't say anything about it until we start pumping the gas in."

* * *

Bobby Day watched the next morning as the huge pumps that were flown in were set up at various points in the city. "You are obviously going to use gas to drive these poor unfortunate wretches out of their tunnels, General," he finally said to Ben. "What type of gas?"

"Laughing gas, Bobby," Ben told him. "When they come out, they'll be happy, jolly good fellows all."

"Is that supposed to be funny, General?"

"I wouldn't even attempt to joke with you, Bobby. You have no sense of humor—none at all."

Bobby ignored the barb. "And when they come out, you'll take them prisoner, right, General?"

"Not likely, Bobby. Not likely. We'll try to round up the kids and turn them over to local people. But we'll shoot the adult creepies as they come out."

"That is monstrous!"

"That is reality, sonny-boy. No one, anywhere, at any time, has ever been able to rehabilitate a creepie— man, woman, or child. And some of the most skilled doctors in the world have tried for years. It just can't be done. But if you would like to adopt a real live creepie for your very own, to love and cherish forever and ever—which would be about fifteen minutes, if that long—you certainly have my permission to do so."

"I don't need your permission to do a damn thing!" Bobby popped right back. "And your humor is really sick, General. Really, really sick."

"I'm really, really sorry about that, Bobby. You certainly know how to hurt a guy. Oh, well. Now if you'll excuse me, I have some creepies to attend to." He turned to Corrie. "Everyone in protective gear. When that is done, start pumping the gas in."

"I don't have any protective gear!" Bobby hollered.

"Then you're going to have a real problem in about a minute or so, Bobby. It won't be fatal, but you'll damn sure wish you were dead."

"What kind of gas are you pumping in there, General?" Bobby hollered.

"It's a mixture of tear gas and blister gas, Bobby." Ben was getting into his protective gear. You see all those Rebels who are backing away and getting the hell gone from this area? You'd better join them and do it damn quick."

Bobby wanted to stay, but his better judgment took over and he retreated, managing to jump into the bed of a truck that was pulling out. He gave Ben the finger, but Ben ignored the gesture.

All the suits were equipped with helmet radios. "Where is Anna?" Ben asked.

"She's safe. I just checked," Corrie told him.

"Check again. That kid's got more moves than a mongoose."

Corrie's laugh was muffled as she double-checked. "All people in protective gear?"

"Everyone is set," Corrie replied.

"Snipers in place?"

"Ready for the shoot."

"This isn't going to be pleasant," Ben said. "So let's get it over with. Start the pumps."

That was the signal for a long and bloody afternoon.

* * *

The Rebels knew they didn't get all the creeps, but they were convinced they had broken the backs of the creepie population in the small city of Gyor. Those citizens who returned to pick up the pieces would have to deal with what was left . . . when and if the surviving creeps finally surfaced.

Bobby Day certainly could hear the shooting that went on for hours that afternoon; but he was not witness to what the shooting was about and knew that if he were not careful with what he wrote and reported, Ben would boot him out of the country and probably clear off the continent.

Bobby reported that the city of Gyor was cleared in a brutal and ruthless way by the Rebels.

"I certainly can't disagree with that," Ben said, and shrugged it off.

The Rebels pulled out and headed south toward the town of Papa, about twenty-five miles away. But their reputation had preceded them and they found the town deserted: no citizens, no creepies, and no punks. It was a dead town.

From Papa, the Rebels went to Sarvar and found virtually the same thing. At the city of Szombathely, population about a hundred thousand before the Great War, the Rebels found many of the citizens of the small city returning.

Winter was not far off, and Ben decided to shut the operation down and winter in Szombathely. The airport, which had been remodeled just before the Great War, was adequate, and the Rebels set about cleaning it up and getting the runways ready to receive aircraft.

"Shut it all down for the winter," Ben ordered his battalions.

"What are we going to do during the cold months?" Anna questioned Ben.

"You're going to school, my dear," Ben told her.

"Shit!" Anna muttered.

Thirteen

One of the first things Ben did was open up the schools and get some sort of city government going. As soon as the people who had been hiding out in the country saw what was happening, they began returning to help out.

Hungary was supposed to have relatively mild winters, but somebody forgot to remind Mother Nature of that. Late fall blew in some perfectly awful weather.

"This is mild?" Doctor Chase bitched. "Hell, it isn't even winter yet!"

"I can arrange for you to go back to the States," Ben suggested.

"To hell with you, Raines. And put out that damn cigarette. Those things are going to kill you yet."

Ben blew a smoke ring at Lamar and grinned.

Lamar gave Ben the bird and left the room.

There were many former schoolteachers among the Rebel ranks, and since Anna absolutely positively refused to attend the newly opened public schools, Ben arranged for tutors to meet with her several hours a day.

"Anna doesn't fit in with those kids," Jersey told Ben. "And she knows that. She may be a kid by age standards, but she's a grown woman by all other precepts. And she has a mind of her own, Boss."

"You're telling me?"

While many of the Rebels enjoyed the stand-down and often wore civilian clothing while relaxing, Anna refused to wear anything other than Rebel BDU's.

"The Rebel Army is her home, Chief," Beth told Ben. "It's her one grip on something permanent. And that is something she has never experienced in memory."

"Besides," Corrie added, "most of the women in the ranks tailor their BDUs to fit a little better."

"Really?" Ben said drily. "I hadn't noticed."

That got him a laugh, for Ben was noted for his eye for the ladies.

Along the front, batt coms reported no hostile action. Behind them, the citizens of the countries the Rebels had helped stabilize were slowly rebuilding and putting a semblance of order back into their lives.

In front of them, to the east, lay the unknown, much of it now buried under a thin blanket of white, for winter had appeared early and it had arrived hard.

Back in the States, there were now four major political parties: the Democrats, the Republicans, Simon Border's Christian Front, and Harriet Hooter's New Left (she had finally been convinced that ASSHOLE was really not much of a name for a political party).

Of the four major parties, Harriet Hooter's New Left had become a force to be reckoned with, for the whiners, the complainers, those who wanted some-

302 *William W. Johnstone*

thing for nothing, the I'll-sue you-if-you-even-look-at-me bunch, those who wanted the central government to take care of them from cradle to grave, those who wanted to meddle in everybody else's business, the hard gun-control crowd, the absolutely positively without a doubt politically correct bunch, and every known pervert in the nation had rushed to join Harriet Hooter and her New Left.

When President Homer Blanton did call for general elections, it was going to be a circus . . . but a circus whose final acts could have disastrous results for what was left of the United States of America.

Simon Border had about twenty-five percent of the voters; Harriet Hooter had about twenty-five percent of the voters, and the Republican and Democrat party each had about twenty-five percent of the voters. It was going to be an interesting election.

"Why don't you retire from national politics and come down to the SUSA and live?" Ben suggested to Homer via radio one early winter's day. "Cecil will find you a job if you want one."

"When I call for elections, Ben," Homer replied, "this country is going to go to hell in a handbasket, and you know it. Is that what you want?"

"I must admit I find the prospect both amusing and tragic," Ben said. "But if you'll recall, it's something that I predicted would happen."

Homer ignored the last bit. "You have a strange sense of humor, Ben. The once-mightiest nation on the face of the earth is threatening to unravel, and you find it amusing."

"The SUSA will not be affected by it, Homer. Not

one bit. Cecil tells me that several of our states need qualified administrators. He suggested you."

"When the people vote me out of office, Ben, I'll consider your suggestion."

"Homer, Harriet Hooter has gathered every kook, nut, radical, weirdo, and pervert in the country to her New Left Party. You lost a lot of your supporters to Simon Border and his Bible-thumping, self-righteous, hypocritical fruitcakes. The Democratic and Republican Parties are fragmented. The only thing holding the USA together now is the nation's police, the military, and a few reasonable-thinking men and women. It's coming unglued, and I'd hate to see you get hurt when it all comes tumbling down."

"There was a time when you wouldn't have cared, Ben."

"You're wrong, Homer. Back when the nation was whole—more or less—I never wanted violent overthrow of America or any physical harm to come to you. Those around you convinced you that I did, but they were totally off base and knew it. You were fed false information right from the git-go. I just wanted you out of office . . . peacefully and constitutionally."

"I like your honesty and bluntness, Ben. I find it refreshing." He paused. "I'm going to try to ride out the storm over here. If I'm not reelected, I just might take up residence in the SUSA and look for a job down there."

"All right, Homer. I'll make sure there is a job waiting for you. Talk to you later."

Ben leaned back in his chair. It wasn't even winter yet, and already he was bored with the inactivity. He smiled as he toyed with the idea of taking a patrol out into the countryside. Then he remembered there were three battalions of Rebels wintering in and around the city—with checkpoints everywhere—and he knew he wouldn't have a snowball's chance in Hell of pulling that off.

At the first hint of spring, he was going to hit Budapest, a city filled with punks and creeps and hardened criminals from all over Europe. Well, he could busy himself mapping out that campaign. That would occupy a few weeks of his time.

He looked up as Anna walked past the outer door of his office. Over the weeks, Ben had grown increasingly fond of the girl. He had entertained thoughts of adopting her but was hesitant to approach her with the idea.

What if she told him to stuff it?

Well, there was one way of finding out.

Now was one of those rare moments when Ben was alone. Jersey was outside, checking on the guards. Beth had gone for supplies. Cooper was at a MASH tent getting treated for a bad head cold. And Corrie was en route to the radio shack to check out new equipment.

"Anna?" Ben called.

She stuck her head into the room. "Yes, General Ben?"

"Come in and sit down, honey. I have something to ask you."